The Grumpy Billionaire

The Grumpy Billionaire

AN EASTPORT BAY BILLIONAIRES NOVEL

TRU TAYLOR

Contents

About

THE GRUMPY BILLIONAIRE

Mara

When we last saw each other eleven years ago, I would have bet everything I owned that Reid Mancini loved me. I knew that because I loved him, too. Madly, passionately, with every fiber of my seventeen-year-old being.

And that was why I made sure after our high school graduation night I would never see him again.

So much for that plan.

My new job in Rhode Island is both good and bad. Good because it's a great step up career-wise. Bad because it's a little too close to home... and to him, the only guy who's ever tempted me to let go and love someone.

Now my first love is all grown up with a full-grown man's size and power and an oversized cocky attitude to match.

With the world's largest social media network to his name, he's got all the fame and fortune he ever wanted and then some—and no doubt a harem-full of willing women falling at his feet.

Oh, and he hates me.

Not that I can blame him.

He has no idea why I abandoned him so suddenly… or how often I still think of him. He won't find out either—not if I have anything to do with it.

Everything would've been fine if he'd just stuck to his famously aloof no-talking-to-the-media policy. But no, he's decided to give his first ever television interview. And he says he'll talk only to me.

If I could turn him down without losing my job, I'd do it in a heartbeat. That's how desperately I don't want to be in the same room with him, talking one-on-one, on camera for God's sake. But in TV news, ratings rule—and hot, hard-to-get billionaires are ratings gold.

So I have to spend a week with him getting the story. It's the only way to keep my job.

I just hope I can keep my secrets in the process.

It's only a week. I can do this. Seven days. Two ex-lovers. One last chance.

Now we'll see exactly how much of a difference a decade can make… and how impossible it may be to leave the past behind.

Enjoy the read…

ONE

Mr. Grumpypants Himself

They say absence makes the heart grow fonder. Not in my case. When Mara left without a goodbye, without a care, I didn't have *a heart anymore.*

So what's a heartless guy to do when the one who got away... comes back?

- Reid Mancini

The guys were already there, stuffing their faces, when I arrived at Nooky's Diner.

I pushed open the glass door, causing the bell overhead to ring out its familiar jingle, and they all looked up. It was like a scene from that old TV show Cheers, only instead of them yelling, "Norm," they called out my name.

"Reid!" Tucker waved one hand over his head to get my attention.

As if I could have somehow overlooked six tall billionaires crammed into the corner booth.

"You made it," he said as I approached the table.

"There he is, Mr. Grumpypants himself," Hap said.

"Don't look now guys, but I think he might *actually* be smiling."

Hap was *always* smiling. He gave me the huge, dimpled grin that had made him a child star and the target of worldwide tween adoration about fifteen years ago, not to mention a very rich man thanks to years of syndication royalties from his weekly show Happy's Family.

My old friend was right. A matching grin *had* overtaken my face. Who could blame me? It was good to see my high school best friends and former housemates again. It had been several weeks since we'd all been together, a fact Hunter didn't hesitate to point out.

"I was getting worried that you were too big for us little people now that StillYours.com is such a huge hit," he teased. "A guy's social media membership surpasses Facebook's, and suddenly he's too good for the regular guys he grew up with."

Sliding into the oversized corner booth, I laughed at the good-natured ribbing and took a look around at the collection of "regular guys," AKA Hunter, who'd founded Chipp, a multi-billion-dollar digital payment processing software company, and Tuck, Aiden, Paul, and Josh who'd helped him with the startup, becoming billionaires themselves in the process.

I'd also taken part in the initial programming and getting Chipp off the ground but now was more focused on my own fast-growing company.

"I know. I know I've been kind of a stranger, and I apologize," I said. "I get caught up in the work and forget how long it's been since I've come down to my house here. Hell, I forget to eat half the time."

"Who cares about that freaking huge oceanfront mansion?" Aiden said. "What's worth visiting is your friends. I mean Hunter and Hap and Tuck moved out of the Billionaire

Bachelor House, too, but at least *they* didn't become ghosts afterward."

Of course he was right, and it wasn't just the work at my Providence-based company headquarters that had kept me away from my seaside hometown. I'd found the distance was helping to accomplish something that time had not.

Here in Eastport Bay, it was literally impossible to escape memories of Mara. Driving along the ocean, sitting on the beach, eating out at Cliff House or anywhere at Brady's Wharf, running across the town's famous lovebirds Romeo and Juliet, the swan couple she'd loved so much.

Mara was everywhere.

Even sitting here at Nooky's, the memories swarmed me. We'd come here often as teenagers. The homey all-night diner was pretty much the only place in town I'd been able to afford to take her back then.

Maybe someday with *enough* time and distance, this place —this town—wouldn't hold so many painful ghosts, but in the meantime, moving my primary residence to a penthouse apartment in Providence, the state's capital, had done me a world of good.

I had absolutely missed the guys, though, and was eager to catch up on what had been going on in their lives.

"Seriously, you guys are saints for putting up with my mopey ass all of these years. But I promise it's all behind me. I'm in a better place now—finally. I'm putting her in the rearview and moving forward. I mean that's what she did with me right?"

I didn't have to explain who I meant by "her." These guys had known me way back when Mara and I had been inseparable.

"Absolutely," Paul agreed. "I mean you gave her a chance to change her mind and come back, but eleven years is long enough to grieve a relationship."

"Hell yes," I agreed. But even now a stab of pain pierced my gut at the thought of how long it had been since I had seen her or talked to her—and how easy it had been for her to forget about me.

"All right, all right, enough about me and my pathetic lack of a love life. Tell me what's going on with you. Who's knocked up their wife lately?" I joked. "How many more babies are we adding to the former Billionaire Bachelor House clan?"

They laughed, but nobody coughed up any baby news.

"No one? Really? I was beginning to think our friend group would be responsible for populating the entire kindergarten class of Eastport Bay Elementary in a few years."

"Don't look at me," Hap said, raising his hands up to the sides. "Even if I had any news—which I don't—Rachel would kill me for spilling the beans before she's ready to."

I looked around the table. "Okay then, anybody else find their soulmate and fall in love in the past few weeks? Any pending engagements I should be aware of?"

My tone was lighthearted, but at the rate these guys had been working, it wasn't that far-fetched of a question. It seemed like all you had to do was walk down Main Street in this town and the love of your life would bump into you and spill her purse, a meet-cute ready and waiting on every corner.

Unfortunately for me, I'd already met the love of my life in high school, and she'd decided she did *not* feel the same.

Mara had left town suddenly without a word of explanation and had refused to see me or return my calls, emails, and letters once I'd managed to track her down.

Maybe I was a slow learner, but I had finally *finally* gotten the message.

"Not yet," Aiden said, answering my question and shaking me out of my morose trip down memory lane. "But I'm always open to it."

Paul spoke up. "I'm thinking of proposing to my new doctor. Everyone else just threw meds at me, but she worked at getting to the root cause of my allergy issues. For the first time in my life, somebody's figured out the right combination of treatments for me. I'm on a new diet and a new histamine drug, and I feel like a different person."

"I *thought* I'd noticed a distinct lack of sneezing," I quipped. "Guess we can't call you 'Sneezy' anymore."

Hunter's brother Jack had nicknamed us the Seven Dwarves when we'd all shared a mansion while working round the clock to launch Chipp. I'd thought it was pretty funny, and once we all considered it, the individual nicknames had been surprisingly fitting.

"Well, I'm still calling you 'Grumpy,'" Paul shot back. "It'll take more than one friendly lunch for me to be convinced that your ogre-ly ways are in the past."

"That's fair," I conceded.

"Since we're getting all personal, I guess I'll mention I'm going in for adult ADHD testing." Josh said. "Maybe you guys will stop calling me 'Dopey' once I get some treatment for that. I can't believe I never figured out what the issue was before, but I took one of those online quizzes and I had basically every symptom in the book."

"That is awesome, man." I clapped a hand on his shoulder.

Hopefully my tone expressed the sincerity of my words. "Believe me, I understand what it's like to be dealing with a challenge for so many years you can hardly even remember what it was like to live without it."

That admission elicited more sympathetic glances than I would have liked. I jumped up from the booth.

"I'm going to check out the pie bar and grab a plate. Anybody else want some?"

Tuck, who ate more than any one I'd ever seen and yet

seemed to always stay thin, put in an order. "Grab me a slice of the turtle cheesecake pie."

"Sure thing. Anybody else?"

"Yeah, I guess I could go for some apple ginger custard pie," Hunter said.

I walked up to the long stainless-steel-topped counter that had anchored Nooky's Diner since my earliest memories of coming here as a kid with my mom on her rare days off.

The owner Pamela Nookson was behind the counter wearing what appeared to be the same apron her dad used to wear back when he'd been a daily fixture at the diner he'd founded and named after himself.

She had a short pouf of blonde hair and a red pencil tucked behind one ear.

"Hey Pam. Busy day. How are you?"

"Well, hey there, Reid. How are you honey? How's your mama?"

"Oh, she's doing great. Thanks for asking."

"Has she retired, or is she still working for the Neely family?" Pam asked.

I bristled at the sound of that last name. It represented both the greatest love and the greatest hatred of my life.

"No, she's still working there... unfortunately," I said. "I've begged her to retire and travel, or chill at the beach every day, or at least move out of her house on their property and into mine—or to let me buy her a better house of her own."

Working to control the frustration in my voice, I explained, "She says Evelyn and the boys need her. I mean, you know she works there, but they're also friends, and Evelyn isn't in the greatest shape these days apparently. My mom's more of a companion now than a maid. As far as I can tell, she plans to work there as long as she's physically able to."

I had more than one reason for wanting my mother to

move out of the tiny cottage on the outskirts of the Neely estate.

First, it was far too small and modest for her with the means she now had available to her, thanks to my business successes.

As far as I was concerned, she deserved to live in a palace and be waited on hand and foot. But she'd steadily refused my offers, saying they were unnecessary and that she couldn't leave Evelyn and her twin sons.

The other reason (the primary one) was that I found it impossible to visit her there at the little cottage I'd grown up in, mere steps away from the extravagant mansion where Mara had grown up.

These days when Mom and I got together, she drove over to one of my houses or we met at a restaurant for lunch or dinner.

"Well, you tell Miss Cheryl that I asked about her. In fact, let me box up a slice of pie for her to go. She hasn't been in here for a while, and I bet she's missing it. Her favorite's the double fudge if I remember right."

"Yes, that's right. Thank you. She'll love that," I said.

"And what kind will you have today, hun?"

I looked over the tempting assortment displayed behind the sparkling clear glass. Nooky's had at least ten varieties of pie available at all times, and the selection changed daily. I made my choice and ordered Tuck's and Hunter's slices, asking Pam to put them all on my ticket.

When I had them in hand, I turned to head back to the table. Motion on the television screen mounted above the bar caught my eye, and I glanced up.

And dropped all three plates.

White porcelain and pie entrails exploded across the checkerboard tile floor, decorating the base of the counter as well as the shoes of a couple of patrons seated nearby.

The worst part? I couldn't even apologize because I was barely aware of the fallout of Pie-mageddon. I couldn't pry my eyes from the TV screen.

"Oh my," Pam declared. "Don't you worry about that, honey. Jordan will clean it up."

She turned and called for a young waitress who emerged from the kitchen with a dish towel in hand.

"Jordan, darlin', can you get a bussing tray and a mop? We've had a little accident out here."

Apparently noticing my catatonic stare, Pam picked up the remote and turned up the volume on the TV overhead. "Is there some kind of emergency on the news or something?"

After a few seconds, her worried expression relaxed. "Oh yeah, I noticed her the other day. That's your little girlfriend you used to come in here with, isn't it? Pearson and Evelyn Neely's daughter. Mary, was it?"

"Mara," I corrected in a husk of a whisper. My throat had gone so dry it was a wonder any sound came out at all.

Now not only was I seeing her face again for the first time in a decade, but I was also hearing her voice.

Other than listening to her voicemail message an embarrassing number of times before the number had been changed and disconnected, I hadn't heard her speak since the night of our high school graduation.

She was doing a report about an upcoming Breast Cancer Awareness Month event, standing in downtown Providence only about a block away from my company's headquarters beneath an enormous pink balloon arch.

Finally managing to rip my eyes away from the screen, I mumbled an apology to Pam and Jordan and the customers who'd been in the splash zone.

"I'll be happy to pay for any damage," I said to one and all.

Pam smirked and handed me three replacement plates of pie. "If we cried over spilled milk—or pie—around this place, we'd never stop blubbering. It happens. How long's Mara been back in Rhode Island?"

I shook my head. "I have no idea."

Pam's face changed, growing less amused and more compassionate. "Oh. I guess you two didn't keep in touch."

I almost snorted at the massive understatement. "No. We didn't."

When I got back to the table, I noticed my friends were all wearing expressions that matched Pam's concerned frown.

"You okay, man?" Hap asked.

"Yeah, sure. I'm fine. Just clumsy that's all." I gave a half-hearted laugh, set the plates down, and slid back into my seat at the booth.

"I saw the TV screen," Hunter said in a serious voice. "I didn't know she was back. I guess you didn't either?"

I shook my head, keeping my eyes trained on the plate in front of me though I no longer had any appetite for pie.

"No, I haven't heard from her."

"Are you going to call her?" Josh asked. "I mean, you guys were so close in high school."

Close. Ha. That's what I'd thought. I'd thought we were two halves of the same whole. Clearly not since Mara and I hadn't exchanged a single word in over a decade.

Imbuing my tone with a sense of cool I did not feel, I said, "Nah, like I said earlier, it's over. I'm moving on."

"I don't know," Hunter said. "There *is* something compelling about the love of your youth. It's hard to get over. And that's not always a bad thing."

"Maybe for you," I said.

It had certainly worked out for Hunter and Kristal, the girl he'd longed for his entire adolescence and had recently made his bride.

"In my case, I'm not even sure it was love," I said, warming to the notion. “More like a combination of raging teenage hormones and stupidity.”

They all laughed. Tucker held up his glass of chocolate milk. “To raging teenage hormones and stupidity—ever may they reign.”

“Hear hear,” Paul said.

“To moving on,” I said in a toast of my own.

All my friends clinked their glasses with mine in a toast, but I noticed them exchanging knowing glances, apparently not buying my show of disinterest in Mara’s surprise return to Rhode Island.

When everyone had gone back to their meals, Hunter leaned over and spoke in a low voice. “Maybe you *should* call her, you know. Set up a coffee or something, just talk to her, get some closure. It would do you good.”

“Yeah, no. That’s not going to happen,” I insisted. “For one thing, she hasn’t answered any of the dozens of phone calls I’ve made to her over the past eleven years, so I don’t think she’ll suddenly decide to pick up the phone. For another, I don't even *care* what happened anymore. I refuse to chase her. I’ve chased her enough for one lifetime already. If she wants to talk to me and explain herself, she'll call. But I'm not going to hold my breath for that. Obviously what we had meant nothing to her.”

As for me, Mara had been *everything*.

She had been my whole world back then.

TWO

Promise Me

Reid-Twelve years earlier

Calling Mara my first love was a disservice to everything else we were to each other. We were best friends, confidants, partners in crime, and when we were much younger, playmates.

We had grown up next door to each other, though you couldn't exactly call us "neighbors." That word implied a certain sense of camaraderie and equal footing that bore no resemblance to the relationship between our respective families.

My mom had gone to work for the Neely family when she was eighteen—and pregnant with me.

The arrangement had been the result of some sort of Catholic charity matchmaking program pairing teenage girls who were "in trouble" with charitable families who were willing to take them in and give them room and board in exchange for help around the house.

In my mother's case, it had turned out to be a lifelong arrangement.

It had taken me years to realize Mom and I weren't actually part of the Neely family. When I was little and had no concept of things like minimum wage and social classes and live-in help, the estate's expansive seaside grounds had seemed just as much my territory as Mara's.

And I'd considered her my equal.

By the time I had grown old enough to understand that the Neelys were the "haves," and Mom and I were the "have-nots," it was far too late.

I was already madly in love with the Eastport Bay power couple's only daughter.

Mara's mother was a socialite who was far more interested in her tennis game and her friends than in her daughter. Her dad, the state's Attorney General, was an aloof, distant figure who was rarely around.

When he was, he seemed to regard his pretty daughter as a possession at best—at worst, he treated her like a campaign prop.

My mom was always busy working somewhere around the property, and Mara's twin brothers were so much younger they weren't suitable playmates, so Mara and I were essentially on our own—which was fine with us. We'd been inseparable.

When we weren't in school, we'd spent our time running around the estate building forts, climbing its iconic European Beech trees, spending time at its private beach, swimming and building sandcastles.

It was an idyllic life for children lucky enough to grow up on New England's "classic coast."

Now that we were older, we still spent nearly all our time together, but the nature of our friendship was different. The change had happened gradually. Our conversations now were deeper, as was my understanding of the impossible gulf separating us socially.

Some of us were a little luckier than others, it turned out.

Mara spent more time away from the estate these days. She

was sixteen, and her parents had her on the debutante circuit, which meant she attended numerous dances and society parties I would never be invited to.

"I hate the whole thing," she would claim. "It's so boring and stupid. I'd rather be here with you."

When she *was* with me, all was right in the world. We took walks along the shore or through the wooded area of the property, rode her family's horses together, or just sat on the rocks near the water reading books or talking or fishing together.

My favorite times were when everyone else was in bed. I climbed the tree beside her house and settled onto the large branch just outside her room. Mara would sit by the open window, and we'd stay up late into the night, talking, watching movies, or listening to music.

It didn't matter what we did—it was all magical. Those stolen nighttime hours were our secret, our own private world.

But I knew it couldn't last. The parts of her life that did not involve me would gradually overtake the rest.

As the daughter of a powerful politician and one of Eastport Bay's premier socialites, Mara would naturally move more and more into her role in society.

Our friendship was bound to fade into the background eventually.

Which was why I didn't let my continually strengthening feelings for her make their way into our intimate conversations. Ever.

One evening when her parents were away at some fundraising gala at Bellevue Manor, Mara and I walked down to the beach and spread out a blanket. We lay on our backs, side by side, listening to music on her phone as we watched the sun go down and the stars come out.

When one of her favorite songs came on, she jumped to her bare feet and held her arms out to me in invitation.

"We have to dance," she declared, a bright smile on her beautiful lips.

"You know I don't dance," I argued, but I could already feel my resolve weakening. Basically there was nothing this girl could ask me to do that I would refuse. Well almost nothing.

I wouldn't kiss her for instance, even if she begged.

Fuck. I should never have even imagined it.

Just the mental image of Mara's sweet pink lips touching mine had my heart racing and sweat popping out along my brow, not to mention what was going on below the belt.

That was another reason I couldn't dance with her unless she was talking about some stupid line dance or something. If I were to take her in my arms and hold her against my body right now, she'd know beyond a shadow of a doubt that my feelings for her had gone *way* beyond friendship or childhood crush.

Thankfully she seemed completely unaware of my condition. And my mad love for her.

"No, I know that you *won't* dance," she said. "Saying you 'don't' dance is just a cop out. I've seen you play tennis. Anybody who can move like *that* on the court is capable of dancing if he wants to. So... I'm asking you to make a decision to dance with me right now."

Her lips curved in a knowing, persuasive smile that did nothing to help the heart palpitations—or the hard on.

"Please," she added in the softest, sweetest tone.

Though my brain knew better, apparently my body had declared mutiny, because I found myself getting to my feet and moving toward her.

The persuasive smile turned into one of satisfaction. She stepped up to me and put one palm on my shoulder. The other she held out for my hand.

Licking my lips and willing my breathing to remain at a

normal pace, I took her offered hand and began an awkward side-to-side shuffle, trying to please her.

She smiled up at me as if I was Derek Hough and about to win the Dancing with the Stars trophy.

"See? You can dance," she purred. And then she took another step closer.

The hand that had been on my shoulder moved up to my nape. Slipping her fingers from my other hand, she clasped both her hands behind my neck.

The maneuver caused the front of her body to press against the front of mine.

At the feel of her curves and softness, all of my self-talk was rendered worthless. The physical evidence of my raging attraction to her was straining the front of my shorts and demanding to be noticed.

Mara didn't say anything about it, but she *did* respond, tucking her hips and pressing her lower half more tightly to mine.

A pleasurable jolt of electricity rolled through my abdomen, and I got even harder. Suddenly I wanted nothing more in the world than to drag Mara down to the blanket and pin her beneath me, tug the strap of her sundress down and kiss the slope of her neck and shoulder, slide the hem of the dress up and feel the silky skin of her thighs, her—

No. Stop. Just stop before you get carried away and ruin everything.

I glared down at her, speaking through clenched teeth. "*What* are you doing?"

Mara gazed up at me with an expression of mock innocence. "I'm dancing with you, obviously."

And then she moved against me in a deliberate, slow rub that caused me to go hard as a rock.

I went still. Gripping my hands on either side of her hips, I shifted her back a step. "I think that's enough dancing for now."

Her pleased grin turned into a pout. "Why?"

"You know why."

Flopping down to the blanket again, I stared out at the rolling waves and dug my fist into the sand at my side, squeezing it with almost enough pressure to produce glass.

Mara came and sat beside me. Far too close.

"No. I don't." she insisted. "There's nothing wrong with us dancing together."

"I doubt your father would agree with that," I said. "He's made it pretty clear that he doesn't want our friendship to turn into anything more."

Her pout was accompanied by a head toss. "Who cares what he wants? It's none of his business who I dance with."

We both knew we were talking about something far beyond dancing at this point. Though if asked, no doubt Pearson Neely would not have wanted his daughter to dance with me either.

"I thought we were friends," Mara said.

"Of course we're friends. You're my best friend. Nothing will ever change that."

"If nothing will ever change that, then why are you so afraid to dance with me?" she challenged. "Friends dance with each other all the time."

"I'm not afraid," I insisted, but we both knew it was a lie.

I was absolutely terrified of what would happen if I ever owned up to my true feelings for Mara, if I ever allowed myself to *keep* dancing with her and to give her the kind of attention she seemed to want from me.

"Well, Harry McAllen isn't afraid to dance with me." The look on her face was the visual equivalent of a dare.

Although I knew she was trying to bait me, I couldn't seem to stop myself from rising to it.

"What's that supposed to mean?" I asked gruffly.

"At the Seaside Cotillion last weekend, he asked me to dance *three* times. And the last time when the lights went down, he moved me into a corner, and he kissed my neck. And then he slid his hand from my back down to my bottom."

She might as well have thrown a torch into an oil drum. My temper flared. As she had known it would.

"That punk. How dare he touch you like that." And then an unpleasant thought occurred to me. "Unless you *wanted* him to touch you?"

I didn't know what Mara did on the frequent arranged dates her parent set up for her. I kept trying to convince myself I didn't want to know.

She and I were friends. That was all we could ever be. A guy like me and a girl like her... it just wasn't reality.

"Of course not, silly." She wrapped her hand around my tensed bicep and leaned closer.

"I slapped him," she said. "I don't like *him.* There's only one person who I'd let touch me like that."

She gave me a significant look, one that contained all the unspoken desire and pent-up feeling between us. "Only one person who I *want* to touch me."

Tensing my entire body in a desperate battle for restraint, I leaned away from her, falling to one elbow in the soft sand.

"Mara... no."

Instead of allowing me to escape gracefully, she followed the motion, leaning harder against me as I fell over sideways onto the sand.

Smiling, Mara crawled over me and pressed on my shoulders until I was on my back and she sat astride my hips.

Our faces were even now. Her wide, dark eyes bored into mine as our rapid breaths mingled.

"I know you feel it, too," she said. "I see the way you look at me. I felt what happened when we danced together... what's happening right now. You want me as much as I want you. Why do you keep fighting it?"

I heaved a couple of heavy breaths, struggling against a nearly overwhelming desire to pull her down to me and sink my hands into her hair. What I should have done was push her off me, but I couldn't seem to make myself do it.

"Because it's impossible," I finally managed.

It was a confession I'd never dared to make before. Now it seemed inevitable.

Might as well get this conversation over with.

Our friendship might not be able to withstand it, but there seemed to be no other choice. Mara was forcing the matter.

"If we ever started something, I wouldn't be able to stop," I explained.

"I'd want everything from you. I already do want everything from you," I admitted for the first time ever.

No doubt it was a huge mistake. So was allowing her to stay in this position, cradled atop my lap, which felt at the moment like it might go up in actual flames.

Move. Just do it. Lift her off you and put some distance between you. Before you do something you'll both regret.

She pounced on my failure to do so and on my unintentional admission.

"You can have it." A fierce light glowed in her dark eyes. "I *want* to give you everything. I want to be everything to you... the way you are to me."

Mara leaned down, attempting to press her mouth to mine. I twisted my head, causing her lips to land on my jaw instead. Clenching it, I dug deep into every reserve of self-control I possessed.

"We can't. And you shouldn't say things like that."

"It's the truth," she insisted.

"For now maybe. If your father ever found out about this,

you know what would happen. He'd fire my mom. We'd have to move. We'd be homeless. She doesn't make enough money to save enough for a house of our own. And my part-time job doesn't pay enough to support us. I would have to quit the tennis team and my after-school clubs like Science Olympiad so I could work more hours to support us. Is that what you want?"

"Of course not, but I would never let that happen." Mara's voice wavered for a moment, but then she set her jaw and lifted her chin. "I would just tell my father he's not allowed to fire your mom. She can live here as long as she wants to—and so can you."

I had to laugh at her ridiculous self-confidence. Her sassy, girl-boss attitude was impossibly cute.

"Oh really? And when did Pearson Neely start listening to you? He doesn't listen to anyone but his campaign advisors and his own gigantic ego."

"I'm his only daughter," she said. "If he *really* understood how important you are to me, there's no way he'd hurt me by sending you away."

"You sure about that, sweet girl?"

"Of course." But her expression wasn't as certain as her tone. "Anyway, he won't find out."

"No. He won't," I agreed. "Because nothing's going to happen between us. Besides you're planning to go off to Columbia next year, and I'm going to URI on scholarship. You're going to meet a bunch of guys in New York and forget all about me."

"I could never forget you," she swore solemnly. "Never for as long as I live."

Though I knew the words shouldn't make me happy, a deep sense of satisfaction filled my chest, warming my insides and expanding like a hot air balloon glowing and rising in preparation for flight.

"New York isn't that far from Rhode Island," she reminded me.

Her expression changed, looking almost sad as a thought occurred to her. "Will you meet a bunch of girls at college and forget about me?"

The truth was out of my mouth before I had time to self-edit or even think about it. "No. I'll never love anyone but you."

Mara's eyelids flared, and her face moved toward me again, but once more, I twisted away, preventing the contact that was starting to feel more imperative than oxygen.

"It doesn't matter how I feel or what I want," I ground out in a voice that sounded like it was made of gravel. "You can't aways have what you want or do what you want to do. You know that better than I do."

For a moment Mara was quiet, just staring at me. Then her body relaxed, and she lifted her head to look around at her family's beach, the rolling waves that moved on and off shore casually as if we weren't having the most critical conversation of our young lives.

She looked back to me and lifted one pretty, suntanned shoulder in a delicate shrug.

"Okay, I guess you're right. But... I want to ask you for just one thing. And then I'll let the topic go. I promise."

Immediately my suspicions were raised. She never gave up this easily–on anything. "What?"

"A kiss."

She said it as if it were no big deal. "Just one. Just kiss me *one* time, and then I *promise* I won't bring it up again."

I shook my head, beginning to protest. "I don't think I can hand–"

"Is it really so much to ask? I just need to know what it feels like," she pleaded. "I've never let anyone kiss me before, and I've imagined kissing you so many times, it's almost all I can think about. I lie awake in my bed at night, pretending you're there beside me. Pretending..."

Apparently her nerve failed before she could finish the sentence. But I knew what she was going to say because my wakeful nighttime hours–and all my dreams– were filled with her, with what I wanted to do with her, for her, and to her.

Oh God. This girl was going to kill me.

Now I *really* couldn't kiss her. I was about to combust just hearing her talk about it.

My grip on her waist tightened, and my arms tensed in preparation to lift her off of me—a feat that was going to take Herculean effort.

But then I spotted the telltale glisten in her eyes.

"Hey don't cry," I begged. "You know it's not because I don't want you or find you attractive. You know I think you're the most beautiful girl in the world."

"I'm not mad at *you*," she said. "I'm just... sad. And mad at..."

She looked around as if searching for words in the seagrass and sand surrounding us. "At life. Fate. The world. My stupid father and mother. It's so obvious we should be together, and I can't believe they can't see it. It's not fair."

Now the tears spilled over, beginning to stream down her face. I couldn't have let go of her if both of our lives depended on it.

Sliding a hand around the back of her head, I buried my fingers in her silky dark locks and pulled her head against my chest, holding her as she sobbed.

"Don't cry," I murmured. "Please don't cry. We'll just... just enjoy the time we have. That's all we can do, isn't it?"

"Can we?"

Her tears soaked the front of my t-shirt now. "I don't think we can even do that. If what you say is true, then it's all pointless anyway. Maybe I *should* go ahead and kiss Harry

McAllen or Jeff Graham—or one of the other boys at school who actually wants to be with me."

A fierce sense of possessiveness and jealousy seized me, unraveling my last tenuous thread of self-control.

The thought of my beautiful Mara kissing any guy but me accomplished what even her tears had been unable to.

I clasped her jaw gently and angled her face up to mine.

"No," I growled. "You won't kiss Harry. You won't kiss any of them. If you ever do, I'll make sure it will never compare to kissing me—because their feelings for you could never compare to the way I feel about you."

I gave in to the demand that pulsed through every part of me and dropped my mouth to hers.

When they met, the pleasure of it was shocking. Her warm, soft lips, the sweet scent of her skin, the happy, hungry little sounds she made—it was almost too much to take.

Small explosions went off across the surface of my skin and deeper, waking the depths of my secret desire for her. Well, not secret anymore. She could have no more doubt about how much I wanted her.

The strokes of her tongue matched mine, sweetly seductive movements drawing me closer, deeper, lighting me up and making me want more and more and more of her.

I would never get enough of this girl—not if I lived to be a hundred and twenty.

Believing there was no chance of ever being with Mara, I'd kissed a few girls before, but this was something completely different. Everywhere she touched me, her fingers left a trail of fire.

It felt like there was something wild in me, some untamed creature that answered only to her call, responded only to her touch.

She was branding me with an imprint so deep it could never be erased.

And I knew. I knew I would *never* be able to say no to her again.

It was stupid. It made no sense. But I was beyond the reach of good sense at this point. Once our lips had met, that was it for me.

I would do anything, say anything, *be* anything this girl wanted me to, and consequences be damned.

If her father wanted to fire my mom and kick us out of our house, then let him. I would figure out something, some way to take care of us that didn't involve leaving Mara.

I had to. Imagining a future without her in it was like picturing a world without air, water, or food.

When the kiss ended and we pulled apart, she looked up at me with wide, wondering eyes.

"That was everything I dreamed it would be," she whispered. "And more. So much more. Promise me we'll never be apart, Reid."

Her tone grew more emphatic when I didn't immediately respond. "Promise me. Say it."

I shook my head, but in keeping with my newfound understanding of my absolute devotion to her, I did as she commanded.

"I promise, sweet girl. No matter what happens.... we will never be apart."

THREE
Take Out

Mara

We'd been apart for more than a decade, but it was impossible not to have thoughts of Reid Mancini now that I was back in Rhode Island.

Even if he'd been just an ordinary guy, he would have been unforgettable… to me.

But he was far from ordinary, and he'd spent the past eleven years proving he was *not* someone to be overlooked, taken lightly, or easily left behind.

"Can that Senator Caine talk or what?" Sheldon asked across the small pizza parlor table. "Did you see that Mancini dude's face? Why'd they even ask him to talk at the State House if Caine never shuts up to let him get a word in?"

"I don't know," I mumbled, watching my favorite photographer inhale the last few bites of his lunch. I really didn't want to talk about Reid's face.

Or his body—long and lean and powerful in the perfectly-fitted, obviously expensive suit he'd worn during the legislative hearing this morning.

Our news director had assigned us to do a package on

the hearing for the six and eleven p.m. newscasts. Its purpose was to advise the lawmakers about policy changes that might attract more businesses to set up shop in our tiny state, and as one of Rhode Island's shining stars of industry, Reid had been invited to share his input.

The press releases had started flying fast and furious as soon as the media-shy internet entrepreneur agreed to speak at the hearing. All four stations in Providence and seemingly every newspaper in the state had responded by sending crews to cover the rare event.

A couple of Boston TV crews had made the hour drive, too, just to get a glimpse of the creator of the web's hottest social media site, StillYours.com.

"I mean, the guy *never* talks on-camera," Sheldon continued, making the enthusiastic hand gestures he couldn't seem to speak without.

"That was our best chance at a sound bite. And you know all Rob is gonna want in the package tonight is words of wisdom from the Tech Titan. I'm gonna have to scroll through about two hours of *blah blah blah* from the senator to get to the good stuff."

He leaned back in his chair, satisfied with his enormous lunch, and wiped his fingers on a paper napkin before balling it up and tossing it onto the red-and-white-checkered tablecloth.

"I can edit it, if you want," I offered.

"Dude—would you? I have two more shoots today before I could even start editing. That would be awesome."

"No problem," I said.

The two of us gathered our paper plates and greasy napkins and stood, preparing to leave the mom-and-pop restaurant and get back to work. I snatched the ticket off the table before Sheldon could reach it.

"No, Mara. Come on. I think I owe you, like, four lunches by now." But he was smiling.

"No. I owe *you*. Do you have any idea how great it is to go out on stories and not be the reporter *and* the photog? You make my job easy. Besides, I'm a *rich* reporter."

I winked at him, and we both laughed at the absurdity of my statement. Television news did not pay well—not until you made it to the top of the ladder at the network or in a big city like LA or New York anyway.

Like everyone at my new television station, Sheldon was unaware of my family history—which was how I hoped it would stay.

I'd supported myself since high school graduation, and I had no intention of using my parents' money or connections to get ahead at work. There was no reason anyone had to know I was part of *that* Neely family.

"You've got a wife and three kids. All I've got is me," I reasoned.

"It wouldn't *have* to be just you if you'd go out with a *nice* guy instead of those himbos you date. I bet you'd like my buddy Ray, or Jason—" Sheldon made another attempt to grab the ticket, which I hid behind my back.

"Hey, leave your buddies—and my himbos—out of it. And you can get the next one," I said.

The photographer sighed and threw his hands up in defeat. "Okay. Thanks. Did I ever mention that you're my favorite reporter?"

"Maybe a couple of times." I grinned at him. "When your belly was nice and full."

Sheldon looked up, over my head toward the front of the pizza joint. The smile on his bearded face grew wider.

"You are not gonna believe who just walked in."

I whipped around to see the restaurant's entrance, and all the air left my lungs in an audible whoosh.

Reid Mancini was standing just inside the front door.

I turned back to Sheldon, my body stiff and suddenly chilled. He was still looking in Reid's direction.

"I can't believe a billionaire would come to Uncle Tony's Pizza for lunch. Shouldn't he be at, like, Capriccio or something?" he said, referring to a swanky high-dollar restaurant on the river near the city's financial district.

I scanned the restaurant's rear wall. "Do you think there's a back door to this place?"

Sheldon finally looked down at me. "Why? We should go talk to Mancini—maybe he'll give us a sound bite about the hearing. It would be a total scoop. Rob will love us."

My entire body clenched at the thought of walking over and speaking to Reid. I may have even winced. "I promise you—he *won't* talk to us."

"Yeah, well I know he doesn't do interviews, but—"

Sheldon's eyes narrowed as he studied my face. "Hey, what's the deal? You know him?"

I nodded, my lips tight. "We knew each other as kids.... and we dated in high school. I can't talk to him, Shel."

"Okay... so I take it things didn't exactly end well." His usually jovial face contracted into a scowl, and the volume of his voice rose with his suspicion. "Wait—did he do something to you?"

Sheldon's spine straightened, and his shoulders went back as he looked behind me again.

I grabbed his arm and whispered, "No. No. Keep it down, okay? I did something to *him*. And I *really* don't want to see him any closer than from across the chamber of the State House."

Now Sheldon's face relaxed into his usual easy smile. "Oh, I get it. You broke his heart, didn't you?"

His tone took on a tint of admiration. "My little Mara—melts the legendary Ice Man and then leaves him cold."

"Don't tell anyone, okay?" I pleaded. "And get me out of here. Maybe if I walk behind you, he won't see me?"

Sheldon shook his head, beaming. "So you want me to be your blocker? I gotta say I'm surprised to see this side of you. The fearless reporter, afraid to face her high school sweetheart."

At my murderous glare, he laughed then pulled me behind his body. "Okay, chicken shit. But you can't hide from him forever. Not in the smallest state in the nation."

As Sheldon walked toward the front door, I shadowed him, staying close and trying not to step on his heels.

I wasn't sure where Reid had chosen to sit, and I didn't want to know. I kept my eyes trained on Sheldon's back like a greyhound after a mechanical rabbit.

"Mara?" A voice from my past, as familiar to me as my own, came from the side, near the service counter.

Crap. He hadn't taken a table after all, but stood near the counter with a white to-go bag in his hand. And he was looking right at me.

Sheldon stopped. I ran into his wide back then stumbled backward a couple of steps, dropping my purse and reporter notebook. I watched my belongings crash to the floor. Then I looked up again.

Crap c*rap.*

There he was, Reid Mancini, right in front of me and far more beautiful than my memory or imagination had been able to grasp. In the years since we'd last stood face-to-face, he'd changed.

He still looked like *him*, wavy brown hair, Caribbean blue eyes you could drown in, tall and athletic in that lean tennis player kind of way. But the years had sculpted intriguing new differences.

The youthful lankiness of his body had been replaced with a broader, thicker masculinity. All the boyish softness of his teenaged face had disappeared and left behind the more angular features of a full-grown man.

The beautifully-shaped lips that had long-ago kissed me and driven me crazy were now set in a grim line, matched by the faint lines that whisked out from the sides of his narrowed eyelids as he studied me.

"Hi... Reid," I wheezed like someone in the middle of an asthma crisis.

"You dropped your..." He motioned toward the assortment of cosmetics and personal items pooled at my feet.

"Yes." I nodded then finally yanked myself out of shock and into action as he dropped to one knee on the dirty floor of the pizza place in his designer suit. It had probably cost more than I'd earn this year.

"No! No—I'll get it." I tried to wave him off. "You'll get yourself... dirty."

Reid ignored my protests and began to gather my things with his free hand.

Oh, those hands. I'd always loved them. I'd studied them for what seemed like hours as a lovesick teenaged girl, running my fingers over the sun-browned skin, so much rougher than mine, admiring the raised veins running across the back and the well-developed muscle between his thumb and pointer finger.

Not to mention what he'd done to me with those hands.

Crapcrapcrap. Get it together, Mara.

He held the items out to me, and I snatched them with a breathless, "Thank you."

Reid picked up my notebook and rose to his feet. "You're welcome. As you may have heard, I'm not above getting a little dirty when it's called for."

He grinned at the reference to his reputation as a ruthless business competitor.

Several social media sites had tried to compete with StillYours.com, and he'd methodically defeated them, driving them out of the lost-love-reunited business one by one.

Now his site claimed the distinction of having more than a billion registered users around the world. Apparently, reconnecting with former sweethearts was big business.

Reid did not immediately give the notebook back to me but glanced down at what I'd written during the hearing. At what I'd written *about him.*

"Serious, soft-spoken, reserved." He handed the pad to me with a quiet huff of a laugh. "You forgot cocky, aloof, and arrogant. Isn't that what they usually write about me?"

"You're not *that* arrogant," I offered, eliciting a bigger grin from him. "I mean... sometimes people misunderstand quietness to mean..."

My voice drifted off into awkward silence as I stared at his bemused expression.

"Yes. Well, thank you for the benefit of the doubt, I guess."

I probably should have offered some sort of glib response, but my mind refused to produce anything other than a sort of confused awe at the reality of being so close to him again.

It was an experience I'd never expected to have. In fact, I had taken great precautions to ensure it would never happen, staying away from Rhode Island entirely, insisting that Mom and Bax and Bowie fly to see me in the various towns and cities where I'd worked instead of my coming here, where there was a slight risk of running into Reid at the airport.

As we stared at each other, the silence lengthened uncomfortably until Sheldon, whose existence I'd completely forgotten in the past three minutes, spoke up.

"Sheldon Santos." He extended a beefy hand toward Reid. "It's nice to meet you, Mr. Mancini."

"Call me Reid."

My ex-boyfriend set his food bag on a nearby table and clasped Sheldon's hand firmly. Then he gave him a cautious smile and glanced warily at the camera slung over Sheldon's shoulder.

"That thing's not loaded is it?"

Sheldon's face took on an affronted frown. "No, man. I wouldn't do that. No legitimate photog would shoot you when you weren't aware of it."

Reid lifted a dark brow. "You'd be surprised what people would do with the right amount of motivation. I hear there's a pretty good price on my head these days."

"Forget what I said about not being arrogant," I said, tilting my chin up to him and arching a brow.

Reid's face broke out into a real smile, reminiscent of the ones he'd worn almost perpetually when we were younger.

He gave me a deferential nod. "Well, naturally, I wasn't suggesting that *you* wanted anything from me. I believe you made your position on that quite clear, Miss Neely. It is still Miss, isn't it?"

"Yes." I swallowed hard, unaccountably nervous. "And I understand you're still single as well. How is it that the world's most successful matchmaker is alone?"

Reid's refusal to do interviews combined with his immense wealth and celebrity-level good looks had caused the national media to pursue him relentlessly. And the fact that he was famously hard-to-get only fanned the flames—among the press and women of all ages.

My own friends had made lecherous comments about him whenever a long-distance lens had managed to capture his shirtless image on a private beach or his tuxedoed form at some hoity-toity high-dollar charity event.

Reid smirked in response to my question. "Well, as you know, my business is devoted to *reuniting* true loves. And one must have *had* one of those to be reunited with one. So, I'm afraid it's not of much use to me personally."

He gave a slight head nod and lifted his to-go bag from the

table. His voice took on the same formal tone he'd used this morning with the legislators on the finance committee. "Sheldon, nice to have met you. Mara—welcome home. I'm sure we'll run into each other from time to time professionally."

And then Reid walked past us out the front door.

"Not if I can help it," I muttered to myself, my face still burning from the casual insult he'd delivered in that nothing-personal tone of his.

"Well—that was interesting." Sheldon blew out a loud breath. "I can see why you broke up with him. That guy's kind of an ass."

"Yeah," I agreed as we left the restaurant and headed toward the news car parked a few blocks away.

Except he wasn't. Reid Mancini had been the best guy I'd ever known.

"And, for the record, dude," Sheldon continued, "No matter what he said—he was blown away by seeing you. No guy looks at a girl like that unless—"

"I know," I interrupted, not wanting Sheldon to finish his thought. It didn't matter. I knew it anyway.

When we'd last seen each other eleven years ago, I would have bet everything I owned, would've bet my mother's life that Reid loved me.

I knew that because I had loved him, too. Madly, passionately, with every fiber of my seventeen-year-old being.

That was why I'd made sure after our high school graduation night I would never see him again.

FOUR
You're in Luck

Mara- Eleven years earlier

The deep, wraparound porch had always been my favorite feature of my family's waterfront home.

Today the space felt suffocating in spite of the continuous ocean breezes. It wasn't the fault of the summer day but the situation that made me feel trapped.

Cricket and Brianna, my mother's closest friends, were here for lunch, and Mom had asked me to sit down for a few minutes and tell them about my college plans.

The two women were usually pretty harmless, chattering about their latest exotic vacations, property acquisitions or shopping trips.

Unfortunately, today the conversation had turned to another topic.

Reid.

He was mowing the lawn, one of his duties here at the estate. Each time he drove the lawn tractor past the porch, the conversation paused, and their eyes followed his shirtless form until the tractor moved out of sight. I could almost see, feel, and smell the lascivious things they were thinking.

It made me feel like tearing my hair out—or better yet, theirs.

Admittedly, he did look amazing. Years of tennis matches and manual labor around the property had layered his lean body with muscle. His tanned chest, shoulders, and back gleamed in the bright sunlight, as did his sweat-soaked dark hair.

"That boy should *never* wear a shirt," Cricket said before literally licking her lips.

"Amen," Brianna agreed.

She stroked the underside of her neck and her chin with her long, manicured fingernails. "I've never considered myself a cougar, but *that* would turn any woman feral."

My mother looked embarrassed. "You two are terrible. He's Mara's age for God's sake."

Cricket winked at me. "Well then maybe *she* should tap that. There's something to be said for hot, simple men."

My gut boiled with protective fury. Reid was brilliant, a literal genius. But this socialite couldn't see that because to her, he was just a "simple" poor guy.

I didn't say all that, and I didn't mention the fact Reid and I had been carrying on a secret love affair for the past year, starting with the night I'd finally persuaded him to kiss me on the beach.

I simply said, "He's my friend."

"That's right," Mom agreed quickly. "Mara and Reid grew up together. Besides, he's not a suitable candidate to be her boyfriend. She's been seeing the McAllen boy. You know his parents—James and Sarah McAllen from the beach club?"

"Looks suitable enough to me," Brianna said, turning her head to follow as Reid made another pass with the tractor.

"Hush. You're embarrassing Mara," Mom scolded. "She'd never be interested in that boy. His mother works for us, and his father—absentee of course—is apparently some low-level mafioso."

Now my ears perked up. I was always interested in anything to do with Reid, but this was new information. I wondered if he knew.

He'd always told me he had no idea who his father was. His mom had never married, raising him alone here at the estate.

Not the least bit dissuaded, Cricket waggled her brows. "Ooooh. An Italian stallion."

"A half-Italian, half-Irish *gardener,*" my mother corrected, her tone filled with disdain.

"I have to agree with Cricket on this one," Brianna said, fluffing her hair then stretching her arms far overhead. "When it comes to men, I say the simpler the better."

"You married into one of the wealthiest families in Eastport Bay," Mom argued.

"I didn't say don't marry money. Lincoln's rich, but he's the most docile, Beta guy around, and frankly not the sharpest knife in the drawer. His older brother runs the family business. Linc just spends the money—on me."

She laughed out loud then turned to me. "You want my advice, Mara? Never marry a powerful man. It's a recipe for misery." Her gaze swung to my mother. "Your mom knows that better than anyone."

Mom popped up from her wicker chair. "Who needs more iced tea? Anybody?"

Apparently, she wasn't interested in getting into a discussion about her own marriage, which her friends—and I—already knew wasn't a happy one.

After listening to their frequent fights (the walls in our house weren't as thick as Mom and Dad thought they were) I'd already decided I'd never repeat my parents' mistake.

Reid was as different from my dad as he could possibly be,

and he was the only one I'd even consider marrying. He was my soulmate.

Once we both turned eighteen, I fully intended to leave this place and be with him, no matter what my parents thought of his "suitability."

High school graduation was only a week away. After that, we'd be free. We could stop hiding our love for each other and have a real, twenty-four-seven, out-in-the-open relationship.

I could hardly wait.

* * *

Graduation Day

He's all mine.

That was the thought repeating in my head as I watched Reid deliver the valedictorian speech to the crowd assembled at Eastport Bay High's football field. I was about to burst with pride and happiness.

This handsome, brilliant, super-sweet guy was all mine, and tonight… I would become all his.

Since that first kiss a year ago, we'd been taking things further and further. Tonight, we'd spend our first full night together alone.

We'd reserved a room at the swanky Eastport Arms hotel where the graduation party would be held. I liked my classmates, but Reid was the only one I wanted to celebrate the occasion with. It marked the beginning of our "real lives" together.

Both of us had received some money for graduation. In fact, Reid had gotten an enormous check from his mysterious absentee father. Pooling our funds, we had enough to at least get us started should the worst happen and my parents forbid me to date him and try to use the threat of cutting me off financially to make their point.

"I'm going to send it back," Reid said as we sat on the hotel room bed, staring at the obscene number on the check. "It's probably dirty money. Who knows what he did to get it? And I don't want *anything* from him."

"So it's true then? He's a mobster?" I asked. Apparently the discussion Mom had shared with her friends on the porch had not been mere gossip.

Reid frowned. "It's true. He just got out of prison. That's why Mom never married him. I'm not sure why she decided to saddle me with his last name. He was sitting out in the audience today—the big, Sicilian-looking guy in the tan suit."

My jaw dropped. "He was there? I didn't see him. Did you talk to him?"

Reid shook his head then glanced at me from beneath lowered brows. His turquoise eyes looked stormy. "I'm from bad stock, Mara. Just like your dad says."

"Screw my dad."

Placing my palms on either side of Reid's face, I made sure he was looking straight into my eyes.

"Seriously. Screw him. Screw everyone. And don't talk about yourself like you're some kind of prized bull—your 'stock' doesn't mean anything. What matters is what's in here."

I pointed to his chest, tapping the tip of my finger over his heart.

Reid covered my hand with his then grasped it tightly, bringing it to his mouth for a soft kiss. "You're unbelievable, you know that? I don't know what I'd do if I ever lost you."

"You will never have to find out."

Smiling and appearing to fight back tears, Reid squinted and looked off to the side in the general direction of a nautical themed oil painting on the wall.

"Sometimes I think it would be nice to have a dad—even a shitty one like him, you know?" he said. "But then I think...

there was a reason my mom didn't want me growing up with him. I don't need his money. I don't give a shit about being rich. All I care about is being with you. As long as I have you, I don't need anything else."

"Then you're in luck."

I gave him a naughty grin as I stood up and started peeling my party dress off my shoulders and down my body, revealing the special underwear I'd bought just for tonight.

"Because you have me. And you can keep on having me... anytime you want."

FIVE

Kryptonite

Mara

It was, hands down, the best night of my life. The next morning was the absolute worst.

Attempting to sneak in at dawn, I'd turned my key in the lock as quietly as possible and slipped my shoes off, intending to tiptoe through the house up to my bedroom without waking anyone.

Unfortunately, it was impossible to wake my parents because they were already awake—waiting up for me.

My father asked me to join him in his office for a *conversation*.

"I want you to stop seeing him—immediately," he said. "Break off all contact."

It felt like someone had hit me in the chest with a fifty-pound medicine ball. "How can I do that? He lives here."

"*That's* about to change."

Reid's dire prediction had come true. He and his mom were about to be homeless, and it was all my fault.

"No. Please. Don't evict them," I begged. "Cheryl doesn't have the money for another house."

"That's not my problem. This is what she deserves for not educating her son properly on his social standing."

He stood from his desk chair then sat down again, clenching his hands atop its surface.

"The thought of you with that... greasy little gutter rat sickens me. His father is a common thug. He's an ex-con for Christ's sake."

"Reid is *not* like his father. He doesn't even know him. He's never even talked to him."

"But it's in his blood," Dad sneered. "Good breeding always shows—so does bad. The kid's a mongrel. I'm sorry I ever allowed your mother to take Cheryl and her little fatherless runt in."

I didn't want to cry in front of my father, but my fury wouldn't stay suppressed, streaming out in angry rivulets down my cheeks.

"I hate you."

Dad shrugged and actually let out a chuckle.

"I hated my father, too, when I was around your age. Especially when he told me I had to marry your mother after she got pregnant with you. 'Neelys do not have bastards,'" he boomed in a mocking voice then snorted. "You'll get over it."

"I won't," I swore. "I'm never going to speak to you again."

His chuckle grew into a laugh. Clearly, he wasn't taking me seriously. "Suit yourself. As long as you don't speak to that boy again."

"Mom will be mad at you if you send Cheryl away," I blurted, growing desperate now that I realized how close Reid and his mother were to being on the street.

My father's face contracted in a smirk. "I suppose you're right. She does love having her little 'crutch' nearby, and there'll be no end of harping about it if I evict the old maid."

He paused for a beat to think then continued. "Here's

what's going to happen. I'm sending *you* away. You'll spend the summer with your aunt and uncle and cousins in Missouri and go directly from there to Columbia in the fall."

I blinked a few times as the shock settled. "When can I come back home?"

"When your ridiculous infatuation with 'the help' is over and you can assure me you won't see that white trash boy again."

My shoulders relaxed marginally, and my head stopped pounding quite so loudly. It wasn't ideal, but it wasn't the end of the world either.

It wasn't like I'd be locked away in a vine-covered fairytale castle, trapped in a sleeping spell. Reid and I could text and call over the summer. Maybe he could even borrow a car and drive out to see me in Missouri.

When freshman year in college started, I'd be in New York, and he'd be at URI. We'd already plotted out the route from Kingston, Rhode Island where his university was located, to Manhattan and knew it was only about three hours by car and by train.

"And before you start thinking you're going to carry on a long-distance 'love affair' and reunite when I'm not looking," my father said, "or worse, run away together—"

He rolled his eyes at the idea. "Let me assure you... my reach is *long*. I can find anyone, anytime, and I have sources of information you can't even begin to imagine. I *will* find out about it if you ever see or even speak to him again. And Mara... *he'll* be the one who pays the price."

My head jerked back, and I had to swallow hard to speak around the boulder suddenly inhabiting my throat. I knew my dad was tough, but I'd never seen him this vicious before.

It was chilling.

"What does that mean?" I whispered.

"It means I'm a very powerful man. I'm the top legal officer in the state," he said.

His tone turned speculative. "It would be a shame for your little crush to get caught up in some legal trouble and find himself locked away in the ACI. It's unfortunate, but a lot of innocent people are convicted of crimes and put in prison. Sometimes inmates die on the inside, killed by other prisoners. And the young, attractive ones... like Reid... they probably wish they were dead. I wouldn't wish it on anyone I cared about—certainly not on someone I claimed to love."

The periphery of my vision went black, the sides closing in until I felt like I was seeing my father through a long, dark tunnel.

"You wouldn't do that."

It was a hope, a prayer, a futile grab at a rapidly retreating lifeline. That sleeping spell and enchanted castle were starting to sound pretty good.

"Oh believe me, little girl, I absolutely would. *If* he lives through that and gets out in one piece—which is a big if—I'll make sure he's unemployable in this state and anywhere else I can call in a favor. His life, simply put, won't be worth living."

Dad left the threat there with a just-try-me look on his face.

I swiped at my own face, burning with hatred but understanding at the deepest level that I was powerless to disobey.

Because I did love Reid—and I would *not* let my father hurt him.

"So I'm supposed to just... disappear? Without a word to him?"

"Write him a note if you must," Dad said. "But make it brief and clear. Don't leave any room for doubt or hope. Tell him you don't love him and have no desire to ever see him again. Tell him you're leaving because you want to see other people, that you want a clean break."

"He'll never believe it," I told him. "He knows I love him. He'll search for me. Eventually he'll find me."

"Then it should be your mission in life to make sure that when he does, you convince him you want nothing more to do with him, that he's better off moving on with another girl—someone of his own class."

"How?"

"You were smart enough to get into three Ivy League schools. You'll figure it out."

And I did. In fact, I rescinded my enrollment at Columbia and went to Stanford instead, hoping the greater distance from home would curb my temptation to sneak back and see Reid.

He was my kryptonite—just talking to him would do me in. I'd fall apart, confess everything to him, including my undying love.

That love would be the death of him—literally.

As predicted, Reid eventually tracked me to California and showed up at my dorm. Thankfully the university's security protocol kept him out.

When I refused to let him come in or to go outside and talk to him, he sent up a note. My self-preservation instinct begged me to throw it away, unread.

But I couldn't. I opened the folded paper and stared at the words he'd written. Even the sight of his familiar handwriting hurt.

My eyes watered so furiously it took me a few tries to read it.

Mara,

I've searched for you for so long, and now that I've found you, I'm not leaving until you agree to see me. I don't know what happened or why you're doing this, but please just talk to me. Or at least listen to what I have to say. I love you. I will always love you. I believe you still love me, too. We can work this out, whatever is going on. If I lose you, I will never be happy. My heart is broken, and only you can fix it. Please, sweet girl. Give us a chance.

I sat on the floor of my room, clutching the note, and bawled. The jagged edges of my own shattered heart pulled toward his like a super-magnet.

And still, I didn't go to him. I scrawled a short response on a sheet of printer paper and begged my roommate Jennifer to take it down to him.

"'Go away?' That's it?" she asked after reading the tear-stained note in her hands. "The poor guy drove, what? Three thousand miles to get here, and all you have to say to him is, "Go away?'"

I could tell she thought it was monstrous of me not to at least talk to Reid, but it was the only way I knew to keep him safe.

* * *

No doubt if that tragic scene had taken place today, all Reid's money would have broken the doors of my dorm down like a gold-plated battering ram.

But back then he'd been just a confused college kid with an empty wallet and a broken heart.

He was alive though. He was safe. I'd accomplished that much.

Even now that we were both adults and he was a self-made billionaire, I worried about his safety... about what my father might do to him.

Dad's power had only grown. After completing his second

term as Attorney General, he'd run for governor and won. In a state as small as this one, he knew everything that went on, and he could get to literally anyone.

Which meant the danger to Reid was still just as real. After all, I was his kryptonite, too.

I'd have to do whatever it took to stay away from him.

SIX

Reid

Pizza? Really?

That was the big emergency that had sent Mara and her camera man running from the state house without sticking around to even ask me questions after the hearing?

Not that I would have answered them. In fact, I'd been gleefully anticipating refusing her request for an interview. Of course I'd say no to *any* reporter who asked, but I'd take particular delight in turning Mara down.

I'd spotted her immediately, though she'd been standing thirty feet away from the podium where I'd spoken. I looked up from my notes, and my eyes had gone directly to her as if guided by a laser targeting system.

She was beautiful—even more beautiful than she'd been as a teenager, which was saying something.

Once during my speech, my eyes had strayed to her, and I'd completely forgotten what I'd been saying. I'd stuttered and had to glance at my notes to get back on track.

Then she'd leaned in to speak close to her photographer's

ear, and I'd literally felt my temperature go up several degrees though the House chamber was freezing.

Were they involved? Maybe he'd moved here with her from out of state, following her to a larger TV market. Maybe they lived together. Maybe they were engaged.

A strange blend of resentment and hostility filled my gut.

I hate him. I hated this man I didn't even know merely because he *might* be romantically involved with Mara.

So much for "moving on."

The pair was standing too far away for me to see her left hand, but I made a mental note to ask my assistant Lee to look into it for me. I certainly hadn't gotten the chance to do it myself.

Mara and the photographer had left the state house before the hearing had even ended, depriving me of the chance to snub her—and inspect that ring finger up close.

I'd instructed my bodyguard Seth to follow them and report back on where they'd gone. With that information in hand, I'd asked my driver Ben to swing by Uncle Tony's for some takeout, claiming to be famished.

Then I'd insisted on going inside to get it myself, much to Ben's and my own surprise.

And now I was parked outside her family's mansion—and my mom's cottage—in the driveway the two vastly different homes shared. It was the first time I'd actually been on the property in years.

And what are you doing here now, *asshole?*

Was I planning to climb up to Mara's balcony like Romeo? Or wait till later when she was asleep like the princess in Sleeping Beauty, sneaking inside to wake her with a kiss?

My breath quickened, and my muscles tensed, a sweat breaking out on my brow.

Of course, I *could* just walk up to the front door and

knock, ask to come inside and then apologize for my abysmal behavior earlier today.

I sat frozen in indecision until my mother walked out onto the front steps of her cottage and waved. Smiling, I turned off the ignition and got out of the car.

"Hi Mom."

"Well, this is a nice surprise," she said. "To what do I owe this unexpected visit?"

Strolling up to the small front porch, I gave her a hug. "No reason. I was in the neighborhood and thought I'd drop by."

She flashed a knowing smile. "So, it has nothing to do with the fact that Mara is home and living next door again?"

"Of course not. She made it pretty clear she didn't want to keep in touch. I'm sure you remember."

"I remember." Mom nodded sympathetically and invited me into the small kitchen where she immediately began making me a sub sandwich.

Setting it on the table in front of me along with some apple slices and a tall glass of iced tea, she took the chair facing mine.

"I remember a boy who couldn't get out of bed for weeks after you tracked her down to Stanford and she wouldn't see you. I remember a guy who cried on my shoulder until you were almost hyperventilating."

Cutting my sandwich in half with so much force I nearly split the plate in half, I said, "I don't need you to remind me of that. It was a long time ago. I'm over it."

"So over it you sat in your car and stared at her house for ten minutes before I walked out and caught you?" she asked.

Her tone gentled and warmed. "Reid, honey, you don't have to pretend with me. I know how you've always felt about her, for better or worse. And this time... I think it would be better to keep your distance."

"I'm planning to."

"Good. Because I think you've turned a corner lately, and I'd hate to see you slide back into that dark place again. I love you both, but the two of you just weren't meant to be."

A spike of objection stabbed me in the gut the way it always had when I'd given myself the same good advice. Something deep inside me refused to believe what Mara and I had back then wasn't real.

Outwardly, I agreed with my mother. "You're right."

"I know I am. Best let bygones be bygones... and let Mara go—for good."

We talked a while longer about anything *but* Mara, I thanked Mom for the sandwich, and she walked me to the door.

"Good night. See you soon. My place next time," I said.

"Goodnight, honey." She kissed my cheek. "One of these days you're going to find the *right* girl. It'll happen. You'll know her when you see her."

Unfortunately, as I walked back to my car, I glanced up to Mara's bedroom window and saw *her.*

Darkness had fallen, and her window shade had been left up. She wasn't dressed for bed. In fact, she might have been getting ready to go out for the night.

Did she have a date?

I'd figured out today at the restaurant she wasn't involved with the photographer, but that didn't mean she wasn't involved with anyone else in the local area.

Suddenly I had the strangest urge to cross the lawn and climb the tree nearest her window, to rap on the glass and just talk to her like we did in the old days. Nostalgia wrapped around my heart like the ivy vines that snaked up the outside of the Neely mansion.

What I wouldn't give to be back in that time, in my

younger body, in that unshakeable—or so I'd thought—friendship with Mara. In her arms, in her bed...

Fuck.

Sliding behind the steering wheel, I slammed the door and started the ignition, spinning the tires to turn away from the house. Away from her.

What the hell was wrong with me? Did I think I was living in some kind of fairy tale? Mara had made it abundantly clear —back then and today—she was not interested in anything about me.

While I was standing beneath her window mooning away over old memories, she probably didn't even remember those things we'd shared.

There was only one way to handle this thing. Forget about her, too. Ignore the fact she was back in Rhode Island.

It was the smart thing to do and the only choice that would allow me to keep at least a shred of my dignity. Not to mention my sanity.

SEVEN
Good Sister

Mara

I watched the taillights of Reid's car the whole length of the driveway until he turned onto the road, and they disappeared into the night.

How could it still hurt *this much*?

When I'd vowed to stay as far away from him as possible, I hadn't been considering the fact his mother still lived next door. Of course he'd come visit her on a regular basis.

And of course he wouldn't knock on the front door of my family's home and ask for me. Or climb the tree and spend the night outside talking to me through the window screen.

See? He's not holding onto old memories. He's moved on. You should do the same.

"Your father called here again."

Turning away from the window to face my mother, I did a double-take. "Mom, *what* are you wearing?"

Apparently, my mom was moving on as well. After thirty years of unhappily-ever-after, she'd left my dad—or rather kicked him out. The Eastport Bay estate had been part of her inheritance, not his, so he now called a townhouse in Providence home, and she was turning our family home into a funhouse.

She'd completely redecorated the house—and herself.

Her hair, which had been a dark brown like mine her whole life, was now blonde. Her forehead was tighter than I'd seen it in years, and her lips were suspiciously plump. My mother had turned into a Bratz doll, the middle-aged edition.

She'd also bought a whole new wardrobe. Boxes arrived on the front porch daily. She said she needed all the new clothes to fit her smaller size which she'd arrived at thanks to her new favorite pastime, attending a disco dancer-cize class at a local gym.

The class instructor, Ricardo, who was about twenty years younger—and almost certainly gay—was her new "boyfriend."

I wasn't sure *he* knew they were an item, but they spent a lot of time together, and Mom talked about him like he was the second coming of Richard Simmons.

"Ricardo's on his way to pick me up. He's taking me out to Rooftop at the Providence G tonight," she explained. "He's a fabulous dancer. Sooooo sexy."

Gesturing to her outfit, which consisted of a fringe-y leather bikini top and matching skin-tight leather pants, she asked, "What do you think? This outfit is very 'now.' You should get one like it."

"I'm not sure I'm 'now' enough to wear that," I said. "I like your shoes."

Her sneakers were glittery gold with large stars on the sides. "These are Golden Goose," she explained. "They're Italian. I'll order you some."

"That's okay. Thanks anyway. Hey, do you know where Bax and Bowie are tonight?" I asked just as the front doorbell chimed. "They were already gone when I got home from work."

"Out with friends, I'm sure," Mom said in a breezy tone. "That'll be Ricky."

She hurried for the door. When she opened it, "Ricky" was not standing outside. An Eastport Bay police officer was.

Beside him were my two brothers who looked a little banged up and a *lot* intoxicated.

"Good evening, Mrs. Neely," the officer said.

"What happened?" Mom asked.

She sounded more irritated than worried. Clearly the boys were alive and relatively unscathed from whatever they'd been up to. Also, she was used to it.

Evidently, my sixteen-year-old brothers were doing their best to win the grand prize in the *Who Wants to Go to Reform School?* competition. This was not the first time they'd been Ubered home by the police department, and they'd recently been kicked out of Eastport Bay High School for pulling one too many pranks.

The final straw had been when they'd somehow gained entry to the school before dawn and hidden hundreds of alarm clocks all over the building—which they'd set to go off at two-minute intervals all day long.

Their fellow students were reportedly very amused.

The principal was not.

Baxter and Bowie had apparently not learned anything from the expulsion. They now attended a private school just outside Eastport Bay—no doubt my dad had pulled some high-level strings to get them admitted in the middle of the fall semester—and I'd become well acquainted with the headmaster there in the past month.

The man placed regular frustrated phone calls to our home about their truancy and/or unruly behavior, and Mom was usually not around to answer them.

The police officer answered her question. "Your sons were in a minor fender bender in Providence, Mrs. Neely—on

Allens Avenue in front of the Wild Zebra *Gentlemen's* Club. They weren't injured, but the BMW they were driving was damaged. I don't need to tell you they're too young to be in any of those clubs—or to be drinking alcohol."

"We weren't drinking," Bowie said, punctuating the obvious lie with a loud, alcohol-scented burp.

Bax offered his best attempt at a charming smile. "I was drinking... but not much."

He held one hand up and pinched his pointer finger and thumb together. The word "much" came out sounding like "mush" instead.

"Get in here, both of you," Mom ordered, and the boys obediently stumbled inside.

To the officer, she said, "Thank you so much for bringing them home. We'll have someone pick up the car in the morning."

She tried to hand him a tip, but he waved his hands in front of him and backed away. "I'm not a delivery driver, Mrs. Neely."

"Ms. Neely," she corrected. "I'm getting a divorce."

"Ms. Neely," he said, accommodating her request with admirable patience. "This can't happen again. Out of respect for your husband—"

"*Ex*-husband."

"Ex-husband," he repeated. "... the Providence P.D. called us and transferred your sons to my custody. But they said next time there's going to be an arrest—or two. I hope you understand the seriousness of this."

"I understand," she said with obvious impatience. She was already looking past him toward Ricardo's waiting car.

Turning to me, she asked, "Will you please handle your brothers? I don't want to keep Ricky waiting. Tell them they're grounded for eternity and that I'll deal with them in the morning before school—and they *will* go to school no matter how hung over they might be."

"Sure. I'll take care of them," I said. What else could I say? "Be careful. Make good choices."

She laughed at my facetious recitation of the things she used to say to me before I went out with my high school friends, back when she was the adult in this equation, and I was the kid.

Shutting and locking the door behind her, I turned and went to herd my brothers from the living room, where they'd collapsed on the sectional sofa, up to their rooms on the second floor.

"Ima just sleep here," Bowie mumbled.

"No. Up. Both of you. I know you're tired, but you'll be glad you're waking up in your own beds in the morning when your alarms go off *for school*."

"School?" Bax whined, sounding like he had at age three after being told he had to take a nap.

I tugged at his big, sweaty hand, encouraging him to get up.

"Yes. You know the place you go on the rare occasions you haven't been banned from the building? Now go. Come on, get up. I want you both upstairs in one minute. I'll be right behind you with some water bottles and ibuprofen."

He got to his feet, swaying a bit, and gave me a big, goofy grin. "I wish you'd been in school with us, Mara."

Bowie also rose, saving me the trouble—and backache—of trying to pull him to standing. "Yeah, I wish you'd been around more. You're a good sister."

Regret squeezed my heart, and guilt leaked from every pore as I escorted Baxter and Bowie up the stairs to the bathroom that connected their bedrooms.

Would things have been different if I hadn't stayed away for what amounted to their entire childhoods?

The twins had been little more than toddlers when I'd left eleven years ago. I felt terrible for missing all their Little League games and school plays over the years.

We'd kept in touch with phone calls and texts and occasional visits, but there was no replacing the years I'd missed. All I could do now was try my best to make up for them now by being the responsible big sister.

"Wash your faces and take two of these ibuprofen tablets each. And drink this water. All of it. If you throw up, do *not* under any circumstances call Cheryl to come clean it up in the middle of the night. Call *me,* okay?"

"Okay, thanks Mara," Bowie mumbled.

"Thanks," Baxter echoed. "Sorry."

I didn't tell him it was okay because it wasn't, but I did wish them both a good night. "Try to get some sleep. I'll see you in the morning—unless I see you sooner."

Going back downstairs to the kitchen, I made a cup of tea and sat at the center island to await the inevitable. My elbows rested on the countertop, my forehead dropping into my hands as I studied the grain of the marble.

How the hell did things get so crazy?

I'd hoped that taking a job in Rhode Island and moving in here would fix whatever was wrong, but I'd been here a month already and things were definitely *not* fixed.

And something was *definitely* wrong. The boys were going off the deep end, my mom was acting like a stranger.

There was nothing wrong with having a good time, but I didn't think she actually was. There was almost a desperation in the way she'd conducted herself since I'd been home. I'd never seen her like this before.

According to Cheryl, it had been going on for a while since my parents' breakup. She'd been the one to contact me when the boys had been expelled from the public school.

Calling the station where I'd worked before Channel 3,

she asked me to come home and check on my mom and brothers.

"I'm getting too old to go pick them up in the middle of the night when they get into trouble," she'd said. "And I hate to say it, but I'm not sure either of your parents are up to handling it. They're each pretty deep in their own troubles. I think she's depressed, and he's checked out, totally in denial about the divorce. I'm not sure what to do, but maybe you will."

I'd never known her to exaggerate, and once I'd gotten here and had a real look at what passed for Neely family home life these days, I saw that she hadn't—at all. I only wish I'd realized it sooner, but it's kind of hard to know what's going on back home when you live two thousand miles away.

Mom and Ricardo came in through the garage door well after midnight, giggling as they entered the kitchen and headed for the fridge.

Like hers, his long hair was bleached blonde, and his skin bore the evidence of a recent visit to the tanning salon. Also like her, he wore leather pants and a midriff-baring top.

Had they intended to wear matching outfits for their "date" tonight?

I got up from the couch, where I'd been reading. "Hi," I said, startling them both.

Mom whirled around, her hand at the base of her throat. "Mara. You scared me. What are you still doing up?"

Her eyes went to the clock on the microwave. "It's late."

"I'm not tired," I lied. It had been a *long* day. "I'm drunk-sitting. Bowie and Bax have each been up twice to vomit, and my money says they're not finished yet. Hi Ricardo."

"Hi Mara. I saw you on TV tonight at five. You just keep getting more gorgeous—bitch."

The line was delivered with a friendly smile, so I took it as the compliment it was intended to be.

"Thanks. You too." His Botox-ed forehead and lip fillers matched my mom's as well.

He smiled, pleased.

"Did you two have fun tonight?" I asked.

"We did." Mom did a twirl in front of the fridge, holding the seltzer bottle she'd taken from it. "There was an amazing DJ."

"And a burlesque show," Ricardo added. "I kept saying, let me up there on that stage. I'll show you some burlesque that'll make your nipple rings quiver."

He laughed loudly and did a silly shoulder shake followed by some enthusiastic twerking. I had to laugh, too. Ricardo was definitely entertaining—I could see why Mom liked being with him, even if she was aiming her Cupid's Bow in the wrong direction.

"You are so bad," she scolded as she laughed. "You'd probably better get going. You're going to have under eye bags for your seven a.m. class—unless you'd rather stick around and help clean up after two puking teenagers."

Ricardo clutched his face and made an expression of mock horror. "Oh my God, my beauty sleep is ticking away." He pretended to rush around in a panic. "Where's my silk pillowcase? Where's my retinol?"

Turning to me, he said, "Bye doll. See you soon."

I got up to give him a hug. "Bye. Drive safe."

Mom walked him to the door where they exchanged air kisses and said goodbye. When she returned to the kitchen, her smile was gone, and her shoulders drooped.

She looked exhausted.

"You okay?" I asked.

"Sure. Why?" She threw a see-how-fine-I-am fake smile over her shoulder as she opened the fridge to put the seltzer back inside.

"I don't know, you seem a little... sad. You've seemed sad a lot lately."

She wheeled on me, all pretenses of cheerfulness dropped. "I'm not sad. I told you we had *fun* tonight. Ricky and I always have fun—unlike your father and me. By the way, you never answered me earlier. Did you hear what I said? He called here *again* today."

Her face twisted into a sneer as she referred to the man who'd sired me.

I plopped down onto a bar stool at the island. "Yes, I heard you. He keeps calling the station, too. I'm sure if he could track down my cell number, he'd call that."

"You didn't call him back?" Her perturbed expression had melted into a hint of amusement.

"No."

The hint was now a full-blown smile. "Good. I don't know what he's thinking calling here. I guess I'll have to change the number—or get rid of the landline."

"Don't do that. It's the only number the boys remember. I'll call him back, I guess, and tell him to stop bothering you here."

"It's okay—I'll just turn the volume down on the answering machine so I don't have to hear it." Mom rested her elbow on the island counter, leaning in and studying my face. "You're the one who seems sad. What's going on? You're not acting like yourself."

Says the stranger posing as my mother.

I don't know why I told her. Old habits die hard, I guess. Maybe because I was exhausted, too? Or maybe I was hoping she'd tell me to stay away from Reid.

"I saw Reid today."

"Oh, sweetheart." She stretched across the counter and covered my hand with hers. "That couldn't have been easy. How was it? What happened?"

"Sheldon and I ran into him at this little pizza place near the State House. We said a few words to each other. I'm fine."

I shrugged and looked down at our joined hands, so similar in size and shape.

"Of course you are." Pride filled her voice as she gripped my fingers. "You're a strong woman, and you don't need him or anyone."

You know those moms who are always asking you when you're going to settle down and get married and give them some grandchildren? Yeah—that wasn't my mom. In fact, she'd probably be thrilled if I never married at all. I knew she wished she never had.

"You're going to make it on your own doing exactly what you want to do when you want to do it the way you want to do it," she said. "And you'll have a man in your life only when and if it *amuses* you."

I had to laugh at the way she drew out the word "amuses," a reference to all the over-the-top villains from the old James Bond movies we'd always loved to watch together.

Remembering better times, I gave a mwah-ha-ha Dr. Evil laugh, and Mom joined in with one of her own.

"Let's check the streaming services and see if anyone has a Bond marathon on tonight," she suggested, her eyes filling with a spark I rarely saw these days. "It's not like we're going to get any sleep with the tequila wonder twins upstairs."

"Good idea. I'll go do a search," I said, banishing for the moment all thoughts of the boy I'd left behind.

EIGHT
Assignment

Mara

My alarm went off way too early the next morning.

I'd been hoping for an easy day—maybe a couple of press conferences or an in-house research day for my upcoming sweeps story.

But my news director Rob called me into his office, and what happened next was literally the last thing I would have ever predicted. I worked hard to keep my jaw from hitting the floor.

"Reid Mancini?" I repeated.

"Yes. Can you believe it? He actually *wants* to do an interview."

Rob's face glowed with fevered excitement and the anticipation of extra-planetary November ratings.

"He's offered to talk about his company and his private life. We can turn it into a weeklong series for sweeps. Every affiliate in the country's going to want this."

Rob jumped to his feet as the realization hit him. "The *network* will probably want it."

My pulse screamed through my veins as I struggled to

wrap my mind around what I'd just heard. "So, he actually called here and volunteered to do the interview with us."

"Well, his assistant made the call. And not with *us*, with *you*. He was very specific about that."

I relaxed marginally. "We probably got punked. You said the assistant was male?" I closed my eyes and gritted my teeth, thinking of my prank-loving photographer friend. Sheldon had to be behind this.

"Did someone verify this with Mancini's office?"

"Of course. The assignment desk called there immediately." Rob took his seat again. "I know—it's hard to believe—but the first-ever interview with the mysterious founder of StillYours.com is going to air on *our station*."

He looked like he might pass out or at least start salivating all over his desk. "Here's the number. You'll need to call and set up a time. I want you to start on this right away. We've only got two weeks till ratings start. I have to talk to promotions. I want to start airing promos."

His words came out at machine gun speed as his frenzied brain planned for the ultimate sweeps story.

"But..." And now the panic started to set in. "But what about my report on modern day mobsters in Rhode Island? I've already set up the interviews. We've already pulled file tape."

"I know," Rob responded in a distracted tone, already picking up his phone to call Sue in promotions, no doubt. "That doesn't matter anymore. I'll give it to... I don't know... Aaron can do it."

"Aaron?" I nearly shrieked. "He can't do it. You saw his report on the measles outbreak."

Aaron Bryson was our main anchor. While a likable, handsome guy who gave good TV, he wasn't exactly brilliant, and certainly not capable of doing a good job with the investigative story I'd enterprised and had already started researching for sweeps.

It's not that I disliked Aaron. In fact, I'd considered him as a candidate for the role of Mara's new himbo. He fit my requirements exactly—attractive, not-too-bright, and *not* looking to settle down.

But he was more suited to the weekly Adopt-A-Stray segment and stories on Tony the Dancing Cop than real journalism. In fact...

"Why can't Aaron do the piece on Mancini? He'd be perfect. And it would be a great high-profile series for him as main anchor," I said.

Rob frowned at me. "Mara. This isn't up for negotiation. Mancini's assistant was very clear. He wants *you*."

I shivered. Why was the station wasting money on air-conditioning in October?

"But—"

"I'm surprised you're not jumping at this," Rob continued. "You told me you want to work at the network level someday. This is the kind of story that will get your name on the radar. In any case—we're not missing out on this because you'd rather do a report on some tired old Mafioso."

He waved a dismissive hand and looked down, punching numbers into his desk phone. Conversation over.

I went to my desk in the newsroom, silently fuming at Rob's remark about my planned sweeps piece and growing warmer by the second. Couldn't they turn on any air-conditioning in this place? It was only October, for God's sake.

I stared at the number in my hands. Mancini Enterprises. I pictured calling Reid's office, asking for his assistant, arranging a date and time to meet with him and get the behind-the-curtain view of the empire he'd built since I'd cut off all communications with him eleven years ago.

Of the life he'd built without me.

My desk phone rang, and I picked it up without thinking, without checking the caller-ID first.

"Mara Neely, Action News Three."

"Mara? Mara, honey, it's Dad. I'm so glad I finally caught you."

My eyelids squeezed together, my face contracting in a grimace. "Hi," I managed to get the word out.

"Hi. It's so good to hear your voice. I wondered if I'd ever get through to you. I've left messages at the house, and I don't have your cell num—"

"What do you want, Dad? This is not a great time to talk."

"Oh, I know you're busy. I don't want to keep you. I can't tell you how proud I am to turn on my TV at night and see you—it's been so long."

"Did you need something?" I asked, fighting to keep the acid out of my voice. The newsroom was open, our desks divided only by low partitions. There was no such thing as a private conversation here.

"The station's not going to give you favorable coverage just because I work here, you know."

"That's not why I called." Dad had the nerve to sound offended. Exasperation filled his voice. "I'm calling because I need to see my little girl. In person."

"I'm really swamped with work. I just got this huge assignment dumped in my lap," I said, which was true if not the real reason for my avoidance. "After work I'm really busy at home with Bax and Bowie."

He chuckled. "I know they're a handful, but boys will be boys. They'll be okay. How's your mom?"

"She's fine," I lied through a clenched jaw.

"I've tried calling her, but she won't talk to me," Dad said. "That's one of the things I wanted to discuss with you, besides just catching up. I think she's going through a menopause thing... or a mid-life crisis. I mean, that long-haired bozo she's hooked up with..."

"Stop. Just stop right there."

I rubbed a hand over the front of my shirt, trying to alleviate the sudden tightness in my chest.

"Mom would murder you if she could hear you blaming your separation on her *hormones*. And she'll kill *me* if I talk to you about her personal life. Mine is none of your business either. You've meddled quite enough for one lifetime."

"Mara. I'm sorry. I don't know how else to say it. I'm sorry you were hurt. I didn't realize you were that attached to the kid—I thought you'd get over him and move on. I only did what I thought was best for you, to protect you."

"No, you did what you thought was best for *you*. What you wanted to protect was your political career. You wanted to be Governor, and you didn't think you could get there as the Attorney General whose daughter was dating the son of a mobster."

My father's silence told me I'd hit the nail squarely on the head. When he finally responded, he didn't deny it, but he did sidestep my accusation.

"The guy wasn't worthy of you," he explained. "He still isn't, no matter how much 'new money' he has. There are rumors he got the seed money to start his company from his father. I hope you're not planning to take up with him again. I can still make his life a living hell, you know. It would be a shame if his business permits got pulled while there was an investigation into—"

I hung up without waiting to hear the rest of the threat. In fact I didn't want to hear *anything* that man had to say. It was a shame to flush a lifelong relationship, but he'd given me no choice.

Even after all these years, it made me sad. I mean, before he'd threatened the love of my life and destroyed mine in the process, there *had* been some good times. Family vacations, doing puzzles together in front of the fireplace in winter, fishing off the pier behind our house.

He hadn't always been a manipulative bastard.

That almost made it worse. If he'd been some kind of monster my whole life, there'd be nothing to miss. And I *did* miss having a father.

I dropped my head and rubbed my left temple where a sharp ache was beginning. The lack of sleep, the surprise assignment switcheroo from Rob, and then my dad's call—could this day get any worse?

A pair of long, thick legs and huge boots came into my view. I glanced up to see Sheldon's sneaky grin.

"So, I hear we'll be spending some quality time with your boyfriend."

"You do realize your testicles are exactly at left hook level, don't you?" I snarled up at him.

Sheldon skipped to the side with a high laugh. "Look out, mini-Mara's on the warpath. Hey, when you're done threatening my man-parts, we've got to get over to the Superman building downtown. Some developer wants to turn it into condos."

"Okay. Let me grab my notes and I'll meet you in the parking lot."

* * *

After work I went home and had dinner with Bax and Bowie, who'd somehow managed to get to school this morning and make it through the day.

At least I assumed they had—I hadn't gotten a call saying they were AWOL.

Cheryl had left a pan of eggplant parmesan and some homemade garlic bread in the oven's warming drawer and a fantastic mixed green salad in the refrigerator. The boys wolfed the meal down, answering my questions between mouthfuls.

"How are your college applications coming along?"

Knowing I wanted to attend an Ivy since the ninth grade, I'd sent in my application on the first day they'd opened to them. My brothers weren't quite as certain about—or as interested in—their college plans.

"Good," Bowie said. "I'm planning to go to RISD and major in finger painting."

I doubted the Rhode Island School of Design offered that particular major—it was one of the top art and design schools in the nation. Nevertheless, if Bowie was serious about wanting to pursue art, I was all for it.

"I see. And do you have an art portfolio to submit?"

He gave me a wide grin, lifted the paper napkin from his lap, and used it to wipe some red sauce from his lips. Holding the smeared napkin out dramatically, he said, "Ta da. My portfolio. Modern art."

I gave him a tolerant smirk. "Glad to see you're taking your future so seriously. How about you, Baxter?"

He managed to stop laughing at his twin's antics long enough to give me a dopey look and a, "Dunno. I guess I'll go wherever Dad pays somebody off."

"That will *not* be happening," I assured him. "Have you applied anywhere at all yet?"

His laughter died off and morphed into a scowl. "College is stupid. I'd make a better living as a plumber."

"Then apply to be an apprentice with a plumber. I'd like to see you fill out a few college applications as well so you'll have some options. Both of you are very smart, and you can be successful at whatever you decide to do. But you do have to decide. No one's going to do it for you."

"Mom and Dad don't care what we do," Bax informed me.

"Why would you say that?" I asked.

Bowie answered for him. "Because it's true. All mom cares about is shopping and going out with her disco dancer-cise friends, and Dad's too busy shaking hands and kissing babies to even talk to us."

Our father was running for re-election. A lifelong politician, he considered a second-term as Governor his crowning achievement. We'd been dragged along to public appearances and campaign events our whole lives as he worked his way up the political food chain, but this time, he was doing it alone.

The most recent polls showed him basically even with his opponent, which no doubt had him worried.

"When the election is over he'll be around more," I assured my brothers.

"I don't care," Bowie said.

"Me either," Baxter agreed. "Mom was right. He's a DINO."

"What's a dino? Dinosaur?"

"Dad in name only," Bowie clarified.

After dinner, I went to my room to make a phone call. Obviously, I couldn't talk to my little brothers about the Reid situation—or anything serious. They had enough on their plates.

I definitely couldn't discuss Reid with my mother—or his mom, Cheryl, as nice as she was—for obvious reasons.

Sadly, my prolonged absence after graduation had distanced me from my high school girlfriends. We'd done the so-excited-you're-back-in-town lunches over the past month, but we weren't on heart-to-heart level anymore.

I needed to talk to Heidi.

Heidi Haynes, Kenley Carpenter, and I had worked together in a tiny market in Georgia where we'd each taken our first reporting jobs after college. Though we were from vastly different hometowns and backgrounds, our shared career dreams and small-market-TV-poverty had bonded us closely.

We'd supported each other through a lot. We understood each other.

And Heidi would understand what I was dealing with now. She'd had her own disastrous first love.

Not that my relationship with Reid had been disastrous—it was more the *aftermath* that had required a hazmat team.

Now that Heidi had found her forever-guy she might not be able to commiserate as much, but I knew she'd really listen.

"Oh Mare, I'm so glad to hear from you," she enthused over the phone. "How's Providence? How's your mob story coming? I got your email about it—sounds so cool. We don't have anything like that in Nashville."

Heidi had left Georgia shortly before I did, finally breaking away from her Blackhawk-chopper-helicopter parents and overcoming a rather unfortunate nervous stomach issue to land her dream job anchoring news in the country music capital.

"My mob story sleeps with the fishes, I'm afraid," I told her, still feeling sour over it.

"Oh no. What happened? Your sources fall through?"

"No. Reid happened."

"Reid? Your old boyfriend, Reid? Oh my God. Do tell," she prodded in that sugar-sweet Southern accent that leaked out whenever she wasn't on-air.

I explained the baffling developments—that I'd run into him at a pizza place, that his assistant had called offering an interview today, and that my boss was forcing me to do the story because an interview with Reid was the "get" of the decade.

"Wait a minute—your Reid is Reid *Mancini*?" She gasped. "And you never told me this? How did it not come up that your ex was one of the world's wealthiest and most famous men? Not to mention super-hot."

"There was no point in discussing it. He was out of my life."

"And now he's back in it," she said.

"Temporarily."

"Sounds like he wants to make it longer."

"What do you mean?" I asked.

"Isn't it obvious? He sees you, sparks fly, angels' voices sing. He's *got* to see you again, so he arranges it so you can't say 'no.'"

"Um, I'm pretty sure that's not it. I did explain to you what I did to him, right?" I hadn't given Heidi *all* the details, but she had enough information to understand that I'd perpetrated the world's most thorough case of ghosting.

"Yes, but it's been eleven years. You were both young and immature, and he wants to see if the old feelings are still there now that you've both grown up."

The suggestion produced an explosion of nerves sizzling all over my body.

"Well, the feelings are definitely *not* still there. And I'm sure that goes double for him," I said. "If anything, he wants to punish me by shoving all his achievements and money under my nose, to make sure I see what a 'big mistake' it was to dump him. You should have seen how hostile he was—he made a point of saying he'd never loved me."

Heidi laughed. "Don't you see? That *proves* he still has feelings for you. Why else would he be sure to get that little tidbit into what—a five-minute conversation? I guarantee you the boy's still got it bad."

"If that's even partially true, there's *more* reason for me not to do the story. I'll just tell Rob tomorrow that I can't do it. He'll have to get someone else."

"I think you should take the assignment, Mara."

Heidi's tone was gentle but firm.

"Remember that little speech you gave me when I was

refusing to give Aric a chance, or even work with him? You told me what I needed to hear, even though I didn't want to at the time. Now I'm telling you—you've got to stop running from your past. Face your fears. Stop pretending you don't have feelings, especially when it comes to guys."

"I have feelings when it comes to guys," I argued.

"Not *that* kind of feelings."

Heidi knew my M.O. when it came to dating, specifically that I only dated guys who had no boyfriend potential whatsoever.

"Speaking of—have you hooked up with any new himbos lately?" she asked.

"Not really, but the hunting grounds are bountiful here —plenty of club clowns and gym gigolos. I just haven't had a lot of opportunity. I stay home most nights with my brothers."

Heidi's tone turned sympathetic. "How're they doing?"

"Well, let's see... Bax is in severe danger of flunking not one, not two, but three of his classes. And Bowie just crashed his second BMW. He's sixteen."

"Oh boy. My three brothers are a mess, but that *really* sounds like you have your hands full. Hang in there."

"I'm trying to. You know what? Let's change the subject. Have you talked to Kenley lately?"

Our friend and fellow reporter had surprised us both by giving up her TV career to move back home to Atlanta. Her long-time boyfriend Mark had gotten sick of the long-distance romance thing and given her an ultimatum. We would be attending their lavish wedding in a month.

"Not for a couple of weeks." Heidi said. "I just assumed Mark probably wouldn't let her out of bed long enough to get the phone. Why? You sound worried."

"Kind of. It's just, she never calls, and when I call her, it's all small talk. You know how she is—when something's wrong she goes all incommunicado. She's chatty when things are good."

"That's true," Heidi said. "I'll try to call her again. I'm sure it's fine, though."

"Yeah, you're probably right—when you and Aric get married, I'm sure we'll never hear from you again—you'll be lost in your vortex of love."

Heidi giggled and denied it, and I hoped it wouldn't be true. I suddenly missed her and Kenley fiercely. "Well, I'd better go. I'm sure the twin grizzly bears are ready for their next feeding. Thanks for letting me whine."

"You're not whining. I understand, and you know I do. It's really hard to take a risk when your heart's been broken."

"Reid didn't break my heart," I insisted, troubled that it was so important to me to make the distinction. "I broke his."

"I meant your dad," Heidi said.

My lungs constricted. I literally couldn't think of anything to say. I was kind of sorry at the moment that I'd told her about what my father had done.

At my lack of response Heidi added, "I really think you should do the story. At the very least, you could wind up seeing your work on the network news. Any of us would kill for that."

"True."

Heidi was right—I'd always dreamed of a career-making story like this one. But could I handle it?

Could I go for what I'd always wanted professionally if it meant spending time with the only *guy* I'd ever wanted?

"I'm just not sure. I'm ninety-nine percent sure when I go in tomorrow, I'm going to tell my boss, 'no.'"

"Well, do what you think is right," Heidi said. "You have good instincts. If you feel *that* sure about it, then that's probably what you should do. What's he gonna do? Fire you?"

NINE
Old Pictures

Mara

"I'll have to fire you."

Rob sat behind his desk the next morning, wearing a warning on his face though I could tell he didn't like what he was saying.

"You just hired me," I protested. "And I do good work."

This was *not* how I'd anticipated the conversation going.

I had come in and rationally explained that I didn't feel I was the best person to cover this particular story, assuring Rob the station and our viewers would be better served if he gave it to a different reporter.

"Well, of course I don't *want* to let you go, Mara," he said. "You know we love you—you're a great reporter and usually very tenacious. And you have local knowledge. But this is the story of the decade. We can't risk him going to one of the other stations. Would you like to explain to me what's really going on between you and Mancini?"

My heart jumped up my throat, attempting to merge with my molars. "What do you mean?"

"I talked to Sheldon. He told me you two ran into the guy this week. Sheldon said you knew him already."

I stiffened in my chair, gripping the upholstered armrests the way I wanted to grab Sheldon's throat.

Traitor.

"Now don't go getting all bent at him," Rob said, taking in my expression. "I was digging. I used to be an investigative reporter myself, you know."

It was confession time. No other way around it.

"Okay then... Reid and I were in—volved. We were involved. We had a relationship. So, you see the problem."

"What problem?" Rob gave me a pleasant smile, tenting his fingers in front of his chin, leaning back in his desk chair.

I blinked. "Obviously there's a conflict of interest if I do the interview."

The pleasant smile teamed up with a matter-of-fact tone of voice. "There's no conflict. There are no allegations of wrongdoing that need investigating. This is a feature, a profile. Do a puff piece. I don't care."

Now Rob leaned forward over his desk. "Just get him on camera and on our air for November sweeps. Before he decides to take his offer to another station."

I stared at him, shocked to see the desperation so plain in his eyes.

When I didn't respond, Rob's shoulders fell. He looked at the top of his desk then raised his gaze to me with a weary expression.

"Mara, I've already told the GM about it—he won't *let* me keep you on if we lose this interview. It'll look terrible on your resume to move on from a new job after only a month. You don't want that. I'm asking again as your boss and as your friend, who would like very much to keep *his* job, please reconsider. My family enjoys living indoors and having food and clothing. Please?"

I stared at the family photos and the crystal Associated Press news award on Rob's desk, turning the situation over in my mind. I didn't want to endanger his job, and of course I didn't want to lose mine over this.

The boys needed me close by, and in her own weird way, I thought Mom did too. And it wasn't fair to Rob and the rest of my co-workers for me to blow off an assignment that could benefit all of us.

Ratings determined how much money a station could charge advertisers. This story practically guaranteed blockbuster ratings—it could make our year financially. I had to suck it up and get it over with.

"I'll do it," I muttered, sounding like one of my little brothers after being ordered to take out the trash. "I'll call today."

Rob's ready smile popped back into place. "That's my girl. There's the future star I hired."

I didn't return my boss's smile. Instead I stood up and walked out of his office like a condemned prisoner going to the gas chamber.

* * *

I didn't call that day.

I meant to. I did. But I managed to stay "busy" all morning and afternoon. And every time I did pick up the phone and look at that number, I was suddenly covered in a vicious swarm of mutant attack-butterflies and had to put it down again.

At home that night I went to the bookshelf lining one wall of my room, glancing over all of my favorite books from middle school and high school and next to them, my old yearbooks from Eastport Bay High.

Pulling one out, I cracked open its cover for the first time since graduating.

Senior year. We'd been featured prominently in this one, Reid and I. We'd both been athletes, and I'd always been the outgoing type, so I was involved in all the student leadership activities.

Reid had been quieter but well-liked, and of course, he'd been in the tech clubs all four years. The fact that we'd been best friends and always together meant we were pictured together on several pages.

We'd even been voted "Cutest Couple" in the Senior Superlatives section.

That was where I turned first. The attack-butterflies made another pass, but I swatted them away and forced myself to look at it. I needed to do this.

If I couldn't manage to face him in old photographs, how would I ever do it in person?

Our faces, so much younger-looking, even just a decade ago, were pressed cheek-to-cheek in the full-page photo. I recognized the emotion sparkling in my own young eyes. I was in love, blissfully planning a future with the sweet-faced boy holding me close.

My gaze shifted to Reid's image, and a familiar pang hit my heart. He looked happy, carefree, confident—and he *had* been so sure of his future and of us. I studied his eyes, a shade of blue so unforgettable I'd never seen it repeated in another human being.

I hated the realization that I'd examined every pair of blue eyes I'd encountered since then searching for it.

Lower down in the photo, a trail of black marker stretched from my chest to his. A heart had been drawn on each end of the line. Reid had done that when I'd given him my yearbook to sign (I'd reserved an entire page in the back just for him).

I'd freaked out at first when I'd seen his marker drawing on the fresh clean page of my new book, but then he filled in the hollow hearts right in front of me.

In the one on my chest he wrote "Reid," and in the one over his own chest, he wrote "Mara, forever and always."

He'd done the same artwork in his own yearbook. I'd stopped freaking out then and given him a very long, very serious kiss.

Slowly, I flipped to the back pages of the yearbook, my heart picking up beats as if I were out for a run instead of curled up on my bed. And there in his small block-lettered print were the words I'd never quite been able to erase from my memory—or my heart.

Reid had filled every inch of that page, telling me everything he loved about me, my brown eyes, my soft hair, my voice, holding my hand, the special looks I gave him and only him. He listed some of the myriad things we'd shared together over the years, first kiss, first dance.

Of course, he hadn't mentioned the most significant "first" we'd shared—on graduation night—our yearbooks had been handed out weeks before that life-changing event would occur.

He'd ended this high school love letter by summing it up in three words, "I love you," and then added two more above his signature, "Always yours."

I slammed the book shut and held it to my chest, dropping my head as the tears started. God, how could it still hurt so much?

I wouldn't be able to do it. I couldn't walk into Reid's office, sit down across from him under the lights and camera and pretend that none of it had happened. I'd have to just polish up the resume reel and start searching for job openings.

Maybe the boys could come with me and start fresh at a new school in a new town.

After I recovered from my crying jag, I wandered downstairs. I should really have been down there with them anyway instead of holed up in my room, wallowing in the misery of my past.

No one was in the living room or in the kitchen, so I went back upstairs. In a miraculous turn of events, they were each in their own rooms, studying or appearing to, anyway.

I headed back toward my own room but stopped in the hallway outside the open door to my parents'—strike that—to *Mom's* bedroom. The light was on, and she was inside, sitting up in her bed.

Was she sick? Most nights she was out at this time with Ricardo.

"Mom?" I peeked inside.

"Come in, sweetheart."

Oh boy. Her voice sounded weepy. Were she and the Disco Queen on the outs?

I pushed the door open and stepped inside. "Whatcha doing? Hey—you okay?"

My mother was surrounded by photographs of our family. Of her and Dad. The images were spread across the fluffy white comforter, and tears streamed down her face.

The irony wasn't lost on me.

Sniffing a humorless laugh, I went to sit next to her and wrapped an arm around her silk-pajama-clad shoulders.

She leaned her head on my shoulder. "I was just remembering... how perfect things used to be."

"Were they?" I asked in all sincerity. "I mean, is any marriage perfect?"

My parents had never seemed all that happy to me, but then, I was a kid, and frankly my dad hadn't been around that much when I was awake. There could have been good aspects of the relationship I wasn't privy to.

"Well, of course not 'perfect,' but it was very, very good... once. It really was. Look at him—your dad was a good man in those early days. So kind, so much fun to be with. I'll never understand what happened, whether it was the stress of the job... or all the political power."

Mom wiped her wet face with one hand and picked up another photograph with the other. It was of the three of us at Six Flags before the boys had been born, sunburned, beaming, and looking exactly like the happy family I'd believed us to be.

"That's why you shouldn't count on anyone," she said, shaking her head at the image. "They can change on you overnight and become a completely different person."

Like Reid had. The man I'd seen at the pizza place had *looked* like my first love, but he acted nothing like the sweet boy who'd stolen my heart.

"Are you saying you don't think people should ever get married?" I asked.

"Oh, you can get married if you want to—just make sure you don't love him," she answered matter-of-factly. "Or at least make sure he loves you more. Never let a man have too much power over you."

I watched her pull another photo out of the box.

"That's why I like Ricardo. He's fun. He's uncomplicated. Brianna was right all those years ago."

"But..." I started to argue but then realized I didn't have a leg to stand on.

I had actually followed that same advice my mom's old friend had dispensed that long-ago day on the front porch. Unable to have the one guy I really wanted, I'd dated only the least complicated of men, the just-for-fun guys. Those I knew were no threat to my heart.

At the moment I couldn't stop thinking of the one guy who was.

"Mom... do you ever think you and Dad could get back to that place? Like in the early days? I've heard he's not seeing anyone."

She laughed out loud. "He keeps asking for another chance, but I really don't see the point. He wouldn't even go to counseling since he was so *famous*, and Rhode Island is so small. He didn't want it getting out that our marriage might be in trouble—wouldn't 'play well' with the voters, you know. Did I ever tell you he pressured me to take fertility drugs before I got pregnant with the boys? 'Voters love cute little kids,' he said. Apparently, more than one polls better than a single child."

Her eyes rolled heavenward. "I was so busy doing what I was 'supposed' to do, I forgot to live *my* life. You have *no* idea what all I put up with over the years."

"I have some idea," I muttered then added, "He thinks you're having a mid-life crisis, by the way."

"I'm having mid-life *fun*, and believe me, I deserve it. I was the 'perfect' wife and mother on and off camera for thirty years. I was an 'asset' to his political career. Unfortunately, that was *all* I was to him."

"I don't think that's true. I think he loved you in his own, admittedly flawed, way. I think he still does."

"How do you know what he thinks, by the way?" she asked, suddenly suspicious. "I thought you two weren't in communication."

"He called me at work, and I picked up without realizing it was him."

I paused a long time before adding, "He sounded really defeated. And sad. He seemed very concerned about you."

Mom's face hardened as she scooped up the pictures and dumped them back into the plastic bin. "Well, he should have thought about *that* when he was acting like a horse's ass all those years. I should throw these all away."

She gave me the box. "Here—sort through and take out the ones you want to keep. I'm going to get rid of the rest."

"Um... okay." I took the box and slid off her bed. "You want to watch something? Or talk?"

"No." She pulled back the comforter and got underneath. "I'm exhausted. I'll see you tomorrow."

Turning over, she switched off the lamp on her bedside table.

"Good night." I stepped into the hallway and closed her bedroom door but didn't go to my own room right away.

I stood in the hall, wanting to go back in to her, wanting to tell her it wasn't right to throw away your entire past, a lifetime of good memories because of a few bad ones. Even if they *were* really bad.

And then I heard the crying. It started low and escalated to muffled wails that ripped at my heart like exposed carpet tacks on bare feet.

And I was angry at Dad all over again. He still had so much power in her life. He hadn't set foot in this house for months, yet he was here, hurting my mother still.

A charred ugliness sparked to new life and smoldered in the center of my chest. She was right. No one would *ever* have that kind of power over me.

And that's when I decided to do the interview with Reid.

In fact, I *wanted* to do it—like I'd never wanted anything in my life. I would not let him determine whether I kept my job or not. He couldn't run me out of my hometown or my home state.

And he couldn't make me feel anything I didn't *allow* myself to feel.

I was a grown-up now. I was a professional, a strong, independent woman. And I was going to give Mr. Reid Mancini, billionaire web entrepreneur, his money's worth.

He wanted an interview?

He would get one.

TEN

Interview with the Devil

Mara

Reid's company headquarters were located in downtown Providence in what had once been the city's original train station.

He'd renovated the aging building, turning it into a workspace that was ultra-modern inside but on the outside still fit with the city's Colonial-era architecture and classic New England vibe.

A jeans-and-t-shirt-clad assistant approached us in the lobby. "Hi. I'm Lee. Welcome. Would you follow me please?"

Lee led us from the front entrance through several fascinating common areas before taking us to a conference room on the fifth floor.

His flip flops cast a soft echo through the carpeted hallway as Sheldon and I followed. He seemed like a nice guy—young, smart-looking, thin in that long-distance-runner way.

I'd expected to be greeted by a beautifully styled receptionist, maybe a cool blonde like you see at big corporations in the movies. But then, that didn't really fit the tech industry vibe, did it?

It certainly wouldn't have fit the Reid I'd known years ago.

The only occasions I'd ever seen him wear a suit, prior to a few days ago at the State House, were his grandmother's funeral and prom, where he'd worn a tux with a red bow tie and cummerbund to match my dress—

"He's on a call. He'll join you in about ten minutes, okay?" Lee gave us a smile and disappeared again, leaving the conference room door open.

Sheldon whistled. "Can you believe this place? Did you see that employee workout room? I wish Mancini would buy our station. I wouldn't mind having an in-house cereal bar and a 'nap room.' And I heard there's a basketball court here somewhere for pick-up games. I want a look at that before we leave."

Sheldon's nose was practically pressed to the glass wall as he took in the state-of-the-art computers and high-definition, flat screen monitors scattered throughout the work area.

"Down boy. Try not to have a man-cave-gasm while we're here." I hoped my flip remark covered my instantaneous horror at the idea of Reid ever becoming my boss.

"Seriously, though. This guy's my hero. He has got some *sweeeet* toys," Sheldon said.

"Well, start your own successful tech company, and you can have it all, too," I teased. "Anyway, let's get set up. I don't want any lag time when Reid arrives. I *really* don't want to have to make small talk with him again."

"Right. I get it," Sheldon said, moving to one of his light cases to extract a stand and filter. "Keep the opportunity for flirtatious banter to a minimum."

I whirled on him. "There will *be no* flirtatious banter. And, by the way, I don't appreciate you outing me to Rob."

Sheldon shrugged. "Sorry, dude. He did his Jedi mind trick on me. I didn't mean to tell him anything, but he started probing, and I don't know what happened. I wandered out of his office with no memory of the previous three days."

I had to laugh. It was hard to stay mad at Sheldon.

"I know. Rob's like that. Well, you can redeem yourself by getting us in and out of here as quickly as possible. After we do the interview, I'm going to just leave and let you get all the b-roll we need, okay?"

Sheldon set the tripod up at one end of the conference table and attached his camera to the top while I paced the room. He glanced over his shoulder at me.

"Wow. It's worse than I thought."

"What?" I stopped, clenching my cold hands together in front of me.

"You are runnin' scared, baby. You were chomping at the bit to get at those mobsters, but look at you—you're terrified of this computer nerd. I don't care what Mancini said the other day... it's obvious you guys were *way* more than teenage fuck-buddies."

Sheldon's last two words still hung in the air as we both turned to see Reid standing in the doorway.

He'd frozen in place, an odd look passing over his face. It was gone so quickly, I wondered whether he'd even heard the mortifying phrase uttered by my soon-to-be-dead favorite photog.

Please, no.

Reid pasted on a cool business-smile and stepped into the room, hand outstretched toward Sheldon.

"No—that sounds about right."

Great. He'd heard it. Loud and clear.

Reid looked over at me. "Right, Mara?"

Heat exploded through my body, reassembling in my face. No amount of foundation could hide it, and I saw in Reid's astute gaze that he'd noticed.

"It's nice that we can be so out in the open about our past

relationship," he continued, his smile adopting a cruel twist. "And it sounds like you've filled in Sheldon here on the full *extent* of it."

He sat in the large leather chair at the end of the conference table, reaching for the lavalier mic in front of him as if he did TV interviews every day.

Having absolutely no good response to offer, I stayed silent and took the chair nearest him, turning my body toward him so that when Sheldon filmed over my shoulder, Reid would be facing the camera.

He was free of expression as he sat only a couple of feet away, but as he clipped the lav onto the front of his shirt, I noticed a slight tremor in his fingers. Well, it *was* his first television interview.

In spite of my annoyance with him and the whole scenario, something inside me softened slightly. I was used to coaxing nervous people through interviews. I always felt so bad when their voices would quaver or they'd break into a forehead sweat under the lights.

Reid wasn't sweating, but he had left the mic cord running sloppily down the front of the light-blue button-down shirt he'd worn with his jeans.

That wouldn't do. Rob would kill me if I conducted this once-in-a-lifetime interview with that distracting black cord so obvious.

I cleared my throat, which had drawn tight the minute Reid entered the room. "Um, if you wouldn't mind, could you just tuck that cord in..."

I motioned to his buttons. Usually I helped people do this sort of thing. "Um, right there... behind your shirt, so it doesn't show."

He looked down at his chest. "Oh, yeah. Sure."

Fumbling with the cord, he tried to figure out how to arrange it so it was out of sight.

A few more seconds of this, and I turned back to Sheldon, pointing to him then to Reid, silently begging him to do it.

Sheldon shook his head and pointed right back at me, mouthing, “No way.”

I turned back to Reid. He’d managed to get part of the mic cord hidden, but more of it was out than in. I had no choice.

“Here—I’ll help you.”

Rising from my seat, I leaned over the corner of the table toward him.

Now my fingers shook as I undid his top button and tucked the cord behind it, trying desperately to ignore the close proximity of our faces and the heat coming off of his skin.

And he smelled amazing.

Much to my dismay, I recognized the cologne he’d worn in high school, a delicious citrusy scent that had always produced a Pavlovian sexual response in me. On the few occasions I’d crossed paths with a guy wearing it since then, I’d practically run in the opposite direction.

I fastened Reid’s top button and moved down to the next, slipping it out of its slot and pushing the cord behind the soft fabric. As I did so, the backs of my fingers accidentally brushed his chest. I went still at his audible intake of breath.

I wasn’t breathing all that steadily now myself.

“Almost done,” I gasped, snapping back into action, moving down to the next button, my trembling growing more pronounced.

“No hurry,” he murmured, followed by a soft laugh.

Determined not to make eye contact with him at this close range, I kept my eyes trained on Reid’s shirtfront. I had to stay in control of the situation. The last thing I needed was to start remembering other times we’d been this close, the last time I’d undone his buttons.

Great.

Now my mind was flooding with images of the two of us together in various states of undress. My internal temperature rose until he could probably feel the radiant heat from my blushing face.

Finally, I had worked my way down as low on his shirt as I dared to venture. *Screw it.* Sheldon would just have to frame the shot tight—I was *not* going to tuck that mic cord into his pants. I pulled away.

"Thank you," Reid said in a low voice.

I did venture a glance at his face then, only to find his eyes were focused on my chest, so generously displayed for him at this angle. He brought his gaze back up to mine.

His eyes, that mesmerizing shade of blue-green, held a naughty gleam. Then I looked down at myself. Great day to have worn a wrap-dress.

I straightened and took my seat, drawing the neckline together belatedly. "You're welcome, Mr. Mancini."

Actually, I'd worn this dress for a reason. Figure-flattering and coral red, Kenley used to refer to it as my you-want-it-but-you-ain't-gettin-it dress. Delivered in her chewy Southern drawl, the phrase had always made me laugh.

Whether because of the strong color or the male attention it usually drew, I'd always felt powerful in this dress. Paired with high nude pumps, it seemed like the perfect outfit to get me through today.

Of course, I hadn't anticipated spending the first five minutes of our meeting with my chest in Reid's face.

I cleared my throat. "Are you ready?" I forced myself to meet his eyes again.

They were narrowed in amusement. His tone matched.

"Oh, I'm *ready*."

Would it be unprofessional to start the interview with a hard kick to the shins? What would a network pro do? I took a cleansing breath, let it out, and started to ask the first question.

Reid lifted a hand to stop me. "Before we begin, I should tell you there are a few subjects that are off-limits. First, I won't discuss—"

"No. No way. That's not how it works. You said you wanted to do an interview. That means I choose the questions, and you answer them."

He cracked a smile. "I see your fiery little temper hasn't changed over the years."

"Do you want to do this or not?"

Reid held my challenging gaze for long moments. Then he laughed, his voice dipping low, giving me goose bumps.

"Let's do it."

I shook off the disconcerting chill and disciplined my voice into its professional on-air demeanor.

"I'm sure our viewers would like to know, Mr. Mancini, why you've decided to do a televised interview now, after refusing them repeatedly since your social network launched."

Reid looked off to the side then smirked in a way that told me I'd just asked the first question on his no-no list.

"I guess the answer to that is I hate talking about myself. I'm a private person. And... I'm not sure why my life would really interest anyone."

I looked down at the notes I'd written based on my pre-interview research on his life the past few years. "You don't think people would be interested in your yacht, your mansion on Oceanview Avenue in Eastport Bay, your vintage Porsche collection?"

His dark eyebrows dropped, and the corners of his mouth turned down. "I've always thought it was rather rude to discuss how much you have. There's always someone with less, there's always someone with more."

"True. But not too many have more than you," I countered. "Of course, you'd have even more wealth if you didn't give so much away. According to my research, you donated more to charity last year than both Warren Buffet and Michael Bloomberg."

Reid shifted in his chair, his pointer finger tapping the glass top of the conference table. "I don't really want to talk about that."

His eyes flicked up to me and back down to his hand.

"Okay..." I dove for my notes.

Usually I was a perfectly adequate interviewer, but the awkward in the room was thick enough to slice and dip in olive oil. I had to put our personal history and that little mic-cord-intoxicating-cologne-fiasco aside and do this thing.

"Let's talk about StillYours-dot-com," I pivoted. "You started working on it your freshman year of college, launched it as a sophomore, then dropped out of U-R-I to run the company when its popularity exploded. You've created several other successful tech-related businesses since then. But StillYours.com is the largest. It's now replaced Facebook as the world's most-used social media site. What was the inspiration behind it?"

The Million Dollar Question. The answer the viewers would most want to know, the one I most wanted to know.

"How does someone so young decide to build an empire around reuniting lost loves?" I asked.

Now Reid looked truly uncomfortable. He turned his neck as if trying to work out a kink, his expression contracting into an unwilling scowl.

When he finally did speak, his voice was tight.

"I never talk about that." His color deepened noticeably.

"Why not?" I asked. This was getting ridiculous.

Reid's eyes pinned me with a hot blue glare. "Because no one would like the answer. The truth would be bad for business."

"How bad could it be? It's not like you stole the idea or something... is it?"

And now the hot glare was in full flame.

"Of course I didn't steal it," he snapped, his public reserve completely cracked. "I tapped into an unmet need. I figured out what people wanted, and I gave it to them. I preyed on all the sentimental suckers who believe in love and buy that whole idiotic meant-to-be shit."

Reid grabbed his microphone and stood up in one swift move, ripping the cord out of his shirt, sending buttons bouncing to the floor and across the long tabletop. He let it drop from his hand and pointed at Sheldon.

"If you air that—I swear on everything I own I'll sue your station until it can't afford to turn on a light bulb. Then I'll sue each of you personally."

His shaking hand moved to point at me, his voice dropping to an ominous whisper. "I. Will. Own. You."

Then he strode out of the room without another word. Sheldon and I looked at each other in stunned silence.

Shel blew out a long breath. "That is one cynical dude."

He removed the camera from the tripod and crossed the room toward his bag. "Well, it was nice working with you."

"What do you mean?" I folded the heavy black tripod.

Sheldon reached for it and lifted it from my hands. "I mean—Rob's gonna have a shit-fit. You're the first reporter Mancini's ever sat down with for an interview, and you pissed him off in under a minute."

"Me? I didn't say anything. You saw—he just blew up for no reason."

Sheldon dropped his chin and lifted his eyebrows. "Maybe it wasn't what you said. Maybe it was that whole heavy-breathing, eye-humping thing you two were doing beforehand."

"What?" I shrieked.

Yanking the power cord from one of the stand lights out

of the wall, I marched across the room to unplug the other one.

"This is all on him. I just asked him regular questions. And I didn't do *anything* different miking him up than I do when I'm helping anyone else."

I stopped and breathed, one hand going to my forehead as I stared at the floor.

"Of course, Rob's never going to accept that. I guess I'll be putting together a new resume reel after all. Crap. I knew this was a terrible idea."

* * *

"Brilliant idea, Mara," Rob boomed as Sheldon and I walked into the newsroom.

We stopped and gave each other a quick side glance. Shel's expression was as baffled as mine must have been.

Rob, on the other hand, looked like a boy at a ninja motocross stunt show complete with pyrotechnics. And dancing girls in spandex.

"Um, which idea would that be?" I asked, wincing.

"Mancini's assistant just called. He said Mr. Mancini had felt a little stilted in the office setting and wanted to reschedule the interview?"

Stilted? If that had been stilted, I'd hate to see enraged.

"Um, yeah," I agreed, going with it. Anything was better than Rob knowing what had really happened and kicking me to the curb.

"And he told me about your idea to spend a day with Mancini first before filming, to let him acclimate to you. Then you'll be allowed to interview him and shoot video not only at his business, but at his estate, on his yacht—unprecedented access."

Rob was practically hopping in place. "Man, it makes me wish I was a reporter again. This is *Sixty Minutes, Dateline* territory here. I'd die for that kind of in-depth interview with someone like him."

I felt a little like dying myself. A whole day? Alone with Reid. Before we even got any video?

After the way things had gone this morning, what more could he possibly want with me?

And after the way things had ended between us eleven years ago, I couldn't think of anything I wanted to do less.

I closed my eyes for a second, then opened them and pasted on a smile for my boss.

"Great. I'm glad you're happy."

Because I'm about to spend a day in Hell.

ELEVEN

A Day in Hell

Mara

"Name please?"

"Mara Neely. With Action News."

"Yes, Miss Neely. He's expecting you." The guard at the gatehouse waved me through.

My dashboard clock read straight up noon on Saturday, as scheduled. I continued on the long winding drive from Oceanview Avenue to the massive stone-covered waterfront home Reid reportedly used only on weekends.

I'd heard he spent his weeknights in a high-rise condominium in downtown Providence, to be closer to work, though Eastport Bay was only a forty minute drive from the city.

Well, if you could afford two luxury residences in the same tiny state, why not?

I parked in the circular courtyard in front of the house and got out. It felt like a world away from Providence. It felt like home.

Seagulls squawked overhead. The light breeze smelled of fresh-cut grass and ocean air, my favorite scent. I got out of the car and walked toward the massive front door, my heels clicking on paver stones that had no doubt been imported from some ancient European city.

The house itself was beautiful—large but not obscenely so—holding true to that particular way the New England rich seemed to have of demonstrating their wealth with tasteful restraint.

I smiled bitterly to myself as I rang the doorbell. It seemed everything about Reid had become more restrained since I'd known him. There had been no trace of the cute, playful boy I'd known in that uptight, bitter-faced man I attempted to interview several days earlier.

I saw a figure approaching through the cut glass panel of the wooden door. A flurry of panic went through me. Reid and I hadn't been able to tolerate a few minutes in each other's presence either time I'd seen him recently. Why would today be any better?

It occurred to me that maybe he didn't want it to be better. Maybe he *wanted* to make things hard on me after the way I'd treated him.

Well, if he wanted to punish me for daring to show my face in Rhode Island again, he couldn't have come up with a better plan—force me to spend a day with him when my life's goal had been never to lay eyes on him again.

The door opened, and there he was—wearing jeans and a vintage Patriots t-shirt, running shoes... and a wide smile.

"Mara. Hi. Hi, thanks for coming. Come in. Please."

He stepped back and waited for me to enter the foyer. Its stone floors gleamed, the high walls accented by paintings and interesting art objects.

Clearly he'd hired a decorator. The Reid I'd known couldn't have cared less if he were surrounded by bare white walls or was living in a museum. But I loved every piece here, as much as if I'd selected them myself.

The house, the art—all of it was exactly what I would have chosen if I'd been the one to become a self-made-billionaire.

"Here, come this way. I thought you might like to have lunch first, before we tour the property and look at possible locations for filming."

Reid's voice was upbeat, carefully polite. Completely at odds with the tension so evident in his face and posture.

I nodded my agreement, and he led me deeper into the house, looking back every few seconds, as if worried I'd change my mind and bolt for the front door.

We turned a corner, and my feet stopped moving without my permission. The entire back of the house was made up of windows. Beyond them, the lawn sloped down to the open ocean.

The view was nothing short of breathtaking, even better than the one on my family's estate.

And Reid had bought this place with his own hard-earned money. It was hard to wrap my mind around it.

While I'd grown up wealthy, he and his mom had lived a frugal existence in their little cottage on the estate. He used to say he didn't care about becoming rich or the trappings of wealth. But his lifestyle now begged to differ.

Well, as my mom had said, people changed. Apparently Reid had changed a *lot.*

He stood waiting for me to catch up, half-in, half-out of a French door that opened to a wide stone patio running the entire length of the mansion's back side. I followed him out onto the patio and to a table which had been set for two and held an array of tempting salads and a dish of what looked like Chicken Piccata.

My favorite.

I looked from the food to Reid's face, and he smiled again. There was a disconcerting little flip inside my chest.

I'd managed to tame my nerves on the drive here, restating

my plan to myself—get through the day, do my job, be calm and professional no matter how much nastiness Reid might direct my way.

But I hadn't been prepared for this—the niceness, the smiling, the fact that he'd remembered my favorite meal.

"Looks good." I cautiously returned his smile and took the chair he held out for me. Maybe it was a coincidence. Maybe it was a bribe. He *did* want something from me after all—an interview that made him look good, instead of like the scornful, ruthless business titan he'd become.

"Did you make this?" I asked, already knowing the answer. I reached for the salad tongs and moved some to my plate. "It looks delicious."

"Oh, no. I don't really have time to cook," Reid answered. "I have… a few people around who help with things like that."

He looked almost embarrassed as he said it, as if there was something shameful about hiring domestic help.

I finished chewing a bite. "Well, the chef's fantastic. And your place is gorgeous. You must love living here."

"You like it?" He smiled. "I thought you might enjoy eating out here on the piazza. I remember how much you always loved looking at the ocean."

There was that damned flippy thing again in my chest.

Stop it, Mara.

He was just being charming to make up for his pissy departure from our interview the other day. But he was right—I had always been a sucker for an ocean view.

The two of us had driven down to Narragansett or out to the Beavertail Lighthouse in Jamestown so often after we'd gotten our driver's licenses. We'd walk on the beach or sit on the stone ocean wall and stare at the surf and talk, hold hands, kiss—

"Excuse me?" I was aware he'd said something, though I hadn't heard quite what.

"I said I really appreciate you agreeing to do this after the way I acted the other day."

"Oh. Well, after your assistant told my boss that it was my idea, I didn't have much choice." I gave him a raised brow and a smirk.

Reid grinned. "Yeah, Lee's a quick thinker. When I told him I'd fucked it up, he said not to worry about it, that he'd fix it."

"He certainly did that."

I lifted the beautiful glass near my plate and took a sip of the golden wine it held. Mmmm, Chardonnay—oaky, buttery—even though that was way out of "wine fashion" these days.

Also a favorite of mine.

"My boss Rob was ecstatic," I continued. "So this was all Lee's idea, then?"

Reid took a bite before answering, keeping his eyes on his plate as he chewed. "Saying it was *your* idea was his idea."

He swallowed and gave me a tight smile. "Spending some time together before we shoot the story was my idea."

"Why?" My heart rate accelerated, waiting for his answer.

He looked right at my eyes, a notch forming between his brows. He let several seconds pass. Then his expression lifted, and he looked out at the water.

"Obviously, I suck at interviews. I thought if we chatted a bit, if you sort of walked me through the process first, when it came time to do the real thing, it would go more smoothly." He turned his gaze back on me.

"If you hate interviews so much, and you love your privacy as you said, why do you even want to do the story? Clearly you don't need the exposure for business reasons. Your site could hardly be more successful. Are you planning a run for public office someday or something?"

Reid choked a laugh as he set his wine glass down, then pinched the bridge of his nose.

"Ow—that burns. No—for God's sake no. I'd never want that. After watching your father and what he put you all through for his political career, that's the last thing I'd be interested in. I just—I thought if I went ahead and did an interview, people would stop bugging me to do it. The answers they want would already be out there, and maybe all the attention would go away. Besides, it's got to happen eventually, I guess. And it might as well be you who does it."

That made sense. To a non-media person.

"Well, I hate to tell you this, but if you do an interview with me, it's more likely to open the floodgates than plug the dam," I said. "The press will see you as fair game, and the phone calls and requests will probably only increase. You may even get paparazzi showing up, depending on what you say."

"Well then, I'll have to make sure I say only the things that show them how boring I am." He looked at his plate then back at me. "Speaking of that... the video from the other day..."

I knew what he was getting at. And realized why he was being so nice today.

"I won't use it. I'll make sure Sheldon deletes it."

The journalist in me cringed at that idea. He *had* said those things, and releasing that clip would cause a sensation.

But the bigger part of me, the part that had been Reid's best friend (and much more) knew I could never do that to him. And I could do a perfectly good story without it.

Reid sagged back into his chair. "Okay, good. Thanks. Now that's something that *might* hinder business for a social media network built around 'true love.'"

"Yeah, *maybe*," I joked back with him. "You know you're going to have to come up with a better answer to that question, don't you? Because I'll have to ask it again. That's what everyone wants to know about you—what inspired your 'genius,'" I teased.

"I'll work on that," Reid said, rising from his chair. "Looks like you're done with your lunch. Want to take a walk?"

He gestured toward several sets of wide stone steps leading down to the ocean's edge.

I pushed back from the table and stood to join him. "Sure. I'd love that."

What I really wanted was to keep going on that topic—to ask if Reid actually thought of people who believed in true love as "suckers." But it was too early, and things were going too well today to go down that road.

And really, even if that was how he saw things, could I blame him? I'd pretty much decided the same thing myself after what had happened with my parents. What was my mom, if not the biggest sucker of them all—still pining away for a man who'd taken her for granted and made her so unhappy?

I fell into step beside Reid, and we walked along the rocky beach together. "This is yours, too?"

"Yep. All the way to..." He pointed at a large white house in the distance, its five tall chimneys visible through the misty marine layer. "...that house over there. Their beach starts where mine ends."

I kicked a stone, sending it bouncing toward the water. "Your beach. Does it feel weird to say that? I don't remember you being that ambitious where money was concerned."

Turning to look at the back of Reid's house, I took in its wide expanse of windows winking in the afternoon sunlight.

"Honestly, no," he said. "I mean, I don't know if you remember, but I never cared anything about money. I just wanted to tinker around online, play with code, build stuff, you know?"

I nodded, and he continued. "It wasn't until... later, that I started thinking about becoming successful or whatever. I guess I felt like I had something to prove. This..."

Holding his hands out to the side, he twisted, gesturing to the private beach, the mansion. "This is what happens when you put on the blinders and focus on your work."

"And when you crush or buy out all your competitors."

He shrugged. "Nobody notices the *second*-place finisher."

Reid resumed walking, pulling away from me and strolling farther down the beach.

I stayed in place a few moments, watching him. I'd never known Reid as someone who clamored to be noticed. And his media-shy behavior in recent years didn't fit with what he'd just said.

As he walked, his head was turned down, moving slowly side-to-side, scanning the area around his feet. And then he bent to pick something up. He stopped and waited for me.

When I caught up to him, he opened his hand. "Want it?"

The annoying flipping sensation in my chest became a desperate thrashing.

In Reid's palm was a dark gray, heart-shaped stone. I used to collect them when we went on beach walks as teenagers, shrieking with delight whenever I'd find a new one.

I still had the collection in a large glass jar in my room at my Mom's house. I hadn't added to it in years. Partially because I'd gone to college and accepted jobs in places far from the ocean.

Mostly because I hadn't really wanted to collect any new hearts—stone or otherwise.

I reached out and took the rock, and Reid closed his fingers on his empty palm, nothing left there but a few gritty grains of sand.

And I knew in that moment, without a doubt, why he'd turned his back so forcefully on the whole idea of true love.

It was my fault.

TWELVE

Itinerary

Mara

The two of us walked back through his immense home toward the front door.

I was already breathing easier, knowing I'd soon be back in my car and driving away. I'd made it—*almost* in one piece.

Now we could schedule the interview, shoot some video, and put this whole thing behind us, each going back to our separate lives.

"Well, thank you for lunch. I know we didn't talk much about the story, but I think you'll be fine," I said. "It's not live anyway. It will all be on tape, so I'll be editing it after the shoot."

As I grasped the doorknob, preparing to leave, Reid put his hand on the door, flattening it against the dark wood, essentially caging me with his body.

Standing this close to him, I was reminded of just how much bigger he was than me, how much more powerful he was.

In every way.

But his voice was soft, asking rather than demanding. "Wait."

He looked down at my face, directly under his in this position. "I want to give you something before you go—it's in my office."

"Okay," I said, quickly sidestepping his arm and walking back into the foyer, relieved to put some distance between us again.

Reid pointed to a sitting room just off the front hallway. "Wait in there, if you like. Have a seat—I'll be right back."

I took his suggestion even as I wondered what he could possibly want to give me. Maybe a list of questions he was prepared to answer? If that was the case, I'd look at it, but I wouldn't agree to stick to it.

That wasn't how interviews worked. Anyway, if he tried to go by a memorized script, he'd come across as robotic or wooden. Neither of us wanted that.

My shoes sank into the plush cream carpet as I entered the small room. I looked down, hoping there was no sand still on them that would leave marks on the pristine surface.

Instead of sitting, I walked around the room's perimeter, examining the photos lining the walls and covering the small tables on either side of the love seat and chairs.

I wasn't sure how much progress we'd made today in getting comfortable with each other again, but the photographs went a long way toward filling in the time gap left by our sudden separation eleven years ago.

For my own sanity, I'd steadfastly resisted doing internet searches on Reid or looking him up on social media. And I'd avoided StillYours.com like the plague.

There were photos of him with various well-known business and government leaders, a framed cover from *Forbes* magazine featuring StillYours.com. There was an article from the U-

R-I student newspaper about the launch of his company, complete with a photo of Reid trying very hard to look grown up, standing beside his dorm room desk and laptop.

Lee was in the photo with him. That's where they must have met—it was evident Reid trusted him—maybe they'd been roommates or something.

I stepped over to another small collection of photos on a tabletop. Reid with his mother. Another with his high school best friends.

And one of Reid with a woman.

I picked that one up to study it more closely. She was dark-haired, tall, almost as tall as Reid, with the exotic eyes and impossible bone structure of a model. In fact, I thought I recognized her from the most recent Sports Illustrated Swimsuit issue.

With her dark hair, wide brown eyes, and olive skin tone, she looked somewhat like me—except of course for the whole model-gorgeous thing. She even had a tiny gap between her front teeth like mine.

Weird. She was like, "Mara Plus—the new, improved version—now with a thousand times more beauty!"

I wondered if she was Reid's girlfriend. Made sense—young, handsome billionaire—supermodel girlfriend—a tale as old as time.

I placed the picture of the lovely couple back down among Reid's photo collection and worked to quell the tide of acid rising in my gut.

This had nothing to do with me. I'd *wanted* him to move on, hadn't I? Why shouldn't he have a beautiful, perfect woman in his life? He deserved it.

And if the girl he'd chosen was basically an upgraded *me*, it was none of my business.

But then, why had he said only suckers believed in love? If

a man couldn't find happiness with that idealized specimen of a woman, who *could* he love?

"Mara."

Reid's raspy voice came from behind me, making me jump.

I turned to face him. "Hi. I was just... looking around."

His lips quirked in a little smile. "Yes, I see that. So, here's the itinerary. Sorry it took so long. I had to print it out for you, and my stupid printer jammed. The thing's as complicated as a fighter jet cockpit. This is why I have assistants at work."

He handed me a crisp sheet of paper.

I reached for it, beginning to read with a growing sense of dismay. "Itinerary?"

"Yes." He grasped my elbow lightly with his fingertips, steering me toward the front door as I looked down at the paper. "For the week."

"The... week? I thought—your assistant said a day. I thought we were going to set up the interview now."

"I'm not ready."

As I stared at him in confusion, Reid continued his matter-of-fact explanation. "I won't do the interview until I feel comfortable, and I'm not there yet."

I glanced again at the dates and times on the paper in my hand, my mind whirling and my belly trembling with a terrible sense of impending doom.

"But we can't—I can't spend a week with you. I have to work. I have a job."

And that's the least of my reasons.

Reid lifted a brow. "I believe your primary job at the moment is securing this series of reports for your upcoming ratings period. I'm willing to bet if we were to call your boss right now and ask him to give us a week to prepare, he'd readily agree. What do you think?"

The question was issued in the tone of a man who already knew the answer.

Of course. In keeping with his reputation, Reid wouldn't go into any battle without already knowing its outcome and being assured of victory.

He had me. He knew it, and I knew it.

I took a half-step back, lifting the paper toward him. "But why? Why are you doing this?"

"I've already told you—I need to feel prepared before I'll be willing to sit down for an interview again."

His voice took on a tone of challenge. "What's the matter, Mara? Is it really so hard for you to be around me?"

"Of course not," I snapped, answering a little too quickly.

"Well then, am I not worth one week of your time?"

His eyes narrowed in annoyance, but just under the surface I used to know so well there was a hint of insecurity.

Was this about what had happened with us? Was he trying to punish me after all?

When I didn't respond immediately, Reid's expression hardened into a sarcastic mask.

"Some people would consider me quite a catch—some journalists, I mean. I've been told I'm the 'get' of the century."

"The decade," I corrected. Why did I find this new arrogance a little bit sexy on him?

He grinned. "Thank you for clarifying. If it doesn't bother you to be near me, then I don't see what the problem is."

My shoulders went back as I tried futilely to close the height gap between us and look him in the eye.

"This is ridiculous, and you know it. I think you'd be just fine to do the interview tomorrow morning."

He shrugged at my noticeable irritation. "Maybe you're right. Maybe I'll just call Tamara Rogers at Channel Ten and offer it to her."

When I refused to take the bait, he withdrew it and

changed tactics, his features softening again into the Reid I recognized.

"One week, Mara. One week, and then we'll go our separate ways and live happily ever after."

He stared directly into my eyes, waiting for a response.

God, those were gorgeous eyes. *Focus, Mara.* I turned back to the door and opened it.

"Fine. Fine, I'll do it. I *will* have to talk to my boss, but I'm sure you're right."

My tone spelled out every bit of my annoyance with him for hijacking my life for the coming week.

"I'm sure Rob will be all-too-willing to rearrange my work schedule to *accommodate* you."

I marched down the front steps toward my car. At the bottom I turned back to him and held up the paper dictating my life's schedule according to his whim.

"Guess I'll see you tomorrow. I hope you're happy."

Reid's face split into a satisfied, amused grin, making him look eighteen again. "As a matter of fact—I am."

His laughter filled my ears and followed me to the car. Only slamming the door shut and driving away gave me any relief from it.

THIRTEEN
Blown Away

Mara

One week. Seven days. I could do this.

I stood in my closet, searching for something appropriate to wear to my first "summons."

Naturally, Rob had eagerly agreed to Reid's demands when I'd called and told him what my high-maintenance interview subject had required.

"We've got a full staff on this week—we can make do without you," Rob had said.

Then perhaps sensing my reluctance he added, "Ratings, national feed exposure, network potential... it's a small price to pay for such a big story, Mara."

"Of course *you* say that—you're not the one paying the price," I muttered.

"Yes, I'm sure it'll be torture for you to spend a week with the world's most eligible bachelor. The other girls at the station are *so* thrilled they didn't get stuck with this terrible story."

His sarcasm came through loud and clear on the phone.

"I know, I know." Any reporter at my station, especially

the single female ones, would've given up every pair of shoes in their closets for this assignment.

"And Mara? Don't let this fall through, okay kiddo? Do whatever it takes, handholding, flattery, promise him whatever he wants—just get the job done."

Whatever he wants?

I flipped through garment after garment in my closet, rejecting everything I came across. I still wasn't sure *what* Reid wanted.

He'd said it was about feeling prepared for the interview. But the Reid I'd known, while a little shy, had never been that nervous about anything.

He'd always seemed so calm before tennis matches, and his teammates on the robotics and Science Olympiad teams praised him for being "clutch" under pressure.

When he'd delivered his Valedictorian speech at graduation, there hadn't been so much as a tremor in his voice. Could he really be that frightened about speaking on camera?

I crossed the room to my dresser and reviewed the itinerary Reid had given me.

Date: Sunday, October 9th

Time: 2pm

Dress: Casual

Note: Please prepare for an afternoon outdoors near the water. It will be sunny with temps in the 70's, but breezy. A jacket may be a good idea.

Did he have his own meteorological service on-call? *Probably.* I smirked. Maybe he'd convinced Rob to give him one of our weathermen as his indentured servant as well.

I finally settled on a pair of navy cropped pants with a navy-and-white-striped boat neck top and my bright yellow lightweight jacket.

My first impulse had been to show up in sweats with no makeup, just to spite him, but then personal pride won out. If

Reid's intention was to show me what I'd missed out on by breaking up with him, then I was going to give him a dose of his own bitter medicine.

I carefully applied my makeup, and instead of straightening my hair as I did for work, styled it in the tousled waves he used to prefer when we were younger. Back in high school, Reid had always wondered aloud why I bothered to use a straightening iron when, in his opinion, my natural hair was prettier.

Anyway, if our "meeting" really was outdoors and breezy, this was more practical.

"Hi sweetheart," Mom said when I came downstairs. "You look nice. Do you have a date?"

"No. Not a date, a work thing."

"On Sunday?"

"Yeah. It's sort of a special assignment. For sweeps." At her questioning look, I confessed. "I'm meeting Reid. I'm going to do the story. I pretty much have to, or I could lose my job."

"Oh dear. I knew it."

I hated the look of sympathy on her face.

"As soon as you told me you'd seen him, I knew you'd end up seeing him again," she said. "You just can't stay away from him, can you?"

"What? No, of course not. I'm only seeing him because I have to. I have to spend a week with him, then we'll do the interview, and that will be that. I'll never see him again. It's strictly professional."

"Poor kid." She shook her head. "You're my daughter all right, a glutton for punishment. We both need to get over the idea that the 'one' exists."

As annoyed as I was, I almost laughed out loud—if she only knew my reputation. Then again, I didn't really want her to know. It served me well with everyone else, but I didn't exactly relish the idea of my mom considering me a "man-eater."

"Mom—I promise you—it's only work."

Her expression was still dubious. "Well, have a good day at *work*. And Mara, as much as I tease you about being just like me, I'd hate to see you end up where I am. Be careful."

Hearing the sounds of a car pulling into the drive, I peeked out the window. It was Reid, sitting in the driver's seat of his Porsche Spyder.

"I will," I promised, then hurried outside before Reid got it in his head to come knock on the front door and escort me down the front walkway with my mom watching, like two tenth graders on their first car date.

"Hi," I wheezed, sliding into the passenger seat just as he opened the driver's side door to get out.

He shut it again. "Hi there. I would have gotten that door for you."

I shook my head with a tight smile. "No need for chivalry. We can go now."

He grinned and started the engine. "So eager. Well, I hope the day I planned lives up to your expectations."

I glanced over at him with a surly look. "I have no expectations. I'm just reporting for duty. The sooner we get going, the sooner it will be over."

His smile only widened as he pulled away from the curb toward wherever he was forcing me to go.

* * *

POP! The cork came free of the wine bottle. I watched Reid's hands as he poured a glass for me, then one for himself.

He lifted the wineglass to me with an expectant grin. "So what do you think?"

I took it and surveyed our surroundings, the sloping grass-covered hills of Easton Park on Atlantic Avenue, the deep blue waves of the ocean crashing on rocks in front of us, and what had to be hundreds of kites flying overhead.

"It's amazing," I said. There was no denying it.

I hadn't been to this park in many years. There had always been at least a few kite flyers here, dotting the park's windswept knolls. But today was different.

The annual Kite Festival was taking place, and I'd never seen anything like it. It was breathtaking.

We'd chosen to view the events from a spot on a hill toward the back of the park. Reid had brought a blanket and a large picnic basket. After spreading out the blanket, he'd slipped off his shoes and invited me to join him on it.

Now we sat together, watching the wind-powered-cart races and the musical kite-dancing performances, where serious hobbyists maneuvered sleek stunt-kites into synchronized swoops and dives and swirls against a cloudless blue sky.

The best part, though, was just seeing the vast array of kites amateur enthusiasts from around the area had brought, managed to get up, and then anchored to the ground so everyone could enjoy the continuous aerial display.

The kites ranged from the simple to the intricate, some beautiful, some humorous. There were birds and fish and insects, a huge octopus with eight wildly flapping legs.

We spent hours having a picnic lunch, discussing his business and my TV news career. As the autumn sun steadily dropped toward the water, I was dismayed to realize how quickly the day had gone—and that I didn't want the experience to end.

Watching the bright colors, the beautiful fabrics rippling in the wind, enjoying the sea breeze and the afternoon sun on my face, I felt as if I'd never grow tired of the spectacle.

Or of Reid's company.

As if hearing my dangerous thought, Reid looked over at

me and gave me a relaxed smile. My heart tightened in an ominous preview of what was in store for me tonight when I was home alone in my bed, reviewing the day.

I tipped my head back and shut my eyes, letting the sun's sinking rays turn my eyelids a fiery red, willing myself to resist the powerful pull Reid had always had on me.

Crapcrapcrap.

This was exactly what I'd been afraid of. I was enjoying our "professional meeting" far too much. All the hard work I'd done over the past decade, training myself not to think of him, not to miss him, was unraveling.

All it had taken to knock a gaping hole in my fortress wall was one sunny afternoon in his presence.

"Still so fucking beautiful."

Reid's soft words yanked me out of my mesmerized state. My head turned to him, eyes opening wide.

The unexpected statement reverberated through me like the quivering of piano strings, long after a key has been struck.

Reid lay stretched out on the blanket, propped on one elbow. He was staring at me, a sad smile playing on his lips.

Apparently, he'd been watching me, studying my profile while my eyes were closed. He glanced down to the blanket, pinching a blade of grass that had found its way there.

Lifting it, he released it into the breeze, and his eyes found me again.

"What happened to us, Mara? What did I do that was so wrong you had to leave and never come back, never take my phone calls, ignore my emails?"

Panic-stricken, I looked away from him, desperately searching through the mental inventory of excuses I'd been brainstorming.

Perhaps if I'd done a better job of breaking things off with him, I wouldn't be facing this situation today. No doubt it *would* have been more effective to tell him of my "decision" via email or phone—there was no way I could have done it face-to-face.

He would have seen through the lies instantly. I'd have cracked and confessed, and he would never have given up hope. He would have continued to try to see me and ended up with his life ruined—or losing it altogether.

At the time, going cold turkey had seemed like the best way to protect him. But now, here we were, years of unanswered questions and hurt between us.

And still, just as back then, I couldn't tell Reid the truth.

FOURTEEN
Public Indecency

Reid

I kept my eyes on the slowly shifting ocean, which now gleamed gold in the sun's waning rays, and waited for Mara's answer.

It was the whole reason for the ridiculous interview-prep scenario I'd orchestrated. I didn't care *what* the reason was—I just wanted to know *why*. And I wanted to know how she'd managed to move on so cleanly when I'd been limping around with a tiny piece of my soul ripped out for the past decade.

"Let's not do this, okay?" she said. "I think today was rather… tolerable, and it would just be better for both of us if we kept the conversation limited to preparing for the interview."

Make that a *big* piece of my soul. I wouldn't have believed there was anything left in the vicinity of my heart, but sure enough, a raw ache surged to life again, my Franken-heart reanimated by the electricity of her nearness.

I sat up and barked a caustic laugh. "Tolerable, huh?"

Getting to my knees, I started gathering the picnic supplies, tossing them carelessly into the basket. Lifting my unfinished glass of wine from the blanket, I poured out the remnants onto the grass before pitching the crystal stemware into the basket, too.

"I'm sorry. For a few minutes there, I thought you'd actually enjoyed yourself today."

Prodded to action by my sour tone, Mara got to her feet and stepped off the blanket so I could fold it. Obviously, the party was over.

"Poor choice of words," she said evenly. "I meant things went well today. Why mess it up by dredging up ancient history?"

I shook my head, my mouth curving in a smile of bitter amusement. "Wow. I didn't believe it was possible, but I guess you really have changed that much. You really are as cold as people say you are."

Her head jerked back as if she'd been slapped. Apparently the remark had stung. *Good.* I'd meant for it to.

"What people? What are you talking about?" she asked.

I gave her a smile every bit as icy as I'd just accused her of being.

"I know a lot about you, Mara. I've got enough money to find out anything I want to know—and I wanted to know what happened to you—for curiosity's sake. I had someone look into you during college, and last year down South."

I paused for a dry laugh. "I used to think I was special, but then I found out I'm in good company—or bad."

"What's that supposed to mean?"

"My investigator's report detailed a long history of short-lived relationships. You have quite a track record of loving and leaving," I explained. "Though, maybe 'loving' is the wrong word."

Grabbing my chin, I struck an exaggerated thinking pose. "I wonder... what word I could insert that would be more appropriate?"

Mara's eyes flew open wide. A half-second later there was a loud crack, and a stinging heat flared in my cheek. Shaking out her hand, she spun around and hiked down the hill toward the parking lot.

I followed her, my heart pounding like I'd run the CVS Downtown 5K through Providence.

Though I'd been trying to get a rise out of her, I was now more than a little worried she wouldn't get into my car again but would instead call a cab.

Or call someone at her station and demand to be picked up.

And to be taken off the story.

Sure enough, when she reached the asphalt, Mara pulled her phone from her jacket pocket, clearly about to call for a ride. Desperation danced in my brain, scrambling my thoughts and cranking up my adrenaline.

Reaching over her shoulder, I plucked the device from Mara's fingers.

"Hey." She whirled to face me. "What do you think you're doing? Give me my phone."

I held it high out of her reach. "Wait. Just wait a minute, okay. I'm sorry. I shouldn't have said that. I was mad."

"Join the club, asshole," she growled, going up on her tiptoes to reach for the phone. "And this interview prep—this is done. You're on your own."

"Will you hold on a minute? I said I was sorry. I didn't mean it."

I stretched my hand toward the sky as she scowled and lunged, trying futilely to get her phone back, no doubt planning to use it to arrange things so she never had to see me again.

She grappled at my wrist, frustration and anger painting her pretty face. It probably didn't help that I was laughing at her.

But I couldn't help myself. She was unbelievably cute, like an irate teacup Yorkie barking and growling at a Great Dane.

"Give it to me, you big bully—I'm not kidding."

"There's that temper again. Your Irish half is showing," I teased.

Mara jumped, and as she came back down off-balance, her chest crashed into mine. My free arm clamped around her waist, catching her and saving her from falling backward and landing on her butt.

Instead of releasing her when she regained her footing, I pulled her tightly against me.

Not *quite* sure why I did it. It wasn't a decision actually—it was more a matter of instinct. Wanting Mara close to me was simply part of who I was.

Our faces were inches apart, her hard breaths and my laughter mixing in the tiny space between us.

The delicious scent I'd noticed on the day of our first interview attempt swirled around me, making me suddenly light-headed. And her mouth—those beautiful heart-shaped lips—were right there.

She stopped struggling. I froze as well—her temper wasn't the only thing aroused at this point, and I was pretty sure she could feel it.

I stared down at her for one charged second more, and then my restraint broke and my mouth crashed down on hers. Honestly, I expected a second slap—but it didn't come.

The aggravation of a few seconds earlier morphed into something entirely different. Mara's soft lips moved with mine, slowly at first but progressing quickly to a mad sort of mutual feeding frenzy, our mouths moving together hungrily as our bodies clung to each other.

This. This was the feeling of my youth, the trembling excitement that had filled me whenever Mara was near, the restless heat that had infused all our physical encounters, culminating in that one perfect night we'd shared before our abrupt ending.

I was a grown man, standing in a parking lot at the edge of the Atlantic Ocean, but I was also a lovesick teenager, swamped with desire for a girl.

This girl. This woman who kissed me with blistering intensity and held me so tightly it felt as if I'd never been out of her arms for a minute, much less for eleven long years.

We went on kissing, and I brought my hands to the sides of her face then pushed them into her hair.

Part of my brain warned this was a critical mistake—Mara had hurt me deeply. She could easily do it again. But I was drugged, powerless to stop what seemed to be inevitable between us.

Her hands came to my waist, moving in long strokes up and down my sides and across my torso. There was no question we were both fully involved now. She was absolutely kissing me back, meeting my trembling energy with her own, unable to keep her lips and tongue and body from revealing the secrets she'd locked away from me these past few years.

She still cared.

She still wants me.

That revelation, coupled with her fervent response and moan of excitement, dismantled my self-control completely.

All thought was ripped from my mind and carried away by the ocean breeze. I pulled her up to her toes, drawing her body more tightly against mine, kissing her with a desperation born of years of pent-up emotion and desire.

Finally, the kiss gentled, and Mara drew back slightly, looking up with dazed eyes.

Her voice was a breath, barely audible. "Reid."

"Mara," I whispered fiercely.

Then I kissed her again, deepening our connection,

plunging into her mouth over and over with greedy, ravenous, hypnotic strokes.

Her fingers delved beneath my hair, caressing the nape of my neck and running over my body, clasping on my shoulders, my back, my arms, as if testing to see whether I was actually there with her or a figment of her imagination.

As my hand coasted over her ass and pulled her against my lower body, a soft pleasure noise hummed from Mara's mouth into mine.

The sound shook me to my core. This wasn't a dream. It was really happening. We were together again in the way I'd longed for daily since the night she'd left town.

And we were about to do it in a parking lot.

I pulled out of the kiss, feeling like a man emerging from a trance.

Still holding Mara close, I lifted my head and surveyed the area around us, taking note of the couples and families folding their kites and packing blankets and coolers into nearby cars. Some of them darted glances at us.

My gaze returned to Mara's kiss-swollen lips, and I gave her a smile of utter satisfaction and fervent desire. "I don't think *this* kind of show was on the Kite Festival brochure."

Dropping my forehead to rest against hers, I whispered, "Let's go back to my house."

As if a spell had been broken, the enormity of what we'd just done seemed to hit her. "No," she yelped, stepping backward out of my arms and bumping into the door of my car.

"It's three minutes from here." I followed her, stepping close again and reaching for her waist with a naughty grin. "Unless you really don't want to leave, in which case I'll gladly risk an arrest for public indecency."

She sidestepped me and almost ran to the other side of the car. I stared at her flushed face over the Porche's roof, taking several head-clearing breaths and slowly gaining mastery over body parts that had *clearly* been neglected too long.

Mara opened her mouth to say something then shut it again and got into the passenger seat without a word.

I opened my own door and dropped into the driver's seat. "I would have gotten that door for you, you know," I teased, repeating my line from earlier today.

Earlier today when I'd had so much hope for this carefully planned outing. Of course kissing her hadn't been part of that plan, but I'd be lying if I said I was disappointed in the turn of events.

"I need to go home now," Mara said through tight lips.

Crossing her arms over her chest, she stared through the windshield at the water across the road.

The frustration of unfulfilled lust simmered just under my skin. Apparently that was where it was going to stay. Mara had shut down on me again. She wouldn't even look at me.

As close as I'd felt to her a few minutes ago, it felt like a huge gulf separated us now.

No. Not again. I wouldn't be able to handle it.

"Mara—let me take you to my house. We need to talk about this."

She shook her head, her body wound as tightly as a new spool of kite line. "No. We don't need to talk. I need to go home. I need to check on the boys."

For a moment I sat staring at her profile. She was clearly grasping for an excuse to get away from me.

"What are you so afraid of?"

"I'm not afraid," she snapped.

Unfolding her stiff arms, she strapped on her seatbelt. "I'm mad at you... for spying on me."

"Welcome to the club, sweetheart," I said. "I've been mad at you for eleven years. All my friends started calling me 'Grumpy' because I was so miserable all the time. Believe me, I didn't *want* to be. I tried to get over it, but it was impossible without any answers about what happened."

Mara still wouldn't look at me, and she didn't respond.

Well, I was through taking silence for an answer. Frustration boiled in my veins, completely eradicating the chill of the October evening.

"You're going to fix that for me, sweet girl," I vowed. "Tonight."

FIFTEEN

Weather and the Red Sox

Mara

Reid backed the car up and pulled out onto Atlantic Avenue. I was terrified he'd drive me to his house against my will—he certainly sounded determined enough.

But thankfully, he turned in the direction that would take us toward my family's home. My shoulders relaxed a fraction.

This was a disaster. I couldn't even *look* at him for fear the traction of those unearthly blue eyes would have me draping myself all over him and climbing onto his lap in the driver's seat, no matter how many young families we might shock and appall. No matter how much danger it might put him in from my father.

What had I been thinking? How could I have let him kiss me—and kissed him back? Which I absolutely had.

I took a deep breath and let it out slowly.

Ten minutes.

Ten minutes and I'd be safely at home. I could run upstairs to my room, lock the door, wash my face, and do my very best to forget the way I'd felt when Reid had kissed me.

And held me.

And made me feel like I was seventeen again and completely out of my mind and in my body the way only teenagers are.

Or so I'd thought. Apparently I was still fully capable of going from zero to a hundred in a few seconds flat. With him, at least.

Once we were underway, he glanced over at me.

"All right. I'm taking you home like you asked. But talk to me," he pleaded. "I'm sorry I spied on you, but after you refused to see me or communicate with me, I didn't know what else to do. You have to understand—I *had* to know where you were and that you were okay. Eventually I accepted you just didn't care anything about me—that you must never have felt what I felt for you. But now... I think it's pretty obvious there's still something there between us."

I folded my arms over my chest again, shaking with a chill from the evening air. "There's nothing to talk about. We were kids. We went to different colleges. We grew apart. It happens all the time."

Reid's finger moved to the dashboard to turn on the car's heater. He huffed an incredulous laugh.

"In one day? You don't grow apart in one day, Mara. We made love on graduation night—"

He threw a hand up in frustration. "We made love, and then I never saw you again. You didn't answer your phone the rest of the weekend. I went to your house, and your mom told me you'd *moved* and refused to tell me where. What is that?"

I couldn't fault him for his confusion. He wasn't stupid. Far from it. He *knew* I'd loved him back then, just as he'd loved me.

Telling our respective parents we were going to the all-night graduation after-party at the swanky Eastport Arms Hotel, we had instead checked into a room upstairs where several years of increasingly serious make-out sessions had culminated in going all the way for the first time.

Several times, actually.

I hadn't regretted a minute of it—I'd been on bliss overload. If he'd suggested eloping the next morning, I wouldn't have said no. But he hadn't of course.

At dawn, he'd left me on the front porch with a kiss, and I'd walked inside to find both my parents waiting up. The chaperone had reported us no-shows at the after-party.

I didn't know what happened at Reid's house, but all hell broke loose at mine. I'd never seen my parents so infuriated.

"What the hell were you thinking, Mara?" Mom had screamed.

I screamed back, brimming with teenaged passion. "I *love* him."

"Love?" My dad had snorted with laughter. "You can't be in love. You're a kid. And he's a loser. It's just your teenage hormones talking. Believe me—that passes. I'm sparing you the consequences you can't see coming."

"He's not a loser. He's brilliant," I'd shouted through tears. "And talented. He's going to conquer the world someday—just wait and see. He'll make more money and have more power than you *ever* had. He's going to make *you* look like the loser, and I think you know it. That's why you hate him so much."

"I don't care enough about the kid to hate him. Pigs will fly the day I see my daughter associated with the likes of a Mancini. They're nothing but greasy low-lifes. You may hate me now, but you'll thank me later."

After our "conversation" in his office, I'd stumbled to the bathroom, gagging from the force of my crying. The entire contents of my stomach came up in a violent heave. I would *never* be grateful to my father over this. How could I be?

He was forcing me to give up the most important thing in

the world to me—or see it destroyed. I had no choice in the matter. If I loved Reid, I could never see him, never speak to him again.

From the corner of my blurred vision, I saw Mom's feet in the bathroom doorway.

"I'm sorry," she'd said softly. "But you need to know your father is only doing what's best for you."

"Like he does what's best for you?" I'd challenged, emboldened by my fury.

Mom's face had hardened. "Mara… if you really do love Reid—you should let him go. You don't want to end up like me, trust me. There are lots of boys out there. Boys who don't have power over your heart. Let him go. It's for the best."

I had never told anyone that story—I wouldn't tell Reid now. As the car snaked along the twisting seaside drive, I stared out the window at the white sails dotting the deep blue bay, feeling numb inside.

"It was for the best." I exhaled an exhausted sigh. "It would have eventually happened anyway. It was better to just —go ahead and get it over with than let our relationship die one of those sad hometown-honey-malnutrition deaths that always happen when people go to different colleges."

"They don't *always* happen," Reid said. ""And allow me to say I strongly disagreed with your idea of what was best for me. Speaking of college, you were supposed to go to Columbia. We would only have been three hours apart when I went to URI. We could have easily kept seeing each other all the time. That *was* the plan, wasn't it? Columbia is the top program in the nation for journalism. Where the hell did Stanford come from? You never even mentioned going there. It took me a *year* to figure out where you'd gone and to track you down."

Keeping my arms crossed, I lifted my shoulders in a tense shrug. "I made a last-minute switch. Stanford had a great journalism program, and California is cool. I needed a change—so I spent the summer with my aunt and uncle in Missouri then went straight to Stanford in the fall."

Reid's grip on the steering wheel tightened. "Right. Well, that still doesn't explain why you didn't just tell me, why you disappeared without a word. It just wasn't like you. *Something* happened, and I want to know what it was. You owe me that much."

This was turning into a nightmare. I'd known coming with him today was a mistake. All the feelings, all the discussions I'd successfully avoided for years... we weren't able to spend one *day* together without them coming out.

How would I ever get through a whole week?

"This isn't going to work," I said, shaking my head emphatically.

"What isn't?"

I looked over at him for the first time since we'd gotten into the car together. "This week. I can't do this. I know you didn't get what you wanted all those years ago. That must be hard for a man in your position—I'm sure you're used to getting your way. But I'm sorry, job or not, you can't force me to talk about things I don't want to talk about. I agreed to prepare you for an interview, not to conduct an autopsy of our 'puppy love.'"

I spit the last two words out in a disdainful drawl—I had to get him to back off.

Reid winced at my deliberate downgrading of our relationship. Then a blank mask fell over his face, and he relaxed back into the driver's seat. He said nothing.

"I'll talk to Rob tomorrow. I'll tell him he can just fire me if he—" I started.

"No," Reid interrupted. "Don't do that. You're right. I overstepped my bounds. We agreed to keep things strictly professional, and I let my... *curiosity* get the better of me. I apologize. It won't happen again."

I narrowed my eyes as I studied him. "So, you're ready to do the interview now... and drop this whole itinerary thing?"

"Oh no. The itinerary stays. But I won't bring up our past again. In fact, we can pretend we just met, if you like. You can go back to calling me Mr. Mancini."

He dropped his tone to a low murmur. "And I'll call you Miss Neely."

The way he said my name was so laced with mocking seduction it gave me a shiver that went straight down my middle and melted warmly in my lap.

"That won't be necessary. Obviously, we know each other too well to go by titles. But if we're going to continue with this, the conversation between us—and everything else—has to stay strictly impersonal."

His face broke into a tolerant grin, his eyes staying on the road ahead. "Nothing but the weather and the Red Sox," he promised.

"And pre-interview preparation," I added.

The grin grew wider. He sent a quick glance my way. "Of course. That's the whole reason we're here, isn't it?"

Something in his tone made me wonder if Reid really understood that as well as he claimed to.

SIXTEEN

Afternoon Show

Mara

Monday's itinerary instructed me to meet Reid at the Eastport Bay Harbor at two p.m. with a seaworthy wardrobe and a pair of sunglasses.

Being prone to motion sickness, I'd always been more of a stay-on-the-beach-and-enjoy-looking-at-the-ocean person rather than a boater. But the idea of spending a day on Reid's yacht made my stomach queasy for another reason entirely.

I'd hardly slept the previous night. Instead, my mind had replayed our kiss over and over again, refusing to stop even when I'd drifted into bouts of fitful sleep. In fact, my dreams carried things even further.

I'd woken up time and time again, restless, sweating, and totally turned on, believing I was in his arms, in his bed. The Reid in my dreams wasn't *my* Reid, the teenaged one, but this new, older and even sexier version.

Unfortunately, being with him had also been even better than when we were younger and had more enthusiasm than experience. How was I supposed to manage being with him today after "sleeping" with him all night long?

I had no choice but to try. Rob had called early in the afternoon to check in, making sure I was sufficiently buttering up our 'invaluable' interview subject.

"Lee tells me the pre-interview meeting went well yesterday. I just want you to know that we all appreciate what you're doing for the station, Mara," Rob said. "The GM is very pleased. And I have Sue already working on some killer promos."

"Sure. Okay, whatever. I guess I'd better go—I have to babysit a billionaire."

"Go get 'em, Mara. I'll check in with you tomorrow."

I showed up for "work" right on time, reporting to the Eastport Bay Yachting Center Marina in the center of the historic downtown area. I found the slip number Reid had given me, and there in the middle of the charming seaside resort was a modern behemoth of a boat. It had company.

Huge yachts lounged side-by-side in the sun like overfed tourists on the deck of a cruise ship. Reid's was by no means the largest, but it was still enormous and probably cost more than the mansion I'd grown up in.

A narrow ramp spanned the distance from the boat to the dock. As I stepped up onto it, Reid's voice called out to me.

"Good afternoon. Ready to come aboard?"

I squinted through the afternoon sun to see him emerge from the rear of the yacht. "As I'll ever be, I guess."

Reid waited for me to reach the top of the ramp, holding out a hand to help me cross. His grip was strong and warm and triggered vivid images from the previous night's dreams. I pulled my fingers away as soon as my feet reached the deck.

As tired and tense as I was, Reid looked rested and relaxed. And hot.

He wore a cream-colored sweater with expensive-looking navy shorts and deck shoes. Seeing him here on his boat, I suddenly realized why he was sporting a tan in the fall. He continued to enjoy time out on the water long after beach season ended for most Rhode Islanders.

"Thanks for coming today," he said. It was almost funny how he continued to thank me for doing something I had no choice about.

"We'll see how grateful you are when I'm puking all over your gorgeous yacht," I warned. "I hope you have a bucket around here somewhere."

Reaching into his pocket, he pulled out a small box. "I've got something even better. Here, go ahead and take these."

He handed me two tiny white tablets. "They're motion sickness pills. By the time we reach open ocean, they'll have kicked in. You should be fine."

"So you remember my little problem." I took the tablets from his hand with a rueful grin.

Reid dropped his voice to a soft tone that was almost menacing. "I remember everything, Mara."

There was a quick skip in my chest. Unsure how to respond to his comment, I ignored it. "Um, can I get another one of those for later?"

He hesitated. "I don't think you'll need it. That's probably enough to last all day."

But I held out my hand, and he acquiesced, dropping the travel-sized bottle into my open palm.

"Better safe than sorry," I said.

Reid showed me around the three-level vessel. "I know boats aren't your favorite thing, but since we'll be doing some filming here, I thought you might like to see the layout, start getting some shots in mind for the—what did you call it—b-roll?"

"Yes. That's what we call the video that goes with a story and fills in the spaces between the sound bites—the interview parts. Sometimes the editor will lay b-roll over the interviews so you hear the person's voice but see something more interesting than a talking head for several minutes."

Although, as I watched Reid's smiling face in conversation, the wind ruffling his hair, there wasn't much I'd personally find more interesting to look at.

Damn it, Mara. Get control of your thoughts.

I tore my gaze away from him, focusing instead on the receding harbor behind us, on the shoreline slipping past as the yacht picked up speed. We passed Brady's Wharf and some harbor-front condos then a Revolutionary War fort whose grounds were now used for the annual Eastport Bay Jazz and Folk Festivals.

"I hope your photographer's not afraid of going out on the water," Reid said.

"Oh, Sheldon will love this," I assured him. "He can't wait for his turn to follow you around."

Reid laughed. "Well, I think *you're* going to love what I have planned for today."

"What are we doing? Fishing?"

I couldn't imagine loving that, but what else did you do on a boat? Anyway, I was here to work, to fulfill Reid's requirement, not to have fun. It didn't matter whether I enjoyed his plans for the day. I rather hoped I wouldn't.

"No. Not exactly," was Reid's cryptic answer.

He refused to elaborate, so I settled in for the ride. We sat in chairs on the lower deck, with Reid pointing out the landmarks we passed—lighthouses, tiny islands, impressive coastal homes with pretentious names and famous owners, places I'd glimpsed from the street side but never from this angle where our view of their impressive properties and private beaches was unobstructed.

After about fifteen minutes, a man joined us on deck, surprising me with his presence. Reid introduced him as his chef, the one who normally worked in his Eastport Bay weekend home.

There was also a captain on board somewhere—Reid promised I'd meet him later.

The chef, Vincenzo, spoke with a thick Italian accent and laid out a gorgeous "afternoon snack" as he called it. To me, it looked like enough food to feed our whole newsroom.

There were fruits and cheeses, sliced baguettes, steamed shrimp and crab legs. He also opened a bottle of Chardonnay in one quick, practiced move, and poured a glass for each of us before disappearing below deck.

The boat turned away from the shoreline and out toward open ocean. "Are we going to Block Island?" I asked.

It was the only destination I could imagine off the mainland, and Reid had already told me we wouldn't be fishing.

He grinned mysteriously. "Just be patient. You'll see."

He was right about the motion-sickness medicine. It was doing its job. Whether from the pills or the wine, I felt good. A bit buzzy, but I wasn't nauseous, and that was all I cared about.

Finally, about two hours out from shore, the yacht slowed and came to a stop. Right in the middle of the ocean. A little flutter of panic chased through me.

I stood up. "Why did the boat stop? Is it broken? Did the engine quit?"

My mind flooded with details of past news stories about stranded powerless cruise ships with failing toilets and boats lost at sea during hurricanes. The skies were crystal clear today, but it *was* fall in New England. Hurricanes happened.

I stood and went to the side, gripping the handrail and leaning over to see the rolling water beneath us.

"No, Mara." Reid laughed. "The boat didn't break." He got up and joined me. "We're here."

"Here? Here where? We're in the middle of nowhere. Why did you bring me out—"

And then something large leapt out of the water and splashed back down about fifty yards from the boat. I nearly fell in my hurry to scramble back from the side.

I crashed into Reid, and my arms slipped around his waist before I could stop and think about what I was doing.

"What was that?"

"That," Reid said with a tone of satisfaction. "Was what we came to see."

He peeled me from his torso and threaded his fingers through mine. He drew me back to the railing, then let go of my hand and slipped an arm around my back, settling a reassuring warm hand on my waist.

"Just wait," he said softly.

I looked up at his face, so close to me in this position. I was about to obey my brain's prudent command to move away from his side when it happened again. A huge form erupted from the water this time much closer to the boat.

It splashed back down, sending a shower of sprinkles in our direction.

I looked at Reid, the realization hitting me.

"A whale," I squealed. "It's a whale. Oh my God. I've never seen one outside of an aquarium. Did you know this would happen?"

He beamed down at me. "I had the captain check in a little while ago with some fishing boats to find out where the pod had been spotted. These are humpbacks. This is their feeding ground. They're out here every day from early summer to late fall."

"Wow. Will it jump again?"

"It's called breaching when they come up out of the water. And it's not just one. There are a whole lot of them under there. Now that the boat's been still a few minutes, we should be able to see quite a few breaches."

The sentence was hardly out of his mouth before it happened again. This time the whale came almost all the way out of the water before diving back under the surface, its wide tail the last part to disappear. Another followed immediately.

I laughed out loud. "They're gorgeous."

"Aren't they? I make a point of coming out to watch them at least once a year. One time we had probably forty of them near the boat. I've seen porpoises, too."

All around us, waterspouts of various sizes broke the surface in frothy sprays, as the pod members took turns surfacing for air.

The experience was like something from a nature documentary. But this was much more beautiful, because we were actually living it instead of passively viewing it on a screen.

It was nothing short of emotional to see such massive creatures displaying their enormous strength so close, to feel the cold droplets of their spray and hear the airy whooshing noise of their spouting, the loud smacking splashes of their tails striking the ocean's surface.

I leaned away from the splash of a particularly nearby breach, pressing into Reid's side and ducking my face into his shoulder. His hand automatically came up to hold my head against him, and we both laughed.

The delights of this new experience, coupled with the pleasure of leaning into the solid warmth of Reid's body, filled me with conflicting emotions—a sense of joy, even peace, but also a disturbing yearning.

Once again, I had the irrational wish that this experience would never end, just as I had yesterday at the kite festival.

Before I'd run into Reid last week, when had I last felt like that?

SEVENTEEN

A Few Too Many

Mara

I pulled away from Reid's side and left the railing long before I actually wanted to.

The answer to my own question was not something I wanted to think about—the last time I'd wished a moment would never end was graduation night, the first and only time Reid and I had made love.

My heart squeezed painfully at just the tiny sliver of memory I allowed to cross through my mind.

"Had enough whale-watching for today?" Reid asked, following me back to our deck seats and glancing over me with an appraising eye. "Not feeling sick, are you?"

I shook my head, trying to keep my expression blank. "No, I'm fine. That was... amazing. Thank you. My parents took me on a whale-watching ferry trip once when I was little, but the ocean was so choppy and I got so violently ill, I couldn't even lift my head to see them."

"I think I remember that story." He grinned. "You want to go in? The wind's picking up out here. If I know you, you're starting to get chilly."

And of course he was right, because he *did* know me. I nodded and stood, accepting the hand he offered to guide me across the deck toward the door to the interior rooms.

"Sunsets are great out here on the water, but it's clouding over today anyway, so it probably won't be a great one to watch," Reid said. "That's okay. There will be plenty of other—"

He stopped himself. "Let's see what Vincenzo has planned for supper."

Reid pointed out the bathroom—the 'head,' he called it—and went to check with the chef and speak to the captain about turning back for shore.

It felt different inside the boat. I was more aware of the motion of the sea rolling beneath us than I had been up on deck. Extracting the small bottle of pills from my pocket, I shook out a couple, swallowing them with water from the sink, just to be safe.

Whatever Vincenzo had prepared, I didn't want to risk it coming back up after dinner.

I washed up and looked myself over in the mirror—windblown, of course, but there wasn't much I could do about that here. Running my hands through my hair a few times, I decided it was silly to even worry about my appearance. I was here as a reporter, not as Reid's date.

It wasn't important for him to find me attractive. Best if he didn't actually.

I left the head and found Reid in the cozy dining room. The table had already been set for us. Low candles burned in the center, warming up the dimly lit room. He'd changed into a pair of jeans with his sweater, bowing to the cooling night air.

"Are you warm enough?" he asked as he waited for me to sit then took his own seat. "I could turn up the heat."

Shaking my head, I said, "No. I'm comfortable. Though I

do feel a little underdressed."

I motioned to the beautiful place settings on the table. They were more appropriate for a meal at the Cliffhouse than for a wild-haired girl in jeans and sneakers.

"You look perfect," Reid assured me. At my wide-eyed glance he added, "Speaking in strictly professional terms, of course."

Vincenzo served our meals, beautifully presented sea bass filets topped with small, cold-water shrimp and capers, creamy artichoke risotto, and the best grilled asparagus I'd ever tasted.

"He cooked all this here on the boat?" I asked after the chef had left the room. "This is better than anything I've ever had in a restaurant."

Reid smiled. "He could make fantastic meals with one pan and a camp stove, but the boat is well-equipped. The kitchen is probably close to one you'd find in a 4-star restaurant. I doubt I'd be able to keep a chef like Vincenzo without spoiling him with all the necessary tools of his trade."

I nodded and finished chewing another mouth-watering bite. Toward the end of our amazing meal, I told Reid, "It's official. You should definitely give Vincenzo whatever he wants."

He sipped his wine and laughed, nodding in agreement.

"What about you?" he asked, his tone casual, but his gaze sharp. "What do you want?"

I gulped the swallow of wine I'd just taken, sending a trickle of it down my windpipe. It took a good half-minute of coughing before I could manage to respond.

"What do you mean?"

"It's been a long time since we've talked about that kind of thing. I know you used to want a career in news, maybe to work for the network someday. The fact that you're here right now shows me that's still true. But you also wanted a big family, a house full of crazy boys running around."

He smiled, no doubt thinking of his own boyhood antics. "Has that changed?"

"Reid," I warned, sensing an attempt to steer the conversation back to dangerous territory.

The two of us used to talk about our future for hours, debating the benefits of various numbers of children. We'd finally decided four would be perfect for us, though we wouldn't start trying until we'd had a few years to get established in our careers.

"I don't think we should talk about that." I pushed the remaining bites of my asparagus around in the buttery sauce, avoiding looking at him.

It was natural, of course, for Reid to want answers about what had happened between us, but I couldn't allow it. Not tonight after the magical afternoon we'd shared.

And certainly not after a few glasses of the excellent wine had combined with the extra dose of motion sickness medicine to soften my senses and perhaps loosen my tongue.

"I'm sorry," he said. "I know I said I wouldn't go there. But I can't help my curiosity. Aren't you the least bit curious about how I've changed in the past decade?"

I ventured a glance at his face. His eyes glowed softly in the candlelight, their blue-green color glinting with the golden reflection of the tiny flames.

Any changes in him had only been for the better—at least on the outside. I quickly looked down again.

"Of course I'm curious. I have been... for years. But..."

"But what?" His tone was coaxing, encouraging me to open up.

Slowly he reached out a finger, placing it under my chin and tilting my face up from its down-turned position. He waited until I made eye contact.

"Tell me, Mara."

"I..." I was starting to get a little fuzzy on my keep-it-professional vow.

Would it really be so bad to just talk to him, tell him about the mind-searing fear that had overtaken me after we'd finally made love and my dad had warned me away from him forever? Tell him about the lonely years that had followed? The emptiness I still felt inside?

It wouldn't change anything between us. I still couldn't be with him. My dad hadn't been making empty threats. He could still do tremendous damage to Reid.

Even if Dad didn't follow through on it, Reid could certainly do damage to *me*. He was the epitome of the dangerously powerful man Mom had warned me against, and if anyone knew what she was talking about, it was her.

No, I couldn't—could *not*—get involved with Reid. We'd survive the week, get the story done, and go our separate ways afterward.

But maybe I *could* have enough courage to be honest with him, just this once, and then carry on with my life.

I would. My heart rushed up my throat, threatening to block the words from coming out.

"I didn't want to know."

Reid's head cocked slightly to one side, his eyes narrowing a fraction. "About me? You didn't want to know *anything* about me?"

"I did, but I didn't." I shook my head. I was getting confused.

The wine, the medicine, sleep-deprivation, the soft rocking of the boat, the soothing rasp of his voice—all of it was working together to push this moment from conversation toward revelation.

That maddeningly soft voice continued to probe. "Because... you were trying not to think about me?"

He reached over and took my hand on the tabletop,

stroking his thumb over the backs of my fingers.

"I tried everything I could not to think about you," he admitted. "For years I dated women as different from you as I could find. Then I tried finding your clone. But I have to confess—even when I despised you, I couldn't get you out of my head."

I averted my eyes, shaking my head, blinking at the fuzzy golden aura around the tabletop candles.

This is bad.

We were doing it again. Our fun whale-watching excursion was quickly turning into another unwanted opportunity to spill my guts to Reid about our breakup and the miserable years that had followed for me.

Whether or not that was what he was going for, I had to stop it here. If I allowed him to get his fingertips any farther under the tight lid on our past, he might be able to pry it all the way off.

Then *everything* would come spilling out.

"I've had too much wine," I announced, attempting to get up from my seat at the table.

Once on my feet, I staggered to the side, the full impact of my alcohol and over-the-counter-pharmaceutical combo making itself known.

"Whoa there." Reid vaulted up and caught me before I fell. "You didn't even drink that much. I don't remember you being such a lightweight."

"I took some more motion sickness pills," I confessed, my voice slurry.

"How many?"

"Two."

Reid groaned. "No wonder you're loopy. With what you already had in your system, that's too much for your body weight. Come on. Let me help you."

He wrapped an arm securely around my waist and led me

down a corridor where he pushed open a door. A flip of the light switch revealed a beautiful stateroom, in the center of which was an enormous, extremely inviting bed.

My head was swimming like the pod of whales we'd seen today. I literally ached to crawl onto that comfy-looking mattress and stretch out. But I couldn't let myself.

I turned around in Reid's guiding arms and attempted to go the other way. All I managed to do was bump directly into his chest in the tight hallway.

"I can't. No. I can't get into your bed," I said to his sweater.

Reid laughed softly. "Mara. Bed is exactly the place you need to be right now. Just lie down for a little while. You can sleep until we get back into harbor. Don't worry—you're not going to wake up naked."

He spun me slowly back around and steered me forward. Too tired to argue, I let him and ended up falling onto the bed's plush comforter more than crawling onto it.

My eyes refused to open even when I felt him removing my shoes and lifting me to tuck me under the luxurious layers of fine bedding.

I was barely conscious when I heard his soft, "Goodnight, sweet girl."

When I answered, I had already started to slip in and out of a dream. He might not have even been in the room still, though in my dream the solid weight of him was tantalizingly warm next to me.

"Don't let me tell you... okay?" I mumbled to the Reid in my dream who was tenderly stroking my hair the way I used to love.

"Tell me what, baby?"

"That I still... I still..."

And my conversation with my dream-lover faded to black as the fatigue overcame me.

EIGHTEEN
Rude Awakening

Mara

Warm sunlight hit my eyelids the next morning, shocking me from sleep to insta-alertness as I realized I'd forgotten to set my alarm.

I sat up straight in bed, ready to jump into action, run for the shower, and get ready for work.

Wait—I wasn't in my room. Not in my bed.

Looking around, I vaguely recognized the state room I'd seen through hundred-pound eyelids last night. I was in Reid's bed.

Crap.

My feet hit the floor, and I looked down at myself, my skin registering the coolness outside the warmth of his exquisite bedding. I was clothed, but not as fully as I had been when I'd boarded his yacht yesterday.

I wore only the black tank top and black-and-pink bikini panties I'd had on under my sweater and jeans.

Crap-crap.

Heart pounding, I searched the room, locating my clothes folded neatly over a chair, and quickly pulled them on.

I made a necessary stop in the head next to my stateroom, making use of the brand new toothbrush and miniature tube of toothpaste I found there, then set out to search for Reid and give him a piece of my now-clear mind.

He'd basically kidnapped me. Taken me out to sea, given me drugs and alcohol, stripped me, and forced me to spend the night.

All right, well it wasn't quite that sinister, but my thoughts grew darker every step I took without finding him.

I checked the yacht's other stateroom. Its door stood open, the bed inside empty and neatly made—had it been slept in at all? Or had Reid perhaps decided to share a bed with the girl stupid enough to let herself be over-served and pass out there?

Crapcrapcrap.

My anxiety grew with every passing minute. I couldn't remember a thing after dinner last night.

Had we done anything? The fact that I'd woken up with *some* clothes on led me to believe we hadn't.

Plus, it had been so long since I'd had sex, my body would probably have let me know. My heart seized as the next question hit me—had I *said* anything revealing?

I climbed the stairs to the top deck, squinting in the bright morning sunlight. There was Reid, dressed in a fresh white polo shirt and pair of jeans, reclining in front of a bountiful breakfast table with his gaze trained on his laptop.

He looked up as I approached.

"Good morning," he said with a wide smile. "Feeling better?"

His smile dropped as I failed to respond. My glare must have answered his question.

"What the hell happened last night?" I demanded.

"Calm down, Mara. Here—have a seat, eat some breakfast. Sorry about the selection. Vincenzo disembarked when we got into harbor last night. I just put out whatever I could find in the refrigerator."

"I'm not hungry at the moment." I scowled at him. "What I *am* is very curious as to why I woke up this morning in your bed instead of mine. In my *underwear*."

"Don't worry. Nothing happened. *You* were the one who took your clothes off. You kept saying you were hot. I tried to wake you when we docked, but you were practically comatose. You definitely couldn't drive yourself home, and I thought it might not be a great idea for me to drive and carry you unconscious into your mom's house."

"My mom! I've got to call her. She probably thinks I'm dead." I felt my pocket for my phone then realized it was in my purse below deck.

"It's okay," Reid said. "I called her last night and told her you were too tired to come home."

My forehead dropped into my palms. "Oh God. That might be worse. What did she say? Did she freak?"

He grinned. "She threatened me with bodily harm in the way only a mama bear can. I swore on my own mother and every body part I hold dear that I wouldn't lay a hand on you. I think she was convinced enough not to call the police, but you should probably check in with her pretty soon—let her know what time you'll be home."

I stood. "Right now wouldn't be soon enough. I'm leaving."

"You're not going to have breakfast?"

Reid lifted a hand and waved to someone behind me. I turned to see a middle-aged guy on the deck of the neighboring yacht.

"Good morning, folks," he called.

I forced a squinty grin for him then turned back to Reid. "Not with you."

"Come on, Mara. A few more minutes. I've got to head in

to work in a little while anyway. It'll be nice to have some company for breakfast for a change."

"Oh, so you don't ply over-tired women with alcohol and anti-motion-sickness pills often, then?"

He grinned at my unmistakable annoyance. "If I wanted overnight company, it's *possible* I could find a woman I *wouldn't* have to drug."

My fingers clenched into fists at my side. "Well, maybe you should do that then. I certainly won't be spending the night again."

"Hold on." Reid stood. "I'll get your purse and jacket for you. And I'll see you tonight after work—seven o'clock dinner still good for you?"

So smug.

"No—it isn't good for me," I snarled.

In fact, it will likely be very, very bad for me to spend another evening with you.

"But I'll be there, since I have no choice."

"Great." He grinned, seeming unaffected by my surly attitude. "Waterplace Park Condominiums. The condo number is on your itinerary."

He retrieved my things, and I snatched them without a thank you, irritated at his sunny morning-person attitude. I stomped down the ramp and toward my car without a glance back in his direction.

Why did every meeting I had with Reid end with him smiling and me running away?

* * *

"So what's on the agenda for tonight?" Heidi asked.

I'd called her from the car on the way home because I wasn't sure I could avoid spontaneous combustion a second longer if I didn't vent.

"I'm supposed to meet him at his condo at seven. There's a Waterfire tonight, so maybe it has something to do with that."

"Ooh, Waterfire," Heidi gushed. "I remember that from when I was at Brown. It's about the only good memory I've been able to hold onto from being there."

Heidi had spent the first half of her freshman year at Brown University in Providence, and it had ended very badly, to say the least.

She'd met the world's most prolific player, promptly fell in love with him, and he'd cheated on her in record-setting, spectacular fashion. She'd run back home to Georgia where it had taken her years to pull herself out of the resulting tailspin.

I left the Eastport Bay Yachting Center parking lot, fighting the urge to look back at the harbor for Reid's boat.

"Yeah, well if Reid's counting on Waterfire's romantic setting to soften me up for the interview, he's mistaken. He's really been pulling out all the stops—no doubt he wants me to see what an amazing condo I passed up on, too."

"Are you sure that's what he's doing—showing off? Because it seems to me like he's wooing you," she said.

"Wooing?"

"Yes—trying to make you fall in love with him—or slip and admit that you still love him."

I barked out a sharp laugh. "Like *that's* going to happen."

"What would be so bad if it did?"

I opened my mouth to recite the long list of reasons why it would be so bad when my other line beeped.

"Hold on." I pulled the phone away from my ear and checked the number. "Heidi? I've gotta go. It's the high school. My brothers have probably set the place on fire—again—or hung the headmaster's underwear from the flagpole."

I clicked back over and took the call. There was no fire—or underwear display—but apparently *someone* had filled the high school's indoor pool with Jello, and those someones bore a strong resemblance to my two easily-identifiable brothers in the security video.

"Does that qualify as senior prank material?" I asked, hopeful but not all that optimistic.

"They're juniors," the headmaster deadpanned. "And they're in *serious* jeopardy of spending their senior years at some other institution—possibly the state juvenile detention facility—if things don't change. I had to hire an industrial cleanup crew to shovel the pool out manually. Thankfully we're on fall break next week, but it'll be two weeks before we can even use it again."

"I'm so sorry for all the trouble, but there's no need to call the police about this, is there?" I urged. "Of course we'll pay for the damage—and the cleanup crew. And if they can possibly help with the cleanup, I'll send Baxter and Bowie right over."

The headmaster sounded somewhat placated. "I'll email you the bill. And please *don't* send them over—they're suspended for the rest of the week, and frankly I'd rather not see their faces right now—or for a long time to come. We've given the boys some... extra rope because of your father. But this can't continue. It was one thing for them to haul in six tons of sand and create a beach—complete with beach chairs and volleyball court—in the school parking lot..."

"I apologize on their behalf," I interrupted.

"And another for them to turn the school's main hallway into a slip 'n' slide," he said.

"I can see why that might have been frustrating and not conducive to a proper learning environment. Very sorry for that as well. Unfortunately, they have access to more money than common sense at this point in their lives. That's why I moved back and took a job here in Rhode Island. I'm trying to create a more stable home environment for them."

He sighed loudly. "Yes well... one more incident and we'll have no choice but to expel them. I don't need to tell you how that would impact their college applications at the prestigious universities I'm sure your parents want them to attend."

"There won't be any more incidents," I promised. "I'll take care of it."

I wasn't sure how, but I would because I *had* to.

"Miss Neely, if I may ask... why am I speaking with you instead of your mother or father? I understand your dad's occupied with state business, but your mother... well, this seems like something that should be a matter of parental concern."

"Believe me, they're very concerned," I assured him. "My mother's... out of town. Trust me, Baxter and Bowie are going to be different boys when you see them again after fall break."

I meant every word of that promise, but the truth was, it wasn't completely up to me. My brothers would have to be convinced of the precarious position they were in and motivated to save their own necks. I wasn't sure I could persuade them on my own—I needed some backup.

And I hated to admit it, but Bax and Bowie needed their father.

Grimacing, I dialed Dad's number. I'd been ignoring his constant calls and messages, but in a state as small as this one, I'd eventually have to see him and talk to him. Maybe today was the right time.

I'd ask him to meet me for lunch, fill him in on the boys' misdeeds, and request his intervention. Besides, I could use a little reinforcing of my armor before seeing Reid again tonight.

Nothing would be more effective for reminding me of why I couldn't be with him than spending some time with my father.

NINETEEN
The Team Dad T-shirt

Mara

When I'd agreed to meet Dad for lunch at Lux Burger Bar, I'd forgotten the choose-your-own-custom-burger place was basically across the street from Reid's Providence condo building.

It seemed like no matter where I went in this state, I was under his shadow. I selected a table in the back corner and sat facing away from the window-view of his shining high-rise.

Dad came in a few minutes later. Several heads turned, and some of the restaurant patrons called out his name, recognizing him instantly as the state's governor.

I, on the other hand, barely recognized him. I mean, I knew it was him of course, but his appearance shocked me. I couldn't believe how much eleven years had changed him. The pictures I'd seen online had obscured the truth.

He was heavier than I'd ever seen him, and his black hair was streaked liberally with gray. He just looked so much... older.

I stood, nervously waiting as he spotted me and approached the table.

"Mara," he breathed, wearing a smile of wonderment. "Wow. It's so good to see you. Can I hug you?"

"Oh. Uh, yeah." I leaned toward him awkwardly as he wrapped his arms around me and squeezed tight.

It was almost surreal to be here with him like this, surrounded by his familiar Dad-smell in an embrace I remembered from my earliest childhood. He hadn't been a frequent hugger, so when I'd gotten one, it had felt extra special.

We took our seats across from each other at the two-top table. I picked up my menu card, preparing to mark it with my choices, but Dad just kept staring at me.

"You look beautiful, Mimi," he said, using the old nickname leftover from a time when I was too little to say my own name and called myself simply "me."

"You look so grown-up."

"Thanks, Dad. It has been a long time, hasn't it?"

A waiter stopped by the table to take our drink orders and waited while we quickly checked off our desired burger fillings and toppings and handed him our cards.

He promised us food within fifteen minutes and walked away, leaving us nothing to do while we waited but talk.

Crap. After the phone call with the headmaster this morning, this had seemed like a good idea. But now that we were here, I had no idea how to start the conversation.

The boys. Talk about the boys. Keep it focused on them.

"So I wanted to talk to you about the boys..."

Dad interrupted. "First I'd like to say, thanks for meeting me. And again—I regret our long estrangement. There's no use warming up to it or putting the subject off any longer. It's the elephant in the room, so we might as well talk about it."

Well, okay. So it was out there then.

I swallowed an enormous lump that had formed out of nowhere the second he'd begun his heartfelt apology. I could see it was sincere. The regret was coming out of his every pore.

"Why did you do it?" I asked.

I didn't have to explain what *it* referred to. He knew exactly why I'd cut him out of my life.

"I wanted to protect you," he said. "At the AG's office, we were involved in a big operation to take down the Rhode Island crime families. Reid's dad was involved in all that, and I didn't want you caught up in it. You were just a little girl. You didn't know any better. That kind of thing... those kind of people... they can ruin your whole life, your future."

"But Reid wasn't involved in that world. He was just a kid. He didn't even know his dad. His mom protected him from that."

"Rhode Island is a small state. You can't escape from who you are here, no matter how much you might want to."

"Who you *are* isn't determined by your DNA," I argued. "It's about the choices you make in life. It's about your heart, your character."

"I don't know, kiddo. A last name can really haunt you, especially here where everybody kind of knows everybody else."

My father's expression morphed into one of horror as something occurred to him. "Imagine if you'd gotten pregnant with his child..."

"I wish I had," I blurted out, shocking myself.

But no, that couldn't be true. A child would have tied me to Reid for life. I *didn't* want to be like Mom, eternally connected to a powerful man who could run roughshod over me and make me miserable.

Dad looked at me with sad eyes. "You still love him... after all this time."

"No." I shook my head vehemently. "I don't. I mean, yes, there's still some leftover attraction. We all have our type, right? That's all it is. I ran into him at Uncle Tony's Pizza. He looked good," I added belatedly by way of explanation.

"I've heard you've been spending quite a bit of time together recently," Dad said in a casual tone.

My heart iced over. Had someone seen us together at the Marina? Or at the kite festival in Easton Park—and reported the "transgression" to my father?

"How do you know that?" I demanded. "Are you having me *watched*? You are, aren't you?" It was a good thing we were having this conversation in a public place, or I might have been screaming like a raving lunatic by this point.

A conversation from the past few days rushed back to my mind, Reid's confession that he'd used private investigators to track me down and report back to him after I disappeared from his life.

It occurred to me that he'd grown up to be scarily similar to my dad, something I never would have expected.

"Here we are—turkey burger with Dijon, avocado, and pickles with a side salad for the lady," the perky waiter sang out, oblivious to the standoff occurring at our table.

"... and Kobe beef with provolone, garlic aoli, and smoked bacon with cheddar tater tots and a chocolate chip shake for you, Governor."

Such a Dad order—high fat, high sugar, and fried all the way.

"Thank you son," Dad said. "Looks great."

"Thank you," I said tightly.

When the waiter walked away, Dad responded to my accusation.

"Mancini's got a reputation as a hard man, Mara. A ruthless businessman. He's not the kid you used to know. You wouldn't take my advice or even talk to me. It was the only way I knew to watch out for you."

"You don't *need* to watch out for me. I'm twenty-eight years old. I can take care of myself. Besides Reid would never hurt me."

And where the hell had *that* come from? Reid Mancini was more capable of inflicting pain on my heart than any man alive, including the one seated across from me.

"There are women in his life," Dad warned ominously.

"And there are men in mine—lots of them," I lied.

Fighting to maintain my composure, I quickly added, "For your information, I've been assigned to interview Reid. That's the only reason we're spending time together. He's being a diva about the whole thing and requiring me to have several pre-interview meetings with him so he can feel 'comfortable.' When the interview is done, I'll never see him again. So you can call off the hounds."

"Sure. Sure, okay," Dad said, clearly unconvinced. "I will, I promise. As long as you promise *me* something."

"What?"

"You watch out for yourself. If you do still have a soft spot for the guy based on your childhood friendship, just keep in mind that people change. And from what I hear, Mancini hasn't changed for the better."

Said the pot to the kettle.

"Don't worry about me. I'll be fine. And if you want a second chance for us to have any kind of relationship, you'll mind your own business and *stop* meddling in mine. I'm very serious, Dad—stay *out* of it."

He held up both hands in the surrender pose. "Fine. Fine. I won't touch a hair on his head."

Pointing my fork in his direction, I added, "*Or* threaten his business interests in the state."

"Or mess with his business interests," Dad repeated in a dutiful tone. "Happy now?"

I snorted a humorless laugh. "I haven't been happy in a long time... but I'm working on it."

His expression caved in, his eyes filling with clouds of

regret. "I really screwed up, didn't I, Mimi? With you *and* your mom."

"Yes. You did. And the boys are pretty messed up, too. That's actually why I wanted to talk to you today. Something has to be done. They're out of control."

"What did they do this time? And how much is it going to cost me?" He was smiling as if anticipating a funny story about his brilliant but wayward sons' latest hijinks.

"It's not a joke, Dad. They vandalized the school's indoor pool. The headmaster threatened to call the police this time. They're getting worse, not better. If they don't turn it around, they're going to make a mistake that money can't fix. They're going to hurt themselves or someone else."

My father's smile fell. For the first time in my memory, he sounded helpless. And *humble.* "Everything I've worked for... all my success...it's worth nothing if my family's not okay. What do you think I should do?"

I blinked away the moisture accumulating in my eyes and looked down at the tabletop, fiddling with the salt and pepper shakers in front of me.

"For starters, you should spend more time with them."

"I want to. I've tried, but they don't want to see me," he said.

"I know. That's what they *say.* I felt the same way. After you... did what you did... I felt like I didn't know you anymore. It killed me to think that someone I trusted could ever hurt me like that. I wanted to punish you."

Dad stared at me with rapt attention as I continued.

"But whether they know it or not, Bax and Bowie *need* you right now—desperately. And they do love you. Even when I was mad enough to refuse your calls, I listened to all your messages. I'm sure they do, too."

"I'm so sorry, Mimi. I never wanted to hurt you," Dad said. "Before, you accused me of thinking only of myself and my political ambitions, and honestly, that's partially true. I did get a little obsessed with the polls."

"A little?"

"Okay, well, I got my priorities pretty mixed up. But like I said before, I never meant to hurt you. Call me crazy but dating a mobster's kid isn't exactly a recipe for happiness."

"I *was* happy. I would have *been* happy with Reid."

The rightness of the words sank in as I said them. "And if we'd stayed together, maybe he wouldn't have turned out to be such a 'hard man,' as you put it. But that's ancient history. We're talking about Bowie and Bax. Do you have any thoughts on how we can, I don't know... scare them straight or whatever?"

Dad rested his elbows on the table and folded his fingers together, thinking. "I have a friend from college who owns a cattle ranch in Central Texas. When we talked a few months ago, he was telling me he runs a program out of there for troubled teens. Sort of like a cross between a dude ranch and boarding school. He says it's a better alternative than a teen boot camp for a lot of boys."

"Sounds interesting. What do they do? Make them muck out horse stalls and stuff?" I asked.

"That would go a long way toward erasing any entitlement issues, wouldn't it?" Dad said. "My buddy said they use a combination of equine therapy, clinical therapy, academics, and nature. They do chores around the ranch, go to classes, do some self-reflection work, help take care of the horses in addition to learning to ride. They do some fishing on the lake there, hiking trails, and they have regular group therapy and individual therapy meetings. Family therapy, too. I could be there for that."

"Do you think you could get them into the program—soon?"

He smiled. "I know I can. All this political clout does have its advantages."

"Right. How silly of me," I quipped.

I'd spent the past few days witnessing what money and power could get you if you really wanted it. Reid had quite handily hijacked my job and my life to suit himself.

"I'm not sure the boys are gonna like it, though," Dad warned. "It'll be hot as hell and damn hard work. They might hate me for it."

"If it works, they'll thank you for it later."

"Yeah," he snorted. "That's what I thought about you, and all it got me was a decade of the silent treatment."

"This is different. And there may be no other choice. They're about an inch away from getting expelled—again. I've tried talking to them. Mom's out of answers—she's pretty much given up. What else can we do?"

At the mention of mom, Dad leaned forward in his seat. "How is she?"

"Sad. Angry. But I don't think she really thinks Ricardo is the answer." I hesitated but then added, "She misses you—the old you, the one she fell in love with."

His brows shot up, and his eyes brightened with hope.

"Do you think she'd let me talk to her? Let me apologize? You think she might give me another chance, too?"

I shook my head, grimacing as I tried to picture that conversation. "I don't know. I mean, miracles happen I guess, but I don't think she's interested. You had thirty years' worth of chances."

"Some of those thirty years were pretty damn perfect. I've got to try," he said. "If I can just get her to listen to me."

As for myself, I was surprised to discover that listening to Dad had helped me. Not to the point of buying the Team Dad t-shirt or jumping on the old true love bandwagon again—that just wasn't going to happen—but something inside of me had loosened a notch.

I didn't know if I could ever completely forgive Dad, but I did understand him a little better.

And being with him again, there was no mistaking that the father I'd once idolized and loved so much was still in there. Just like my mom did, I missed *that* guy. I wanted to keep seeing him.

Wasn't it better to have an imperfect father in my life than no father at all?

Before we left the restaurant, I decided the answer was yes. We promised to see each other again soon, and this time I hugged him. It felt good to be in his comforting arms and to let him back into my heart.

As for Reid—he wouldn't be getting anywhere near *either* place tonight.

TWENTY

Dangerous Ride

Mara

I handed my keys to the valet and walked toward Waterplace Park Condominium's glass-encased lobby.

The air was fragrant with wood smoke from Waterfire, an artistic display of cedar-filled braziers running the length of the two rivers, which intersected in the middle of Providence.

As Reid's condo was right on the river, I'd had to fight a good bit of traffic getting here. On Waterfire nights, downtown was always crowded with couples and families and groups of students, walking the sidewalks along the rivers, listening to the unique mix of instrumental and world music, sampling treats from vendors or just finding a spot to sit and people-watch.

They came to breathe in the amazing scent and enjoy the beauty of the wood fires glowing atop the dark waterways.

The condominium towers overlooked Waterplace Park, a circular basin where boats, filled with wood and volunteer event crew members, circled and changed direction so they could head back up the river and make another pass, refilling fire baskets as their flames started burning low. The whole event lasted several hours.

It must have looked amazing from Reid's balcony far above.

Before opening the lobby door, I stopped to look up at his building. Several residents were already out on their balconies, enjoying the night air and the spectacle below.

From my vantage point, their bodies were dark silhouettes against the reflective surface of the building. The tips of two cigarettes glowed in the darkness as one couple smoked together above me.

"Thinking of scaling the building?" A teasing voice came from nearby. "I recommend the elevator. It's a long way to the top. And I'm not sure you're dressed for a climb."

Reid walked toward me from the open lobby door, smiling, and looking heart-stoppingly handsome in a pair of dark slacks and a luxurious soft-looking black blazer with a cream-colored dress shirt underneath, a couple of buttons unfastened at the neck.

"Pretty dress," he said, reaching me and brushing my cheek with a meaningless, but still unexpected, greeting kiss.

Breathe, Mara, I disciplined myself, forcing a non-lustful smile. "Of course you'd have the penthouse."

"Actually no. Mine's one floor beneath it—some Hollywood actor bought the penthouse for his kid who's going to Brown—but I do have an incredible deck. The view is great. I'll show you later, before we eat. I thought we might walk down to the river first. Will you be okay to walk in those heels?"

"Oh sure, whatever. That's fine."

"It's probably been a long time since you've gone to a Waterfire." He placed his hand lightly against my lower back as we descended the stairs from his condo plaza to the river walk.

"Although I guess there may have been one sometime

when you visited home from school," he speculated. "Or work."

"There may have been, but I haven't gone to one since... high school," I said.

When you and I went together. Back then, the two of us had walked hand in hand along the river, taking advantage of the shadowed spaces under the bridges to steal kisses, feeling anonymous in the crowd.

Reid gave a soft laugh. "Me either. It's right outside my door, and I never make time to go."

"What *do* you do with your free time, Mr. Mancini? Inquiring minds want to know," I said, using my TV voice and holding an imaginary microphone under his chin.

He laughed and grabbed my hand, enclosing it in his with a brief squeeze. He let it drop, and we started walking the perimeter of the basin, watching a performance artist juggling fire batons for the crowd as he perched on a platform over the water.

"I work," he finally answered. "Pretty boring, I guess, but it's the truth."

"But you must go out at night." I held my arms out to both sides and twisted. "You're surrounded by world-class restaurants, theaters, nightclubs. What's the point of living downtown if you don't go out?"

"To be close to work?" He screwed his face up into a comical that-sucks-doesn't-it? expression. "I do enjoy the restaurants. I take clients out frequently."

I noticed he said "clients," not, "women." My mind went back to what my father had said and to the photo of the stunning girl on display in his Eastport Bay mansion.

"What about dating?" It was a struggle to keep my voice casual as my heart pulled a sneak attack, drumming hard enough to compete with the Waterfire music.

Reid stared at me for a minute, his eyes reflecting the flames behind me.

"Sometimes," he said softly and resumed walking.

"Anyone special?" I continued prodding, angry at myself for asking, but dying to know the answer.

"I'm not being nosy," I rushed to add. "That's a question I'll have to ask during the interview. Viewers will want to know."

"As you may have noticed, I haven't exactly ever cared about satisfying the curiosity of viewers."

"You do now. The interview was your idea, after all. So, cough it up—is there someone important in your life?"

Good, Mara. Light tone of voice, pleasant expression. Nothing personal.

He waited a few seconds before responding, stopping in place and staring out at the glow of the fires on the river basin.

"You probably wouldn't want to talk to the women I've dated—they'd tell you I was an aloof bastard." He laughed softly, then paused before adding, "There is this one girl..."

Crap. I knew it. The supermodel Mara-upgrade.

"I never talk about her though. Some things..." Now he turned and looked at me. "... are going to remain off-limits during the interview, I'm afraid."

"You can't tell me what not to ask, you know. That's not how journalism works. Power of the press and all." I gave him a cheeky grin.

He answered it with a smirk. "I didn't say you couldn't *ask* it. I'm just not going to answer it."

We rounded the entire basin and ended up across the river from his condo. A line of people stood waiting for a chance to board one of the long black gondolas that floated slowly up and down the waterway.

When we were younger, Reid and I had always talked of

renting one, but as teenagers, we'd never been able to afford the steep price of a ride.

He walked to the front of the line, whispered something to the ticket agent, and slipped a hand from his pocket into the other man's partially concealed palm. Then he turned and gestured for me to join him.

As I walked over to meet him, a murmur went up from the small crowd, who seemed to be realizing en masse they'd just been cut in favor of a customer with deeper pockets.

"No, Reid," I hissed. "We can't."

He grinned and ignored my objection, evidently accustomed to using his wealth to bend the rules.

Growing ever more aware of the holdup we were causing in the proceedings, I shook my head and stayed put. It wasn't so much that I objected to his methods, though they were wrong. I didn't want to get into that boat with him.

I literally didn't think I'd be able to stand taking that long-dreamed-of romantic gondola trip with him when our relationship was no longer of the romantic sort.

As a girl, I used to imagine him proposing to me on such an occasion, in the way teenaged girls dream of that sort of thing. Drifting down the fire-lit river on a "business trip" just wasn't the same. The thought of it was too sad.

Turning, I beckoned to the next people waiting in line, a couple of young lovers, about the same age as Reid and me. They approached us with wary expressions.

"This looks like a special occasion for you," I said, and the young man nodded. "We'd like to treat you—your ticket is already taken care of. Enjoy."

As their identical looks of shock transformed into smiles of delight, Reid turned to me with a head-shaking narrow-eyed grin.

"And you said I always get *my* way."

The couple walked ahead of us onto the small boarding

dock. The woman climbed into the waiting gondola, and the guy turned back to us and mouthed, "thank you."

He pulled a small box halfway out of his jacket pocket, blocked from his date's view by his body, and showed it to me with an excited secret grin, then hid it once again before joining her in the boat.

The sad irony hooked into my heart and twisted like barbed wire snagging a piece of clothing.

I turned away from the too-romantic picture, looping my arm through Reid's to pull him with me.

"Look at that—you really are a matchmaker—you just didn't know it," I teased.

"And you," he countered with a nod in my direction, "must not be as sour on love as you've claimed to be. I hope they get one hell of a ride for the price I paid."

"I only did that because someone could have recognized me from the news," I lied. "It wouldn't represent the station very well for one of their reporters to cut the line for a gondola at Waterfire. They'd tweet about it and slam me on social media. Public Image 101. You should take notes here."

"You're right. What was I thinking?" Reid laughed and reached toward me, perhaps to take my hand.

I chose that moment to spin around and face him, walking backward just in front of him.

"You know what? I'm hungry," I announced. "Didn't you promise me some dinner?"

"I believe I did," he said, and together we walked quickly past all the lovers enjoying the beautiful night and went upstairs to his condo.

TWENTY-ONE

Fires and Fortunes

Mara

His place was, of course, spectacular.

Wide open and sparely furnished, it still reeked of money, from the gleaming wood floors to the soapstone kitchen counters, to the luxurious white drapes framing floor-to-ceiling windows that looked out over the city skyline.

"Can I take your jacket?"

Reid held out a hand as I peeled off the vintage leopard-print coat I loved and saved for cool-but-not-cold nights like this one.

I'd rescued it from going to the trash years ago when my grandmother, God rest her soul, had been cleaning out her closets.

Wearing it always made me feel very Audrey Hepburn city-chic. I could picture myself walking the streets of Manhattan in it someday when I eventually worked my way up to the network.

"Thank you."

Now that we were away from the shield of the crowd, my

nerves kicked into high gear. I handed Reid the coat and walked straight toward the window wall.

Mr. Mancini had a knack for choosing views. Either that or they just automatically came with money.

Beyond his deck, the city lights twinkled and made the colonial-era city look magical, a tasteful blend of historic and modern. The rivers far below were dotted with firelight.

Lights glowed on the deck as well. A line of candles flickered down the center of a long teak table.

Suddenly, the warmth of Reid's body was close behind me, his hot breath tickling the back of my neck as he spoke.

"Dinner is served. Come right this way."

He walked a few steps away to a glass door embedded in the giant window and pushed it open, holding it for me until I had crossed the threshold.

I looked back over my shoulder at him. "Maybe I should have kept my coat. I didn't know we'd be eating outside."

"Patience," he advised.

He reached up and turned a knob on a tall metal cylinder near the table. It had an umbrella-like attachment at the top, the underside of which began to glow orange, sending toasty waves of heat down over my place at the table.

"Would you prefer 'Summer day at New England beach' or 'July in Fresno?'" he asked.

"Oh, give me Central California. Fire it all the way up. As long as I'm being spoiled by a personal deck heater, I may as well get my money's worth... or your money's worth, I should say."

He gave me a dazzling smile and joined me at the table. "You should be spoiled."

"No, I shouldn't. I'm not a high-maintenance girl."

"I know. That's why you deserve a little spoiling. You've earned it."

Reid lifted a wine bottle from a bucket stand next to the

table and filled first my glass then his, continuing in a casual tone.

"In the course of my... research, I found out you refused to take your parent's money and put yourself through college instead. Interesting choice," he said. "Since then, you've been working your ass off, making it on your own with no help from anyone."

I smiled at his unexpected praise—and his fishing expedition. He was digging, trying to figure out why I'd suddenly rejected my parents' financial help.

"It's no more than most people do." I took a sip of the buttery sweet vintage, adding, "You've earned everything you have, too—and look at this—*you* have it *all.*"

Lifting my other hand, I gestured around to the pricey apartment, the incredible view.

Reid studied my face for a minute, drawing his lips inside his mouth then rolling them out. The move left them slightly damp and very soft-looking.

"Not everything," he said.

I gave a nervous laugh, dragging my gaze away from his mouth back to his eyes.

"What more could you possibly want? Your own island? A jet?"

He looked down and laughed, refolding his napkin in his lap.

"Oh my God. You have a jet, don't you?"

He held up his thumb and forefinger an inch apart. "Just a small one. For work. But I don't have an island, so I'm still a regular guy."

He laughed, realizing how ridiculous that sounded.

"You were never a regular guy," I said, then immediately wished I could suck the words back into my mouth like a popped bubble of chewing gum.

Reid's alert gaze focused on me. "What do you mean?"

I shrugged and darted my eyes away, lifting the lid of one of the platters filling the table. "Nothing. Just—I always knew you'd do something great—that you'd be a success. Ooh... your chef made Chinese food."

"No, actually, I had my assistant pick that up from Jacky's downstairs. It's a Pan Asian place. I remember you used to like that once upon a time."

"Still do," I said, digging in with the serving spoon.

Reid filled his own plate with stir-fried vegetables, rice, and crispy spring rolls. It looked like Lee had gotten some of everything on the menu. There were scallops with noodles, chicken teriyaki, steamed fish, even sushi rolls.

After a minute of eating, Reid spoke. "I'm surprised to hear you say that about me. I thought maybe you figured... I wasn't going to amount to anything."

When he looked up at me, his expression was marked with a vulnerability I hadn't seen in him since the first time he'd admitted to liking me as more than a friend.

I set my fork down. "Reid. Why would you say that?"

Now it was his turn to shrug and act nonchalant. "I don't know. I didn't know what to think. You disappeared. I tried to fill in the blanks."

Oh God. He thought I'd left him because I didn't believe in him? That I thought he would turn out to be some kind of loser?

Nothing could have been farther from the truth, but it was a truth I could not allow myself to tell him.

"No, Reid." I shook my head. "Please don't think that. It wasn't about you. You were wonderful. I did what I thought was best... what I had to do."

Oh God—I sounded like my Dad. Wasn't this almost what he'd said to me earlier today?

"So... what changed?" Reid asked. "Why did you 'have to' do it? You just... stopped loving me?"

Oh man. Here we were again. Back on the subject of our breakup. Reid didn't seem even close to letting it go, and of course I couldn't explain.

I gave him a pleading look. "Reid..."

He leaned back in his seat and put on a wide unnatural smile. "I know—I said I wouldn't bring up this stuff. I'm sorry. Forget it. Spring roll?"

He lifted the appetizer toward me with a serving fork, and I nodded, though I didn't know how I'd eat any more than what was already on my plate.

Safer to stuff my mouth than to open up my heart to him.

We dialed it back to small talk for the rest of the meal, discussing a few aspects of how Sheldon might shoot the story, talking about mutual friends of ours and where they'd ended up.

When I finished eating, I pushed away from the table and walked to the edge of the deck. I peered over the glass safety wall and railing down to the river which flickered with bright orange flame.

The crowd appeared to be dwindling. I shivered in my thin dress, registering the difference between the night air here and the artificially warm environment the patio heater had created around the table.

"It's nice out here, isn't it?" Reid draped his blazer over my shoulders.

It still held the warmth and scent of his skin and elicited a new shiver from me for reasons that had nothing to do with the outdoor temperature.

I risked a glance up at his face. "Thank you. Yes, you're very fortunate to be able to enjoy this every night."

"Actually..." He raised a brow and gave me a crooked, guilty-looking smile.

"Don't tell me you never come out here."

"Not often," he admitted. "I'm usually pretty beat when I get in from work. And..."

The pause was so extended, I thought he wasn't going to finish the sentence, but he did. "It's not the same when you're alone. Do you know what I mean?"

I nodded, understanding instantly. The more stunning a view was, the more beautiful a song, the more special an experience, the more you wanted to share it with someone.

Well, not just anyone. I should know. I'd shared all the moments of my life these past few years with "just anyones."

Anyone but him.

"I'm honestly surprised you spend so much time alone. I thought..."

"What?"

"Well, I thought for sure you'd have someone in your life. You said there was a girl?"

Reid looked away from me, down toward the remaining Waterfire lovers lingering on the sidewalks below.

"She's been away."

"Oh. Yes, I guess she would have to travel a lot."

When he looked back at me quizzically, I continued, "With modeling. I'm sure she has to travel for photo shoots."

Reid gave me a baffled glance, and I answered his unspoken question.

"I figured it out from that picture at your house in Eastport Bay. She's gorgeous. Sports Illustrated Swimsuit Edition, right?"

He opened his mouth, then shut it again and looked down with a little laugh. Reaching over, he tugged the sides of his jacket more closely around me, releasing another intoxicating wave of cologne from the fabric.

God, I could get drunk on the stuff.

His fingers held onto the edges of the jacket, stroking it lightly up and down. "You warmer now?"

I nodded. "Yes, thank you."

He slipped his hand lower, into one of the jacket pockets and pulled something out. "You forgot your fortune cookie."

The small cellophane-wrapped treat rested on Reid's palm.

"Ooh, I love these." I took it and started to pull the plastic apart. "Where's yours? I refuse to be the only fortunate one here tonight."

Reid reached into the pocket again, retrieving another cookie. "Here we go. Should we play the 'in bed' game?"

I wobbled back on my heels, suddenly off-balance in spite of taking care not to drink too much wine tonight.

"What?"

He laughed and reached out to steady me with a hand on my arm.

"You've never done that? You know... you read your fortune and add the words 'in bed' to the end. Tell me it's not just me and my friends who do this."

"Oh. Yeah. No, I know what you mean. Heidi and Kenley and I used to do that, too. Usually it makes no sense whatsoever."

"That's the point."

Reid opened his cookie and started to laugh, loudly this time. "Ah ha—listen to this—YOU WILL SOON RECEIVE EVERYTHING YOU HAVE LONGED FOR... in bed."

He gave me a suggestive eyebrow waggle.

I had to laugh, too, though I felt my face flame without the benefit of the patio heater, thank you very much.

"Okay, now you," Reid said, gesturing to the unbroken cookie in my hand.

Suddenly I was terrified to open it.

"I think I'll save it for later," I said, attempting to stuff it back into the pocket of his blazer.

"Oh no—who's the one who just said 'I'm not going to be

the only fortunate one, tonight?' Open it, chicken. It's probably some stupid Confucius quote."

"Watch your mouth, computer genius. Confucius was a brilliant philosopher."

"Okay, well then, lay the brilliance on me."

He waited with an expectant expression while I cracked open the cookie and pulled out the tiny slip of paper hiding inside.

The words printed there made me gasp. I tossed the paper over the balcony's edge.

"Hey," Reid shouted.

Stretching an arm over the railing, he grabbed for it, but the breeze had already carried it out of reach.

He turned back to me with a perturbed expression. "What did you do that for?"

I improvised. "It's... good luck to throw your fortune away and not tell anyone what it says."

"No, no. I told you mine. You have to tell me yours."

"You can't make me." I grinned and backed away from him like a naughty kid trying to avoid bath time.

He prowled after me, wearing a predatory grin that set the nerves in my stomach to a slow simmer.

"Come back here you little sneak. I'm not letting you get away with this, and I can *definitely* make you tell me."

"How? Are you going to throw money at me, Mr. Moneybags?" I continued to back away. "You can't always get your way. Nothing can make me talk when I don't want to."

"You don't have to tell *me* that. But there *is* one tactic I haven't tried yet." He raised his hands and wiggled his fingers in a mock-threatening tickle gesture.

I gave a little squeal and turned to flee, reaching the patio door and flinging it open before running through his apartment in a doomed escape attempt.

Reid's stride was much longer, I had on heels, and he

knew the layout of the place, whereas I'd never been here before.

I ran down a long hallway. He caught up to me as I burst through the doorway at the end. I shrieked with laughter, even before his fingers made contact with my very-ticklish rib cage and underarms.

Damn him for remembering my every weakness.

I writhed out of his grip, only to have him grab me again and tickle me without mercy. "Please," I wheezed between breath-stealing laughter, wiggling, squirming, trying in vain to get away from his strong, teasing hands.

"Come on, Mara. Tell me. Don't force me to up my game." Reid laughed through his threat. "You're going to make me resort to extreme measures."

"I'll never tell," I vowed as I broke away from him and ran further into the dark room, which now that I got a look at it, appeared to be the primary bedroom.

Oh crap.

Reid caught me again and hauled me back against his body with one arm wrapped around my waist.

"Okay, I warned you," he said.

And he planted his lips on the side of my neck in a wet, open-mouthed kiss.

TWENTY-TWO

Practice

Mara

I struggled once more, a weak half-hearted effort, then my body melted back against him. I was breathing hard from the combination of running and struggling and what he was doing now.

His mouth traveled up and down my neck, caressing and teasing the sensitive skin and absolutely demolishing all my thoughts as his hands gripped my hips and held me in place.

The protest that had been on my lips dissolved in a wave of hot bliss as Reid's mouth worked its way past my ear to my jaw.

I should stop him.

This was exactly where I had vowed not to go. But my traitor body had mutinied against my rational mind. It just felt too damn good. He felt good.

He'd always known exactly what to do to make *me* feel good, to break down my defenses.

And then I was turning in his arms. Was he doing it? Was I? I didn't know—maybe we both turned me around to face him, but suddenly I was right where I wanted to be, lifting up onto my toes, with his mouth moving over mine and his hands dropping to my waist, pulling me closer.

His jacket had fallen from my shoulders during our tickle-fight, and his hands slid around to my back, running up and down, gliding over the silky fabric of my dress.

The kiss went on and on as I lived in a state of suspended reality.

My hands shook with the desire to touch him back, to hold him. Finally I gave in—I was already in deep trouble anyway.

My fingers went to his chest, finding it solid and more developed than it had been when he was a boy back in high school. Now Reid was a man, fully grown and displaying the whole potential of his athletic build.

I slid my hands down the front of him, pressing my palms against the fascinating terrain of his abdomen, so firm and segmented with muscle.

His body was at once comfortingly familiar and excitingly new. It was still him, but it struck me that there was more of him, in all the right places.

My touch seemed to multiply Reid's excitement. He made a small grunt of enjoyment as my hands roamed over his torso, and his kiss changed, becoming harder and deeper.

His body was tensed all over, the muscles growing rock hard, as if he were preparing for battle of some sort. His hands moved to my head, burrowing under my hair and holding me in place for his kisses.

As if I could go anywhere.

It was like I hadn't been kissed in years, and yet it felt like yesterday that I had been a lovesick teenager wrapped in the arms of this same guy.

Reid and I had learned how to kiss together, starting out awkwardly and getting better with practice. Lots and lots of practice.

Maybe it was because we'd gotten together so young, but something had happened to me back then that had apparently ruined me for the rest of my life.

Reid had infused my existence at the cellular level. I hadn't really been able to enjoy kissing anyone else since.

He, on the other hand, had become an even better kisser in the years we'd been apart. And that meant...

I pulled my lips away, a shred of sanity returning to my overwhelmed brain. That meant *he* had been practicing. Naturally.

"What's wrong?" Reid shifted his mouth to my neck, torturing my hungry nerve endings with his persuasive mouth.

Of course he had been with other women. He was a grown man, a gorgeous one at that, and—oh yeah—he had a girlfriend.

And I had... had... something—right—I had promised myself not to get involved with Reid again. With anyone.

I pushed at his chest, and he released me, watching in bewilderment as I backed away, shaking my head.

"What's the matter?" he asked.

"I just... I can't, we can't do this."

He gave a half smile and rubbed a finger over his kiss-swollen lips. "Seemed like we were doing pretty well there to me."

I looked around his bedroom for my coat and purse. Which of course were not in his bedroom.

What was *I* doing in here?

What an idiot I was. I turned and speed-walked back down the hallway to the great room where I located my coat draped over the sofa back and my purse on the counter.

I grabbed them and headed toward the front door.

Reid followed me. "Would you mind telling me what's going on? One minute we're making out like we're going for a gold medal, and now you're leaving?"

"That shouldn't have happened. I didn't want that."

He was close on my heels, then in front of me just as I reached the door. Leaning his back against it, he folded his arms across his chest. He was breathing hard.

"Bullshit. You were just as into it as I was—I could feel you responding to me."

"Move please. I need to go home."

"Mara..." Reid threw his hands up in apparent exasperation. "Come on, don't leave. Let's talk. It's obvious we want each other. Why are you fighting it?"

He reached out and wrapped his hands around my upper arms. I shrugged out of his grasp, but I stopped trying to leave. He was right—at least once our time together should end without me running away.

I had to face this—to address what had happened between us, what kept happening, what could never happen again.

"Okay—yes—there's still some... residual attraction left between us. But it doesn't mean anything. I'm not... interested in you like that. And you shouldn't be interested in me."

"Really?" He didn't seem very impressed with my explanation. "Why the hell not?"

"Well, for one thing you have a girlfriend."

For another, I treated you like garbage and left you, without a word of explanation.

Why would he even still want me? "And... I have someone in my life, too."

Reid narrowed his eyes and analyzed my face, searching for the lie and probably finding it.

He lifted his jaw in a dare-ya kind of way. "Who?"

I scrambled for a name—one of the himbos I'd recently met at the gym who'd offered me his number and asked me to use it whenever my schedule would allow.

"Bruce."

"Bruce," Reid repeated, plainly suspicious that I'd pulled the name from thin air.

I tilted my chin up in defiance and continued lying. "Yes. We have a date tomorrow night at Café Nuovo."

His eyebrows dropped, and his lips pulled into a scowl. "You're supposed to be with *me* tomorrow."

"No. Maybe you should check your own itinerary. You wanted me to come to your company headquarters for a tour in the afternoon and discuss good video opportunities there. The itinerary said nothing about tomorrow night."

Reid bit his lip, his gaze traveling to the ceiling and back down to me. "Yeah, you're right."

I took my minor victory and ran with it, seeing an opportunity to put some much-needed distance between us.

"And as it turns out, Sheldon is going to go in my place," I said. "He's the better one to handle that anyway. I'm going to a medical appointment with my mom tomorrow."

That much was true. However, I had fudged on the timing a bit. The meeting was early in the morning, not that Reid needed to know that.

Some of the tension left his face. He was calmer now, the testosterone surge subsiding the same way my racing hormones were finally settling back into their reservoirs.

He shifted away from the door, making way for me. I started to reach for the handle, but he stopped my motion with a hand on my shoulder, which then coasted down my arm.

"Mara."

"What?" I forced myself to meet his eyes and tried to keep mine from revealing anything.

His gaze and his voice were soft. "What did your fortune say?"

I turned toward the door. "I can't remember. Something stupid."

Leaving his condo, I sprinted down the corridor to the elevator, unable to stop myself from looking back once as I waited.

Reid stood in the doorway, hands resting low on his hips, wearing the disgruntled expression of someone unused to being told "no." I wondered if this was a first—a woman leaving his place at night, rather than doing the morning-after walk of shame.

The elevator doors opened, and I stepped inside, slumping against the interior wall and hanging on to the handrail with both hands. I should have been satisfied—I hadn't run away this time, and Reid hadn't been smiling.

Instead, it felt like that time a couple years ago when I'd noticed my diamond earring was missing while standing near a storm drain, that empty sensation of losing something you know will never be found again.

TWENTY-THREE

Himbo

Mara

I jumped up from the waiting room chair as the doctor's office door opened.

Mom had been with her for two hours, and I was dying to know what was being said on the other side of that wall.

"Please come in, Mara." The psychiatrist smiled at me and held the door to her office open wide. "Your mother has indicated that she'd like for you to be informed about her treatment plan."

"Yes, of course. Good. Thank you," I said, stepping into the cozy space and taking a seat next to Mom on a pleasantly worn leather loveseat.

Dr. Weinberg sat in a swivel chair opposite us. She was a large woman, not unattractive, the kind often described as being "handsome."

She was comfortably dressed in pants and a turtleneck with a sweater vest. Her smile was warm, almost grandmotherly. I could picture her knitting in her free time.

"Well, as you know I'm sure, Evelyn has depression," she said. "After talking to her today, I believe she's been battling it for several years. Now it's reached the point of affecting her decisions and interfering with daily life and perhaps even becoming incapacitating."

I nodded, in shock but also relieved to hear the doctor put a name to it and to see her so calm and confident as she began to explain treatment options.

"The good news is things are about to start getting better. There are medications and therapies I believe will really help your mom and allow her to resume the life she once had and enjoyed. But to begin with, I think Evelyn would benefit from spending a little time at an inpatient facility."

I sat forward on the sofa cushion, my pulse jumping to attention. "You're going to have her committed?"

The doctor stretched out a hand toward me.

"No. No, nothing like that. This is completely voluntary, and she can choose to leave the clinic at any time. The place is quite lovely—it feels more like a spa than a hospital. It's not far from here, near Boston. I'll make sure you get a full tour of the facility when you arrive, and you'll have a detailed schedule of her daily activities. There's a liberal visitation policy. And as I said, she can choose to check out at any time, but I'm recommending a five-night stay to get her solidly entrenched in new habits and make sure her medications are perfectly adjusted for her."

"Are you sure that's really necessary?" I turned to search Mom's face, combing it for any signs of compulsion or reluctance. "Is this what you want?"

It all seemed so drastic to me.

She gave me a soft smile and nodded, taking my hand and squeezing it. "I don't want to keep being like I am, Mare-Bear. This sounds good to me. I want my life back, and if this is the way to get it, that's what I want to do."

We continued discussing what would happen after Mom

came home again and how to handle the insurance claim for a treatment facility of this sort.

Dr. Weinberg promised to help with every aspect. I thanked her and rose to leave, still shell-shocked that I was about to drive Mom home, not to stay, but to pack a bag for a five-day absence.

By late that afternoon, I was driving back home from the Boston clinic alone to get ready for my "date" and thoroughly dreading it.

I'd called Bruce the previous night right after leaving Reid's condo. He'd readily agreed to meet me at the restaurant in Providence at seven tonight.

Now I regretted my decision. After the day I'd had, there wasn't one ounce of me that wanted to go out, with him or anyone. But I had to.

It would be just like Reid to have one of his little minions spy on me to find out whether Bruce really existed or I'd made him up.

And I had to do *something* to put an end to the growing pull between us. I had to go out tonight and prove that I didn't still have feelings for Reid, that I had moved on, that there really was someone else in my life.

Even if in all actuality that someone was a dope with a pretty face and nice trap muscles.

* * *

Okay, well his biceps were pretty nice, too. I watched them bunch and flex in his tight shirt as Bruce cut into a fourteen-ounce New York Strip.

We'd been seated at an intimate corner table in the down-town Providence restaurant.

He looked up from his plate and gave me a happy smile,

gesturing with the hunk of pink-and-brown beef suspended on the end of his fork.

"I'm glad you called. I didn't think I was ever gonna hear from you. When you told me that story about having to spend time with your little brothers, you know, I thought you were just blowing me off."

I managed a fake laugh, trying not to cringe at his mention of Bax and Bowie, who'd left for the "bad boys ranch" with Dad this morning. I was worried about them. And Mom.

And every time I thought about going home to that empty house tonight, I felt like some bereft little kid.

My family was falling apart. I could no longer downplay what was going on or tell myself everything was going to be okay. I didn't know that. And the worst part was I had no control over the situation.

I was doing all I could for them, and still everything was a mess. I felt so alone.

"So, like I was saying, I'm saving up my vacation and sick leave days to take a trip," Bruce said. "I really need to get out of this place this winter, go somewhere warm. Hey, you should come with me—you got a passport, right? Maybe we could go to like, some island or something?"

I gave Bruce a tight-lipped smile and nodded. I literally couldn't think of anything I wanted to do less than go on a trip with him, no matter how good he might look in board shorts. But we had to talk about something during dinner, so I played along.

"Where would you go if you could go anywhere?"

Bruce's face became animated. He was kind of sweet, actually, like a goofy kid.

"Well, I've never been to Mexico. I saw the beaches there on Girls Gone Wild Cozumel, and they are *sweet*. And I always wanted to go to Jamaica and try the bona fide ganja, right from the motherland, you know?"

He pantomimed smoking a joint, nodding his head with a druggie-looking smile on his face.

Correction—there *was* something I wanted to do less than go on vacation with this guy—try the bona fide ganja from the motherland. I looked down at my watch.

Impossible—we'd only been here *thirty* minutes?

"Where would you go—if you could choose anywhere?" he asked.

"Oh, I've always wanted to see Australia."

Reid and I had decided that was where we would honeymoon, and we'd even been willing to have a winter wedding so we could travel there during that continent's warm-weather season. Those had been childish dreams and plans, put behind me long ago. But I did still wish I could see Australia at least once in my life.

"Yeah, that could be cool," Bruce agreed in his cheerful way. "I've never been to that part of Europe."

My fork froze in mid-air as I debated over whether to correct him.

Nah. It wasn't worth the effort. If he ever ended up going there, I assumed he'd find out he was on the wrong continent when his plane touched down. Taking a bite of my seared tuna, I gave Bruce a wide-eyed nod.

He went back to sawing his steak, happily chattering between bites.

"I thought after dinner we could go dancing at this great club I know. My buddies and me go all the time—you're gonna love it. And wait till they see me walk in with the hottie reporter from Channel—"

"I don't think I can tonight," I interrupted, wrinkling my nose apologetically. "I'm pretty tired."

No way was I spending my after-dinner hours with Bruce. I only had about, oh... a half hour more patience left in me before I'd have to claim headache and leave the restaurant —alone.

"Oh. That's okay. We can just go back to your place or something. My roommate is having a party at our apartment tonight, and we wouldn't have any privacy."

He gave me a smile that I thought was meant to be seductive, and then I realized what he was saying.

My jaw might have fallen open. Did he actually think I was going to sleep with him tonight? In spite of my carefully cultivated reputation, I wasn't that easy.

And that was besides the fact that Bruce might literally be the last man on earth I'd ever have sex with. I was so annoyed I started to tell him so, but before I could speak, another voice intruded.

"Mara."

Low and pleasantly rough, it could only belong to the absolute last person I wanted to see at this moment.

TWENTY-FOUR
Rainy

Mara

Reid stood beside our table. Not alone.

By his side, clasping his hand in her skinny acrylic-tipped fingers was the girl from the photo.

She looked exactly like the kind of woman billionaires dated. Her wispy body was sheathed in a clingy turquoise mini-dress that dipped low in the front, revealing luscious cleavage attached to some expensive-looking breasts, and leaving little else to the imagination.

Her dangling earrings brushed the perfect skin of her cheeks. Long, dark hair swung in a straight sheet past her shoulders.

Hmmph. So much for Reid's claim of preferring wavy hair. She wore makeup but probably didn't need it, as she was one of the most physically perfect women I'd ever seen.

Bruce must have agreed because he nearly spit out the mouthful of beer he'd just taken. His face displayed the glazed expression of a man who thought he must be dreaming.

Reid, on the other hand, appeared almost bored. Of course, he had this perfect creature to himself all the time.

She probably wasn't even the first supermodel he'd dated.

"Hi," she said in one of those soft, high-pitched baby-doll voices men seemed to love.*I hate her.*

"Hi." I stuck out my hand and stretched my mouth into a smile. "I'm Mara Neely."

After she gave my fingers a weak clasp, I gestured to my star-struck date. "This is Bruce Franconi."

"I'm Rainy," she cooed, then turned to introduce my lifelong love to me. "This is Reid."

He looked down at her with a patient expression. "We already know each other, pumpkin, remember? That's why we came over to say hello."

"Oh, right." She emitted this little Cartoon Channel giggle, and based on the look that came across Bruce's face, I thought he might just take a knee and propose.

Reid's face was now sporting an amused grin. "So this is Bruce."

He reached across the table and gripped my date's hand, appearing no less than delighted to meet him. "I see you two are finishing up here. How was your dinner?"

"Fabulous," I said in a deadpan tone.

"Great, man. You should totally try the New York Strip. You been here before?" Bruce asked.

Reid answered that he had, and Bruce continued his impromptu restaurant review. "Yeah, this place rocks. I knew I had to bring Mara to someplace swanky, you know, cause she's like, kinda famous and all classy and whatnot."

"Oh yes," Reid agreed, clearly fighting to suppress a laugh. "Only the best for her."

Knowing him like I did, I could tell he wasn't referencing the dining establishment with that little remark. He was talking about my date.

He saw right through him. He thought Bruce was a joke.

Well—I thought his girlfriend was a silicone-filled, one-calorie-from-starvation nightmare. I reached across the tabletop and stroked Bruce's hand.

"Oh—you're too sweet. You know I would have gone anywhere with you, though."

I could tell I'd surprised Bruce from the way his eyes widened. But he got right with the program.

He grabbed my hand, running a thick thumb vigorously over the back of my knuckles and giving me a totally unsubtle wink before turning back to Reid and Rainy.

"I'd ask you guys if you wanted to go dancing with us after dinner, but Mara and I are just gonna head back to her place, make it an early night. She's just about ready for bed, aren't ya, hon?"

I fought to hold in a gasp, while Reid's bemused expression was instantly replaced with a glare. He issued a tight-lipped reply without looking at me.

"Well, it was great to meet you, *Bruce*. You have a good night."

I almost felt sorry for scrawny little Rainy as he whipped her around and dragged her to their table.

Not as sorry as I felt for myself, of course. My ex was sitting down to dinner with a ravishing supermodel.

I was still here with Neanderthal Man's slightly less-intelligent cousin.

"Listen, Bruce. I think I'm gonna go on home. Alone," I hastened to add. "I really had the day from hell, and I wouldn't be good company for anyone tonight."

His dopey sweet face fell in disappointment. "Aw, can't we just stay a little longer? I wanted to get dessert."

I reached over and covered his beefy hand with one of mine. "You should do that. Don't let me be a party pooper and stop you, okay? And dinner's my treat."

"No way—" He started to argue.

"No. I insist. Dinner tonight was my idea. I'm going to

give my credit card information to the server, then give my parking stub to the valet. You just stay and enjoy dessert. In fact, have two."

Bruce's smile returned. "Okay then. I'll get the next one. You get some rest. I'll call you tomorrow."

"Great," I called over my shoulder, already heading for the front of the restaurant. Thank God I hadn't ever given him my number.

Wonder how long it'll take him to realize that?

Dating himbos had its advantages.

I stood out in front of the tall glass and chrome office building that housed Café Nuovo, waiting for the valet to bring my car around. I hoped it got here before Bruce realized my "oversight" and followed me outside to correct it.

On the other hand, he was probably chin-deep in a lovely chocolate mousse right about now.

"Don't let that gorilla go home with you tonight."

The growling voice came from behind me.

I spun around and nearly bumped into Reid's chest. "What? I don't—what are you—"

"I don't want you going to bed with him." His voice crunched the words like ice cubes.

I stared at Reid for a second before replying, "*You* don't want… you can't tell me…"

Looking around for his date, I snapped, "Where's Rainy? Isn't she waiting for you to finish her mini crab cake appetizer? Surely she can't eat the whole thing by herself."

He tossed a hand back toward the restaurant in a dismissive gesture. "I told her I was feeling queasy all of a sudden and couldn't eat. She's in the ladies' room. I've already called a cab to take her home. I'll call one for Bruce, too."

Reid pulled his phone from his jacket, fully prepared to act on the offer.

I put my hand on his arm, stopping him. "He brought his own car. What's going on here?"

The sound of tires on pavement caused us both to look up.

"Your car's here. I'll drive." Reid walked briskly around to the driver's side and took the keys from the valet, slipping him a twenty before I could even answer.

The ecstatic valet practically skipped around to the passenger door and opened it for me. I didn't get in. I leaned over and spoke to Reid, who was now sitting in the driver's seat.

Of *my* car.

"What the hell are you doing?"

"I'm taking you home." This was the tone he probably used at work—the CEO giving orders no one would dare disobey.

But I didn't work for him.

"I can take myself home. And what about your car?"

"I'll get it later."

His voice became less commanding and more pleading. "Please get in, Mara. We need to talk."

I held my position and stared at him. He revved the engine. Finally, I threw up my hands and got in before he decided to drive off without me and leave me to bum a ride with Bruce. I'd rather have walked back to Eastport Bay than done that.

When the valet had closed my door, I turned to Reid. "What are you doing? What if Rainy comes out and sees us driving off together? She's going to think—"

"I don't give a shit what she thinks." Reid pulled away from the curb, just as Rainy came out of the door.

I looked back over my shoulder and saw a taxi pull into the spot we'd just vacated, then turned back to Reid.

"Okay... so you've commandeered my car. Talk."

TWENTY-FIVE
The Real Deal

Mara

"Let's go home first," Reid said, pulling out of the parking lot.

"Whose home?"

Low-grade panic set in at the thought of being alone with Reid in his condo again only one night after I'd lost control of myself and made out with him.

"Mine. I wouldn't mind seeing your mother and brothers again, but not tonight."

"We can go to my house. They're not there. Take me home, and then I'll call *you* a cab. Or you can walk next door to your mom's place."

He laughed. "We'll see."

Forty minutes later, we'd made our way from downtown Providence to Eastport Bay, and Reid pulled my car into the circular driveway in front of my family's home, or at least what was left of my family. I unlocked the door, and he followed me inside.

He helped me out of my coat, hanging it on a hook in the

mudroom as if he were here every day. Well, he used to be, and it hadn't been that long ago.

Nothing much had changed in the house since the days when we'd hang out in the living room watching TV, waiting for my parents to go to bed. Then we'd make out on the couch, taking things as far as two teenagers dared with strict Catholic parents right upstairs—

Okay, not helpful. Let's keep our little trips down memory lane G-rated, shall we?

Reid walked into the living room and looked around, touching a small end table as he passed.

"Wow. It looks the same. I don't know why I didn't expect it to. It's just... weird."

I entered the dim room and clicked on another lamp. I knew exactly what he meant. It was strange for me, too, to see him here after all these years.

In one way it seemed natural and right, and in another—well, I just hadn't expected it to happen—not tonight, not ever.

"So, where's your family?" Reid asked, sitting down on the sofa in the same corner he used to prefer.

"Um, the boys are away at... ranch camp. And mom is..."

It was a simple question, but answering seemed impossible. I was mortified to feel tears forming behind my eyelids.

Surrounded by the busyness of the restaurant and Bruce's inane chatter, the reality of what had happened today had been easier to put out of my mind.

Here in this large, quiet house, where my mom and brothers *should* be, my emotions felt as fragile as snowflakes.

Suddenly, I was glad not to be here alone.

"She's sick, Reid," I finally said. I sat down next to him.

The confusion on his face turned to concern as he processed. He sat forward, placing a warm hand on my forearm.

"Cancer?"

"No. Nothing like that. I guess we're lucky compared with that. She has depression. But it's pretty bad. It's been going on for a while. I checked her into a place today. She has to stay there a week."

Now the tears were getting the better of me. I reached up and swiped at my eyes, turning my face away from Reid in embarrassment.

"Hey," he said softly. "It's going to be okay." He slipped an arm around my shoulders and pulled me against his solid side.

It was such a familiar gesture, especially here in this place. He didn't seem like a high-powered CEO or a billionaire tonight. He seemed like *my* Reid, the boy I'd turned to when the class mean girl had tormented me, when the stress of SAT prep had been too much, when my mom had driven me crazy.

He was the one I'd always trusted to be on my side, no matter what.

I relaxed and leaned into him, laying my head on his chest, breathing in his wonderful scent, allowing myself to be comforted.

"My mother told me Evelyn was going away for a week, but I thought she meant on vacation," Reid said. "That's why Mom decided to go visit her sister in Arizona this week. Where's the clinic? Is it local?" he asked.

As he held me and stroked my hair, I told him a little of what the doctor had said, told him about the facility, about how hard it had been to drive away this afternoon and leave my mom with strangers. I also told him my fears about what would happen when she got home.

And what I feared would happen if she didn't come home, if she needed longer term care.

I wasn't ready to be a mom—especially to two teenage boys who needed someone who actually knew what she was doing instead of clueless big sister as a stand-in.

Reid's free hand tunneled under my hair and found the nape of my neck, massaging out knots I'd just now realized were there.

"Poor girl. You've been dealing with a lot. I'm sorry. I didn't realize how bad it was with your mom. My mom said Evelyn was 'sowing some wild oats,' but I didn't realize she was struggling. I would've tried to help."

I sniffed. "What could you have done? I didn't even realize something needed to be done until recently. I thought she was just going through some kind of mid-life crisis thing, and it would sort of harmlessly play itself out."

"Well, I would have wanted to help."

Tears slipped from my eyes in a fresh stream as I started admitting the full scope of my misery.

"I should have been here, Reid. I abandoned my family. I went off and did my own thing, and everything here just fell apart."

He dipped his head down to see my face. "You were a kid living your life—you're supposed to go out and do your own thing. Don't feel guilty about that, Mara. Holding your family together was your parents' job, not yours."

"But I should have been braver," I said. "I should have stood my ground. I should have fought for what I knew was right instead of running away and hiding."

Reid's hand stilled on my neck. He shifted and leaned away just enough that he could look at me eye-to-eye.

"Running away? From what?"

Oh crap. This was bad. I was a vulnerable mess tonight. My emotions were broken open and leaking everywhere. Reid shouldn't be here to see this.

And he really shouldn't ask me any questions, because in this state, there was a chance I would answer them. I had to change the subject.

"Why are you here? Why did you say you don't care what

Rainy thinks? Is that how it is for the women in your life—you just do whatever you want, and they have to put up with it?"

He gave me a rueful smile. "Pretty much."

"Don't you... love her?"

He stared at me a few seconds before answering. His voice was hard. "I've already told you—I don't believe in love. Infatuation? Sure. I had that with Rainy once, but it wore off pretty quickly. It always does."

He hesitated before continuing. I could see the decision-making process going on behind his eyes.

"We're not together anymore. Rainy and I broke up a few months ago. She's been bugging me to get together and talk things over. I called her today and offered to take her to dinner, so we could talk."

"But you *didn't* talk. You followed me outside." A terrible suspicion crept up on me. "And you brought her to Café Nuovo. You knew I'd be there with Bruce."

A guilty grin developed on Reid's face. He leaned forward, his elbows resting on his knees. One hand went to the back of his neck, rubbing as if he'd slept on it funny.

"Yeah. I guess I... I wanted to see for myself."

"See what?"

"If what my investigator said was true—I wanted to see the kind of guy you're dating now."

I stiffened, already knowing what his evaluation of Bruce had to be. "That's none of your business. And you can't tell anything by looking at someone."

Although hadn't I judged Rainy the same way?

Reid laughed. "Give me a break, Mara. The guy practically has S.T.U.P.I.D. tattooed on his forehead. How can being with some goombah like that be stimulating for you?"

I looked at him straight-on and raised an eyebrow. Reid

already assumed I was sleeping with every himbo I went out with. It was much safer to let him go on believing that.

His expression darkened. "Well, all right, if that's all you care about, then I guess a guy with muscles on top of his muscles would *service* your needs adequately. But what about above the neck? It just doesn't seem like the girl I used to know."

"I've changed. You've changed, too. It happens."

He shook his head in disagreement. "There's no way you've changed that much. I think the real you is still in there somewhere under that front you put up. You can fool everyone else, but you can't fool me. I know you."

He leaned toward me as he said it until only inches remained between our lips.

My heart slammed against my sternum. I was in trouble. He did know me. And he knew exactly how to break through my defenses, exactly how to seduce and confuse me until I couldn't remember how the "new" me was supposed to feel or act.

His face was so close, so beautiful. I wanted desperately to kiss him.

No. I couldn't let it happen again.

Each time Reid held me in his arms he managed to pry another scale from my armor. I sat back against the couch cushion, restoring the space barrier between our faces. Grabbing a throw pillow, I wrapped my arms around it, holding it to my chest.

My tone was flippant. "What is it you think you know, genius?" I was ready to debate anything he might come up with.

One of Reid's eyebrows went up as he saw the challenge in my eyes and accepted it. "I think you don't care about any of these guys. I think you don't even like them all that much. I think you're fucking them as a distraction."

The expectant look on his face told me that was a random shot—he'd thrown it out, fishing to find out how far I actually went in these frequent, casual relationships.

That hook was going to come up empty. I ignored it. "A distraction from what?"

Reid slowly moved his upper body toward me, his gaze lasering in on mine. "From the way you really feel. From what you want more than anything."

My breathing shallowed. He was so close to the truth it was scary. I didn't want to know his answer to the next question, but it left my mouth anyway, barely a whisper.

"And what do I want?"

"You want it all—home, family, kids—you want love. Not that half-assed thing you have with all your boy toys. You want the real deal."

I shook my head slowly in denial, my heart beating in heavy, almost painful thumps as he continued moving toward me, a slow-speed chase with his eyes locked on mine, bringing his face ever closer.

His voice became dangerously soft as he finally reached me, his whisper brushing my lips.

"You want me."

And then he kissed me.

TWENTY-SIX
Confession

Mara

And, oh how right he was. I kissed Reid back, wanting him more than I wanted oxygen, more than I wanted safety in that moment.

Knowing he saw right through my façade into my soul stripped away all the fight in me. What was the point? I had never been able to fight my attraction to him.

That was why I'd had to physically leave the state and never speak to him again. Apparently, that had been a futile effort, because my addiction to him had actually gotten worse instead of better.

My hands went to his face as the kiss went on, greedily gliding over his cheekbones, his temples, sliding into his thick hair, so silky against my fingers.

With a low groan, Reid deepened the kiss and pushed me down to the couch cushions until I was on my back. He covered me with his body, even bigger and harder than it used to be. And I did nothing to stop him.

It felt incredible, intensely satisfying, necessary. Here on this couch where we'd made out countless times, my barriers were falling like the red maple leaves outside my house. I just couldn't fight it anymore. I didn't want to. I wanted him.

And though Reid no longer believed in love, he clearly still believed in lust, in that undeniable attraction that had always burned between the two of us. He possessed my mouth, his kisses becoming stronger, deeper, giving me a preview of what his body wanted to do to mine.

Even before he'd started kissing me, my nerve endings had gone into launch sequence. Now the booster rockets were firing. Every inch of my skin screamed for his touch. I writhed beneath him, lifting against the delicious hardness of his body.

Reid supported his weight on one arm, and his other hand hungrily explored my curves while we moved together, falling easily into a maddening slow rhythm.

After a few minutes of this he disengaged from my mouth, his voice sounding ragged. "God, Mara. I want you so much I don't think I can stand it anymore. If you're going to stop this, do it now. Tell me to go. Because otherwise, I'm going to make love to you—right here, right now."

His words evaporated my thoughts into a puff of steam. I'd almost certainly be sorry later on, but at that moment, I wanted exactly what he'd just threatened.

"No," I answered him in a rough, lust-soaked voice.

Reid stopped moving, his hand stilling on my body as he stared down at me with piercing eyes.

"Not here," I whispered. "My room."

Reid still didn't move. He stared at me as if stunned. I nudged upward, and then he did lift off of me, getting to his feet and pulling me up by the hands.

"Are you... are you saying yes?"

I nodded. As long as I was making this mistake, I might as well go big.

"Yes."

He grabbed my hand and pulled me to the stairs. We

walked up together toward the place he'd never been allowed by my strict, protective parents. And they had been so wise to keep us from being in my room alone together.

No doubt we would have taken things all the way much earlier if we'd ever been given the privacy and opportunity to do it.

At the top of the stairs, Reid paused. I stepped ahead of him and walked down the hallway to my room, pushing open the door and glancing back at him.

His smile nearly stopped my heart. It was so full of desire, remembered and brand new.

"Ah, the mysterious bedroom," he said, stepping inside for the first time ever. "I feel a little like Indiana Jones entering a hidden temple filled with treasure."

Walking around the room, he studied the mementos I'd saved and the photos on my walls.

Did he notice there were none of him? I'd taken them down and stashed them in a box at the back of my closet years ago.

He touched a trophy on one of my shelves, ran his fingers over old concert tickets and the high school ring I no longer wore then stopped when he came to the clear glass jar containing the stone hearts I'd collected from our beach walks.

"Did you put the new one in here?" At my answering nod, he smiled and then asked, "Have you… added many in the past few years?"

"None," I said softly. "I wasn't looking for them."

Reid's eyes narrowed, and his lips gathered into sort of a puckered grin. He'd liked that answer.

Slowly approaching, he slid his arms around my waist, looking down at me and drawing me close to his body.

"I'm sure you came across more than a few willing hearts in all your… travels," he murmured, his voice husky.

"Maybe," I said. It was true.

The more determined I'd been to keep things casual, the more interested guys had seemed to be in pushing me to get serious. Who knew? The key to making guys commit was having no desire to do so yourself.

From what Reid had said, he clearly believed there had been many guys in my life—and in my bed.

It was time. If we were going to sleep together, and it seemed inevitable in this moment, I needed to tell him the truth about the others. I mean, he was probably worried about contracting some sort of disease from me.

"I didn't sleep with them."

"What?" Reid's momentary look of confusion shifted to shock.

I took a breath, gathering the courage to admit what I hadn't told Heidi or Kenley or anyone.

"I didn't have sex with those guys. Not even close. I just... let everyone think that, because it kept me safe."

I sat down on my bed, and Reid sat beside me, staring at my face with an expression so alert he looked like someone who'd had a few too many Red Bulls.

"Why would you want people to think that?" he asked. "How would that keep you safe?"

I shrugged. "Once you get a reputation for playing around, for dating dumb, pretty guys and being sort of 'Wham bam thank you sir'... no one expects anything else from you. I didn't want to get involved with anyone in college. Or in any of the towns I worked in. I wanted to just do my thing and have fun with my friends, keep things casual. Right at first, freshman year, I went out with a couple of nice guys. But they wanted to get serious after a while. They wanted *relationships.* So I started turning down the nice guys and saying 'yes' to guys who weren't looking for anything serious."

"Wow," Reid said, looking at me with a sort of awe. "I

have literally never heard a woman say anything like that. So... how did you avoid sleeping with them, then?"

I lifted my shoulders and let them fall. "I just didn't. The first time we'd go out, I'd say I wasn't ready. A date or two later, I'd say I just wasn't feeling it, and we'd never go out again."

"Weren't they pissed?"

"Probably. But I didn't care. I'm sure everyone assumed we were having sex. I didn't care about that, either. It suited my purpose to be seen as a serial boyfriend recycler."

Reid nodded his understanding. "And these guys, these 'himbos' as you called them, they weren't about to contradict that assumption because it would make them look bad if other guys knew they hadn't closed the deal with you."

"Exactly."

"Wow," Reid said again, clearly trying to wrap his brain around this revelation. "So then... you haven't slept with anyone since..."

I hated the hopefulness in his voice. "No, I have. There was one guy freshman year at Stanford—one of the nice ones. We went out a few times. I liked him. Of course he wanted to, and I thought that if I slept with him it might... help me."

Reid's eyes focused in on mine with a ferocity that was almost intimidating. "Help you how?"

And now we enter the danger zone, ladies and gentlemen.

Did I dare to tell him the truth? No matter how hard I'd tried to hide from him, I couldn't seem to help myself. I took a deep breath, my heart thrashing like a drunk resisting arrest on one of our news clips.

"I thought it might help me... to get over you. That if I slept with someone else, it would maybe erase the memory of being with you." I swallowed. "But it didn't work. In fact it made things worse... so I gave up on that."

There was absolutely no sound in the room. Reid stared at me as if in a trance.

"Mara," he whispered. His eyes were fierce, as if he were on the edge of losing his last shred of control.

"All this time... I thought you didn't care at all. I was so disgusted with myself for not being able to get over you when you'd moved on so easily. I hated you for being able to just turn it off like a switch, for walking away and never looking back."

"I tried," I confessed. "I tried so hard not to look back. I've been running so hard."

"Why?" His voice was a choked cry. He sounded like a man who'd reached the end of his own strength. "Why did you run away from me?"

Those stupid tears were back. One slipped down my cheek as I answered him.

"I didn't think I had a choice. I was scared, Reid. You know how my father felt about us dating. The morning after graduation, after we—well, he found out. He told me I couldn't see you anymore. He said if I did... he would hurt you."

I choked a little on the painful lump in my throat and had to swallow before continuing.

"He meant it. I could tell he did. He said if I saw you again, if I gave you any hope, he'd have you arrested and convicted and sent to prison on some kind of made-up charges. He said he'd make sure you could never find a job or a place to live. I didn't know what to do. I knew if I told you, you'd just try to find a way for us to keep seeing each other. You would have said it was worth the risk. But it wasn't... not to me. I couldn't risk your life—your entire future just because I selfishly wanted to be with you. I loved you too much for that."

His voice was ragged with intensity. "Oh God, Mara—I

thought you didn't care. I thought you were bored of me. It never occurred to me that you were trying to protect me. I wish I'd known."

He grabbed me and held me to his chest, stroking the back of my hair with firm, barely controlled motions. "All I ever wanted was you. Even after you left me—I tried to want other women, I tried to move on. But I couldn't. I still wanted you. Only you."

And then he tipped my face up to his and kissed me as if both our lives depended on it, as if this was our last chance to taste each other, touch each other. Maybe it was. I didn't care.

All I cared about was that moment with him. It was everything I'd longed for these past eleven years.

I brought my hands to his heated cheeks and held his face to mine. I let my tongue move with his, tasting, testing, communicating things I still wasn't ready to say.

Maybe he would hurt me. Maybe I would hurt him. Right now it didn't matter. All that mattered was getting closer to him, getting him inside of me where he belonged.

My fingers went to the front of his shirt, fumbling with the buttons as our mouths devoured each other. I was shaking, making unsteady progress, managing only the top three buttons before Reid broke apart from me for a second and sat back, ripping the shirt over his head.

I sighed with satisfaction, relishing the feel of his hot, smooth skin under my fingers, sliding them over his shoulders and back and down the tightly segmented muscle of his sides.

It was intoxicating to touch him like this. I felt like an addict in the middle of a spectacular slow-motion fall from the wagon after years of sobriety. My senses were overrun as his mouth went to my ear, my neck, kissing me everywhere.

It wasn't enough. I squirmed, restless for more contact, more closeness.

Clearly reading my signs, Reid searched under my hair

behind my neck for the clasp of my halter top, working with it for a few seconds before it opened. He peeled the top down. Then his hands were right where I wanted them most, cupping the tender fullness of my breasts, soothing the aching tips with his palms and gentle fingertips. I moaned as he urged me back on the bed and fastened his mouth around one nipple.

The wet heat and pleasure of it seared down to my core. I pulled his head against me, urging him to continue, to go further, to taste and take all of me now that my surrender was complete.

I didn't want to stop, could not stop until I felt every part of him against my bare skin and held him inside my body. The memory of our one night together had sustained me this far, but now I'd have at least one more, and I planned to enjoy and remember every moment.

"I want you Mara," Reid growled, moving his mouth down my body, devouring me like a man who'd survived on beef jerky for years and had been offered prime rib. "I've got to have you, in every way. I've waited long enough."

"Yes. Yes." I arched my back, lifting myself to meet his mouth and roaming hands, desperate for him, consumed by a desire that approached insanity.

I wanted to kiss him again, needed his gratifying weight on top of me. Gripping his shoulders, I pulled him up until his face was over mine.

Reid kissed me intently until he felt my lower body pressing against him in an increasingly insistent rhythm. I told him with my body, my hands, my mouth that I was ready.

Suddenly he pulled his lips away from mine. "I don't have anything," he said in a dismayed whisper.

"What?" My lust-addled brain had no idea what he was saying. I strained upward toward his mouth, wanting him to kiss me again.

"Condoms. I don't have any protection. I didn't expect to need something like that tonight." He sniffed a short laugh.

"So you didn't intend to kiss and make up with Rainy, then?" I grinned.

"No. That was just an excuse to go to the restaurant so I could see Bruce."

I wrinkled my nose at the mention of my ridiculous date's name.

"Who?" I joked. When Reid smiled, I added, "Well, there was only that one other person for me, years ago. So, I'm safe."

He kissed my nose. "Of course you are—I wasn't even thinking that. I've always used a condom," he volunteered, his voice growing hopeful. "Every time. Even that one night with you, if you'll remember."

I giggled. "How could I forget?"

As it was the first time for both of us, we'd actually read the instructions on the package and put it on him together. We'd been terrified of getting me pregnant.

The same memory seemed to have popped into Reid's brain. "What about..."

"I'm on the pill. I started using it a couple years ago to help with my skin. Don't worry—you won't have to share your billions with some unplanned 'love child,'" I joked.

Reid looked at me, his expression going through several changes before he opened his mouth. Even then he started to speak but then seemed to think better of what he'd been about to say.

Eventually, he smiled and said, "You—are the one person I've never worried about that with. As I said that day at the pizza place, you made it very clear you didn't want anything from me."

I let my gaze drift down his powerful body suggestively then brought my eyes back up to meet his. My hand ran down the length of his torso.

"Well, there is something I want from you right now."

Those unearthly blue eyes of his flared and burned into me, his expression telling me he intended to give me everything I wanted. And then some.

There was no further question where this was going. After eleven long years of separation, Reid would be a part of me again, at least for tonight.

He lifted off of me and stood at the edge of the bed. Pulling my skirt down my legs, he dropped it to the floor then watched with hungry eyes as I removed my panties. He took off his own pants and underwear and socks, then rejoined me on the bed, kissing and touching me all over.

When I thought I couldn't stand another moment of waiting, Reid positioned himself and entered me in a torturously slow, delicious slide.

Every nerve in my body came alive in a new way as I held him inside me. And then he began to move, slowly at first, building speed and intensity oh-so-gradually. There was none of the discomfort and awkwardness of our first time. My body had been tested, and Reid had undeniably gained experience.

At the twisting pain that thought caused me, I quickly put it out of my mind. It didn't matter. He was here with me now. he was mine for tonight. I moved with him, wanting to give him every bit as much pleasure as he was giving me.

Reid whispered to me as he loved my body in deliberate, luxurious strokes. "God I've missed you, missed the feel of you. You're so tiny, so tight, you feel so amazing. I never thought I'd get to have you again."

He froze and squeezed his eyelids tight. "Hold on. Be still for a second. I don't want this to end too soon—I want to feel this forever."

After a few seconds, he began the rhythm again. The sound of his voice, the same voice I'd missed hearing so much, speaking to me in low worshipful tones, telling me how beautiful he found me, how incredible I felt under him, around him, had me thoroughly turned on.

Within minutes I was on the verge of a climax. I moved against him more strenuously, urging him to give it to me faster, harder.

"Wait Mara," he tried to protest, and then he must have realized I was close because the pace and strength of his drive picked up.

"Yes, baby," he urged through gritted teeth. "Yes, come for me. I could always make you come, with my hands, with my body grinding against you, even with all our clothes on, remember? But you had to be so quiet back then. Now I'm going to make you scream. Scream for me. Say my name."

I did. My voice was ripped from my throat as he pushed me over the edge, relentlessly driving the climax higher and higher.

"Reid. Oh my god—Reid."

With my name on his lips, he drove forward one more time and went rigid, shaking all over with the force of his pleasure.

After a minute, the tension left his body, and Reid rolled to the side, pulling me with him, keeping our bodies locked together.

TWENTY-SEVEN

No One Like You

Reid

I couldn't move.

Correction—I didn't *want* to move. Ever.

For the first time in a long time, I was exactly where I wanted to be, with exactly the person I wanted to be with.

Mara lay with her head tucked between my chest and shoulder, one arm and one leg thrown bonelessly across my body. I felt warm, heavy, and better than I had in years. Maybe better than I had in a decade.

"That was... that was... wow," Mara breathed. "I didn't think I'd forgotten anything."

I ran my hand over her hair to her back again and again, laughing softly.

"Apparently, I must have, or I would have tracked you down to the ends of the earth and never left your doorstep no matter what you said. In fact, what the fuck have I been doing the past ten years, starting a business and working all the time? I should have been spending my time stalking you until you agreed to sleep with me again."

She laughed, her ribcage moving against my side. She

pressed her face into my neck, kissing it softly before responding.

"I'm sure you weren't lonely."

I drew back enough to see her face. "I was. I mean, yes, there were a few girls, but... nothing like this, Mara. No one like you."

She pressed her nose into my neck again, kissing me but also hiding her face. Apparently, my admission had pleased her. Maybe it was stupid to have said it, but it was the truth.

There had never been anyone like Mara. There never would be.

My arms stayed tight around her, a hum of contentment vibrating in my chest.

"Thank God you came back. I was turning into a hard bastard," I admitted. "I couldn't make myself care about anyone or anything, really. I kept hoping it would get better, but it didn't. And then when I looked up in Nooky's that day and saw you on the news..."

I let the sentence die. I'd just admitted I'd been lying when I'd told her I didn't believe in love. It had only been a vain attempt to cover how much she'd hurt me.

And now she knew it.

She didn't call me out on it though. She pushed up onto one elbow and looked down into my eyes. "So, do you think you're acclimated enough to let me do the interview now, Mr. Mancini?"

I grinned and nodded. "Ah, I see what this was all about—you really go *all out* to get the story don't you, Miss Neely?"

"Anything for the 'get' of the century." She laughed, her eyes flashing with humor.

Rubbing my jaw and looking up at the ceiling, I cocked my head to one side. "I don't know. I'm still feeling a little camera-shy. I think I *might* need some more coaxing. It might take all night, in fact."

Mara laughed again. "You are a hard nut to crack, Mr. Mancini."

"I'm definitely *hard.*" I gave her a naughty grin.

Sliding my hand around the back of her head, I guided Mara's mouth down to mine, and damn if her kiss didn't put me right back into that "just one more time" frame of mind.

I'd intended to get up and get dressed, to order an Uber and go back to my own house. Instead, we made love again and fell asleep together in Mara's bed, in her childhood room, that hallowed ground I'd never dared to tread.

That rule had been the perfect representation of our history together—I'd been allowed in her life but only so far.

Tonight, she'd let me in all the way, but as we drifted off to sleep, I was afraid of what the morning would bring. Would she shut me out again?

Had I gotten this far... only to lose her once more?

TWENTY-EIGHT

Morning Glory

Mara

The next day I woke to the strange sensation of something tickling my nose, my lips, my cheeks.

My eyes opened to see Reid's smiling face hovering over mine.

"Good morning." His rough early-hours voice greeted me. "I always wondered how pretty you'd look first thing in the morning. Now I know."

Memories of the night's activities rushed back to me, and I felt myself blush. "I'm pretty sure that's not true. My makeup must be a mess. I never sleep in it. And I was crying last night."

I reached up to wipe under my eyes, trying to remove the smudges that had to be there, probably a futile attempt and certainly too late. "And *someone* barely let me get any sleep. How long have you been awake, watching me?"

He stroked my cheek with a fingertip. "Long enough to know that you're the most gorgeous woman I've ever seen, smudgy makeup or not."

That got me moving. I slid away from him, heading

toward the bathroom attached to my room. Seeing my toothbrush there at the sink, I groaned. Ugh, I'd been breathing morning-breath at him while he watched me sleep.

Then I glimpsed myself in the mirror, and I had to laugh.

When I peeked back into my room at Reid, who was now sitting propped up against my headboard, he smiled at me widely.

"You are such a liar," I said. "I'm a disaster."

Turning on the water, I grabbed my toothbrush, not sure which aspect of the disaster to address first.

Reid's happy voice called out. "You're stunning. In fact, I want to take you out to breakfast exactly as you are. Don't change a thing."

My response was garbled by bubbly toothpaste foam. "Yeah right."

I took a washcloth from the vanity then leaned back and looked at him again. "Only if you go just as *you* are."

Reid rolled out of bed and strolled toward me, completely naked and looking unbelievably hot. In the light of day, I was actually in awe that I'd had sex with this tight, powerful body in front of me.

"I think that's a great idea," he said. "Oh wait, I should put something on."

Stealing the washcloth from my hand, he draped it over his front, creating the appearance of a flag flying in all its high-mast morning glory.

He started toward me. "Okay, I'm ready to go. But *you* are a little overdressed, Miss Neely."

I backed into the small bathroom, squealing as he grabbed me. "Leave me alone, idiot. I've got to clean up."

Reid ignored my protest and grasped the bottom of the t-shirt I'd slipped on before going to sleep last night. He pulled it up over my head, leaving the two of us facing each other, naked except for the silly washcloth dangling between us.

"I'll help you clean up," he said in a low, sexy voice.

Lifting the washcloth, he rubbed it softly over my exposed body, bending down to kiss me. He stopped before his lips made it to my mouth.

"Hey, can I use that toothbrush?"

I took the opportunity to slip out of his reach and climb into the shower. "I don't know. I might get your cooties."

Reid gave me a mock-threatening grin. "You might get more than that if you keep flashing me that sweet little ass."

With a giggle, I yanked the shower curtain closed. "No. We can't. I have to get ready. I'm going to see Mom this morning at the clinic, and I don't want to miss morning visitation hours. I need to make sure she's okay there, and her afternoon's filled with appointments and meetings and stuff."

As I turned on the water, I could hear the sounds of Reid brushing his teeth.

"Want me to go with you?" he offered through a mouthful of foam.

I answered a bit too quickly. "No."

Purposely making my voice less frantic, I added, "Thanks anyway. I should go alone. And don't you need to go to work? Your company's probably falling apart this week while you've been 'preparing for your interview.'"

"It'll survive a few days of neglect. Why start your own company if you can't take some time off every now and then? And by that I mean I've never taken any time off before now."

The hot water ran down my body, which was growing warmer for a whole different reason. Reid was acting different.

The man with a workaholic reputation had just admitted blowing off work. To be with me. And he'd offered to go with me to check on my mother in a mental health clinic.

What did he think was happening here?

Being with him last night had been amazing, but I wasn't sure it should go any farther than that.

Obviously, we were still into each other, but that didn't change the same basic problem that had led to our breakup in the first place.

My feelings for him ran too deep—just like my mom's had for my dad. That gave Reid the kind of power over me I'd sworn I'd never allow any man to have.

Crazy, desperate love had led my mom into a depression so deep she could no longer function. Because you couldn't count on it to last. In fact, how could it? It hadn't lasted for my parents. It hadn't kept Dad from changing into a near-stranger who pursued power and fame over family.

Reid was perhaps even *more* powerful than my father had ever been. The fact was, you couldn't predict what another person might do. Even a person as good as my dad had once been. Even a man as wonderful as Reid.

The question was where to go from here? I'd already proved I couldn't resist him.

"Can I see you later?" he asked.

I stopped rubbing shampoo through my hair. My self-protective instinct screamed, "No."

My mouth said, "What did you have in mind?"

"I was thinking dinner and a movie."

So... he was dropping all pretenses of preparing for the interview. Tonight, we'd be spending time together, both fully aware of our reasons. An actual date.

Not willing to acknowledge how big this was, I mentally rehearsed my answer a few times before speaking. "Sure. Sounds good."

The shower curtain swished open, the room's cooler air rushing in around me.

"All right then." Reid smiled and leaned in for a wet, soapy kiss. "I'll pick you up at five."

He took one last sweeping glance over my body before closing the curtain.

"Feel free to wear what you're wearing now. It looks great on you."

TWENTY-NINE
As You Wish

Mara

By the time Reid was supposed to pick me up that night, I'd figured out how to handle him, or us, or whatever you wanted to call this thing we'd begun.

I'd thought of little else all day, except for during the short time I'd been able to spend with Mom at the clinic.

She already looked more like her old self, more rested, healthier. And her doctor there said she was right on schedule to be discharged Sunday.

Driving away from the place, I breathed a sigh of relief over that and then immediately resumed fretting over my new problem.

Many women wouldn't consider a relationship with a hot young billionaire a problem. But for me... it was like that Indiana Jones treasure Reid had jokingly mentioned.

Being with him was beautiful and sparkly and exciting and valuable... but it was also rigged with booby traps and danger. I could so easily fall back in love with him—maybe I'd never even stopped loving him.

Okay, I still loved him. Admitting that just made it worse.

As long as he wanted to spend time with me, I would find it just about impossible to say no. To anything.

But there was still the very real possibility that everything Mom had warned me about was true—that it was too dangerous to be with a powerful man I actually loved.

I finally decided I'd keep seeing Reid but be realistic. Expect the worst. Look at him like one of my himbos—okay, he wasn't dumb in the least, but he *was* beautiful, and definitely temporary, just like they all were.

This thing between us would eventually end, and I would face that with my eyes wide open. I wouldn't be surprised. I wouldn't be hurt.

As long as I could hang onto at least one little piece of my heart.

My entire heart surged as I heard the sound of Reid's car stopping in front of the house. When I opened the door, he was already there on the sidewalk, carrying a gorgeous arrangement of tulips—my favorite.

"Thank you," I said, ridiculously pleased, my grand plan already in severe jeopardy. How exactly was I supposed to maintain any sort of control over my heart with this guy?

He drove to the Cliffhouse in Eastport Bay, a charming ocean-front home that had been converted into a world class restaurant and inn years ago.

We were early for our reservation, so we crossed the Inn's gorgeous sloping lawn to two white-washed Adirondack chairs that had been placed side by side. Many other sets of chairs had been arranged on the lawn, all positioned to face the sun setting over the water.

"Wow. It's beautiful." I turned to see Reid's face fully engaged in that heart-melting smile of his. "The bridge looks so pretty from here."

"I owed you a sunset," he said, lifting a hand to the view.

We sat down together as a cocktail waiter appeared and

took our drink orders. The evening was warm for October, but I was still glad to have brought the sweater wrapped around my shoulders.

Everything about this setting was chill bump-inducing. The lights of the Eastport Bay Bridge twinkled on the horizon and doubled themselves, reflecting in the rippling waters below.

A virtual parade of sailboats drifted past our vantage point, heading for the harbor, so close to shore we could see the faces of the people aboard.

I leaned back in my chair, taking in the beauty of it all, enjoying the crisp, pink Rosé Reid had ordered for us. He reached over and lay his hand palm-up on the wide armrest of my chair.

Without a thought, I placed my hand in his, and his fingers closed over mine. It would be so easy to let the rest of my life entwine with his like this, to let him cover and envelope me, just the way I'd planned long ago.

"Mara?"

I turned away from the pinkish-purple sky to look at his face. He was absolutely stunning in the last of the day's light.

"You're really quiet. Thinking about your Mom?"

"Yes," I lied, happy he couldn't read my mind.

"Everything's going to work itself out, you know."

"You're quite the optimist, all of a sudden," I teased.

"I have to admit I'm finding a hidden reservoir of positive feelings I didn't know were still in there."

He looked down at our joined hands and rubbed a thumb lightly over my fingers. I got the distinct impression he'd been waiting for an opening to tell me what was on his mind.

"A few weeks ago, I could see my whole life stretched out ahead of me, and it all seemed just kind of... long, you know?" he said. "I was driving myself so hard, but I didn't really know what the end goal was. I wasn't really looking forward to anything. I didn't really care about anyone. Now... it all feels kind of... new. Like this—"

He lifted a hand toward the gorgeous view. "This is the best fucking sunset I've ever seen in my life."

"It *is* pretty good." I laughed, and he joined me.

The light in his eyes when he looked at me revealed everything I didn't want to know—Reid was ready to pick up where we'd left off eleven years ago.

Somehow, after I'd run away, refused to talk to him, acted like I'd never loved him, he was ready to take a risk on me again. How did he do it?

I turned back to the view, saying nothing, afraid of what might come out if I did. I was all made-up and hair-styled and carefully dressed on the outside, but inside I was a mess.

My silence didn't stop Reid. Now that he'd decided to talk, he was on a roll, and his earnest tone of voice was making me all kinds of freaked out.

"Last night was amazing, Mara. I haven't been able to think of anything else all day. I was useless at work."

He laughed and went back to caressing my fingers, sending sparks of pleasure shooting up my arm. "I think the reason I couldn't get excited about the future before... was because *you* weren't around."

Ohgodohgodohgod. Where was he going with this? It was *way* too close to that fortune I'd thrown to the wind a few nights ago.

Could I just get up and run away? No. I'd look insane, and these heels were too high for running. I stared at him as he swallowed and continued in that scary-sincere tone.

"Everything's changed for me in the past few days. I feel like I'm... alive again. And I don't want that to end after this week. You probably already know this, but just in case it's not obvious, I still—"

"Your table is ready, Mr. Mancini." A suit-clad maître d'

stood beside Reid's chair, beaming down at us with his best serving-the-billionaire smile.

I sprang out of my chair as if it had become suddenly white-hot. "Yes, thank you."

Saved by the wait-staff. That had been close.

Reid scowled, but stood as well, taking my hand and following the maître d', who'd be pushing up daisies on the hillside if looks could kill.

The dining room was lovely but crowded. Our dinner conversation was light with no further threat of frightening declarations. After dinner, we drove back into the center of Eastport Bay, where Reid managed to find a rare open parking spot on Main Street near Brady's Wharf.

Though it was a Wednesday night, the area was hopping with tourists. People strolled along the ancient brick-lined street, streaming in and out of the plentiful bars and restaurants.

Reid took my hand, leading me toward the historic Eastport Cinema. I'd always loved the place. The Greek Revival-style art house had been built in the 1800's and now featured indie films, classics, and unique cinema events like fundraisers, birthday parties, and weddings.

When we got close enough to read the marquee, I stopped walking and let out a sigh. It read, "Closed for Private Event."

Turning to Reid, I poked out a pouty bottom lip. "That's too bad. This would have been a great place to see a movie. It's okay. We can just go back into Providence or drive over to Warwick and see what's showing."

I tugged at his hand, anticipating a walk back to his car.

But Reid's feet stayed planted. He tugged back at my hand, pulling me toward him and the closed theater.

"What are we doing?" I asked, allowing him to lead me.

He gave me a mischievous grin. "Let's sneak in."

My protest was cut off when the theater door opened, and

the manager greeted Reid. "Good evening Mr. Mancini. Welcome. So glad you and your lovely guest could join us."

Reid looked back over his shoulder and gave me a wicked grin. Shaking my head, I stepped into the theater, which was empty except for us and the manager and, I assumed, a projectionist somewhere. We selected seats in the center of the middle row, and the lights went down.

"What are we seeing?" I whispered, expecting the latest first-run film or, knowing his clout, some coming-soon blockbuster that wasn't even in theaters yet.

Reid put a finger to his lips. "Shhh. The movie's about to start."

"You are too much," I leaned over to kiss him on the cheek.

Reid turned his head so that my kiss landed on his mouth instead, and he took advantage of the pre-movie darkness to kiss me in a way that would've been completely inappropriate had there been anyone else around.

After a minute he pulled back and whispered. "No—I'm just right—for you."

I opened my eyes, taking in the straightforward, emotion-filled look on his face. The attack-butterflies had found me again. They were dive-bombing my insides.

Music filled the theater. The screen lit up, saving me from having to respond. As soon as I heard the little kid's cough and the bleep-bleep noises of an outdated video game, I recognized the movie. I turned to the screen and gasped.

Yes, I was right—The Princess Bride. Based on Reid's self-satisfied expression, he knew he'd done well.

I looked back at the screen, amazed, moved by his gift. I'd watched the video at least a hundred times in high school. Reid used to tease me about it, even called me "Buttercup" at times, and of course I would play along and call him "Farm Boy."

He'd rented this theater so I could see my favorite movie on the big screen for the very first time.

Squeezing his hand, I blinked back tears. Then I settled in, prepared to be carried away by the sappy, epic, hilarious story of never-ending, time-and-separation-defeating love.

As the on-screen grandfather's storytelling dissolved into images of Buttercup and Westley's falling-in-love scenes, I found myself mouthing the lines I knew by heart.

I was surprised to hear Reid's low murmur beside me, reciting Westley's lines along with him.

"I will always come for you," he said, his eyes on the screen.

"But how can you be sure?" Buttercup and I answered.

"This is true love. Do you think this happens every day?" Westley and Reid asked in unison.

My voice almost choked with tears as I recited my next line, the one Buttercup says when she believes her first love is gone forever, "I will never love again."

Oh God. Who did I think I was kidding? I loved this guy. I was *never* going to get over him.

If he loved me, too—which I sincerely hoped he didn't but was afraid he did—I was going to open myself up to a world of pain. I would fall for him even harder than before. Because he was even more impossible to resist.

I couldn't stop it. It was going to happen.

I hated this.

As I sat through the rest of the movie, I simultaneously anticipated and dreaded Buttercup and Westley's romantic reunion. When Buttercup learned that Westley was still alive and still loved her, she would make the vow I could no longer live up to in my own life... "I will never doubt again."

I did not recite it with the movie's heroine.

I *did* go home with Reid to his mansion afterward though.

"I can go in a little late tomorrow," he said as he unlocked the door for us and led me straight upstairs to his bedroom.

He spent the night making me feel like that on-screen princess, worshipped and adored. And as I loved him back with my body, how I wished I *could* live that fairy tale.

But this was real life. I'd already seen how happily-ever-after ended, and it wasn't pretty.

Reid and I were only at the reunion scene in our own story, and no one could predict—for sure—that there would be a happy ending for us.

THIRTY

Reality Calling

Mara

I spent Thursday and Friday nights with Reid as well—he admitted he did need to make up for some lost time at work during the daylight hours.

On those days, I went in to work at the station though Rob had told me to take the week off from my regular reporting duties—probably out of guilt.

I needed to stay busy. I couldn't stand being alone at home, worrying about how Mom was doing, worrying about the boys, and repeatedly going back and forth in my arguments with myself over Reid.

On one hand, I was in paradise. We still clicked on every level. I could talk to him like no one else. He got my sense of humor, and I got his.

He challenged my thinking. He made me feel beautiful. All the years I'd spent away from him seemed to melt away in his presence.

And then of course, there was the mad chemistry and unbelievable sex. I was happy. I could tell he was happy too.

On the other hand, no matter where we were or what we

were doing, a little voice inside my head whispered on a continuous loop, "It can't last. Even though it's perfect right now, it can't last. Nothing ever does."

All the while we were laughing together or walking hand in hand or making love, something inside of me held back, struggling to keep from slipping over the edge into the abyss of "all in."

My ringtone woke me on Saturday morning. I sat up in Reid's bed, looking around the main bedroom of his condo, blinking in the late morning sunshine.

He lay beside me, still sleeping—after all his hard work last night he deserved it. His gorgeous body was sprawled across the pillow-top king mattress, the twisted white sheet barely covering his body and leaving his yummy abs (I'd tasted them last night to make sure) exposed.

Fighting the urge to run my hand over them, I slid out of bed and searched for my bag. I wanted to find the phone and silence it before it woke him. I grabbed the purse and dashed for the hallway.

By the time I dug it out, the phone had stopped ringing. The screen showed a missed call from Kenley.

I immediately hit the call-back button. I hadn't heard from her in weeks, and like Heidi, I'd started to worry. We usually spoke at least once a week. She hadn't returned any of my calls or texts.

"Come on, girlfriend, pick up." I opened the door and stepped outside onto the deck just as she answered.

"Hello? Mara?"

"Kenley! How are you babe? I'm so glad to hear from you. I've been calling."

"I know. Sorry," she said, her voice so subdued I hardly recognized her.

"What's the matter?" There wasn't even a question of *if* at this point. Something was wrong.

"Oh, Mare... my life is over." She sobbed. "Mark called off the wedding."

I sat down at the table. Hard. "Oh my God. I'm so sorry."

Kenley's wedding date was only three weeks away. Heidi and I were to be bridesmaids, and I'd already started wondering if I should invite Reid to fly to Atlanta with me and attend as my plus-one.

"What happened?"

Kenley's voice was caustic when she answered, though her thick Southern accent could probably make even the foulest curses sound sweet.

"He said *God* told him not to marry me."

"God? What the hell?"

"I know—right? He's been acting strange, you know, kind of distant for a few weeks, and I thought it was cold feet or something," she said. "I mean, I had some of that myself, wondering if I'd done the right thing quitting my TV career to move back here to be with him, wondering if we could really spend our whole lives together."

As I listened, I got up from the chair and walked over to the balcony railing looking down on the city's morning hustle. The view wasn't nearly as romantic as it had been on the night of Waterfire.

"But he came over two days ago and asked to talk to me," Kenley continued. "He said it so calmly, so matter-of-fact, like he was Moses and had just been hanging around talking to burning bushes—like he had no second-thoughts about breaking it off with me. He said God told him we shouldn't get married. And then, I was like, 'Okay, well, maybe He did. Who am I to argue with the Almighty? Maybe it wasn't as meant to be as I thought.'"

There was a dramatic pause. "And then I found out the truth."

Oh, this was going to be bad. "What was the truth?"

"Last night I was missing him so much I drove over to his house to... I don't know, just sit in my car and look at it, I guess, maybe get a look at him through the window—God I'm pathetic. And then I saw him."

"Through the window?"

"No, coming home. It was late, like ten-thirty. And there was a woman with him." Her voice was thick, on the verge of tears.

"That asshole. I'm going to kill him."

"They looked like they were coming home from a date, all dressed up. They were holding hands, and she went inside with him. She stayed all night, Mara."

"Oh Kenley, you didn't stay outside of his house in your car all night did you?"

She started crying. "I did. I know it's pitiful, but I had to see. I had to make sure. And now I've got a huge mess to deal with. I've got to tell everyone to cancel their travel plans and call the caterers and florist and reception hall... I don't think I can stand this."

"Email me the numbers. I'll call everyone. I'll take care of it. And I'm still flying to Atlanta to see you. And to kill Mark. Maybe I can change my ticket and come sooner."

Then I thought of my mother, who'd be getting out of the clinic tomorrow and would no-doubt need me to be around. Maybe she could come with me? I didn't know if she'd be up to it.

Ugh—this timing sucked.

"No. No, Mara—I don't want you to drop your life so you can come and mope around with me," Kenley protested. "Heidi says you're working on some big story?"

"Yeah, but it's nothing I can't leave if you need me."

In fact, a day or two away from Reid might help me think straight.

"So you told Heidi?" I asked. "What did she say?"

"She wants to kill him, too." Kenley gave a weak laugh. "I have some tough friends."

"You have friends who love you. And obviously, Mark didn't deserve you. I know that doesn't help very much at the moment, but you'll see it's true. Someday you'll feel sorry for that skank that *God* told him to leave you for."

Kenley laughed for real now. "I hope you're right, but I can't exactly picture it right now."

There was a long pause.

"I just thought I knew him better than that. Really *knew* him, you know?" she said. "He was the last person I'd ever have expected this from. I can't believe he changed so much from the guy I used to know."

Though the sun on the deck was warm, the words sent an icy chill through me. That was exactly what I'd thought about my dad the night he forced me to break up with Reid.

Reid had changed, too— a lot. I probably didn't even realize all the ways he'd changed since our teenage days. We'd been apart a long time.

Shivering, I walked back into his living room and retrieved my coat from the couch where I'd dropped it last night. I wrapped it around myself, covering the white t-shirt I'd borrowed to sleep in.

I told Kenley I'd look into changing my flight and that I loved her, and we hung up.

"Going somewhere?"

Reid's voice in the quiet room made me jump. He emerged from the hallway rubbing a hand through his sleep-mussed hair.

He looked absolutely edible, wearing just a pair of shorts. As he crossed the room toward me, his eyes travelled from my leopard-print coat to my naked legs underneath, all the way down to my bare toes. He gave me an appreciative smile.

"You'll need a bodyguard if you plan to leave like that. I volunteer."

"Uh, hi." I struggled to emerge from the instant funk Kenley's call had dropped over me. "Good morning."

"Good morning to *you*." Reid reached me and leaned down for a kiss, his mouth finding my neck instead of my lips when I twisted my face away.

"Morning breath," I muttered by way of explanation.

"Nothing about you ever smells bad," he said with a smile. "Who was that you were saying those elusive magic words to?"

The smile remained, but there was a slight edge to his voice.

"Kenley. Her fiancé called off the wedding."

"Oh. Wow. It was just a few weeks away, right?"

"Yes. She's devastated. I'm going to Atlanta as soon as I can get away."

"Sure—if you think you should." Reid stepped into the kitchen and started searching through his K-cup collection. "Want some coffee?"

I shook my head, slightly annoyed at his lack of outrage. Of course he'd never met Kenley, and he *was* a guy.

"Well, she's lucky," he said in an off-hand tone as he loaded a little plastic cup into his countertop brewing machine.

"Lucky?"

Now I was *all* the way annoyed. I could hardly believe my ears. I'd just told him my friend was devastated. Had he no empathy at all?

"She just got *dumped*, practically at the altar," I said.

"Right. That sucks. But it could be worse. It could've been the day of the wedding, or they could've gotten married and *then* realized it was a mistake later."

I let out a breath. *Finally.* The man was talking some sense.

Maybe this thing with Kenley was what we both needed to

shake us out of this lust-riddled La La Land we'd been inhabiting for the past week. It was about time reality made a return appearance.

"I couldn't agree more," I said, beginning to gather my clothing from last night. It was strewn all over the condo—we hadn't quite made it to the bedroom.

Reid stopped his coffee-prep to watch me. I noticed his stillness from the corner of my eye and glanced up at him.

His eyes had narrowed. His lips twisted in a riddle-solving look of concentration. "When you say you *agree*... what exactly are you agreeing with?"

"I agree that she's lucky to have gotten out of that relationship before something worse happened. She could have married Mark and thought they were happy only to have him leave her a few years from now... or even ten years from now when they could've had a couple of kids. I mean, you can never really know someone or what they're capable of."

"And we're still talking about Kenley and Mark, right?" Reid asked.

"Of course."

Locating my lacy pink bra halfway under a slipper chair in the living room, I got down on my knees to reach for it.

"But the principle applies to anyone, really. The fact is, you can't predict the future, and you can't count on *anyone* completely."

When I stood up, I saw that Reid had walked around the counter and was close to me. He put his hands on my upper arms, halting my underwear hunt.

"Mara. Look at me."

When I finally managed to meet his eyes, Reid continued, "You can count on me."

I nodded and dropped my gaze to his chest.

He slid a finger under my chin and lifted my face to his again. "You. Can. Count. On. Me."

And then he kissed me in a way that very much made me want to believe him. If only I could.

Reid pulled away, pressing his forehead to mine, his blue eyes clear and beautiful in the morning light. "What are we doing today?"

I backed away and resumed my panty search. "Well, Mom's coming home tomorrow, and I need to clean the house, do some laundry, go grocery shopping. I want everything to be ready for her. It'll probably take all day."

Realizing it sounded like a brush-off, I added, "Somebody's been 'making rather merry' this week and procrastinating on her chores."

I gave him what I hoped was a convincing smile.

He studied my face intently. "But you'll come over tonight? And sleep over?"

"Oh, here they are." I pulled the elusive panties from between two couch cushions. My tone was carefully nonchalant. "I should probably get some sleep tonight. I'm not sure what kind of shape Mom will be in, and I want to be rested in case she needs me."

Reid stood with his hands gripping the back of the couch, his lips forming a tight line. I walked over and gave him a quick peck on the cheek before going into the bathroom to get dressed.

THIRTY-ONE

Take Two

Mara

Sunday afternoon I drove to Boston to bring Mom home. It was amazing what a difference five nights and six days could make.

She looked and sounded like... herself. It scared me to realize just how far away from that she'd gotten in recent months.

We went to fill her prescription for an anti-depressant which she'd started taking at the clinic and looked over her schedule of therapy appointments. She would go every day for a few weeks and then cut back to a couple days a week if all went as planned.

"So, what do you want to do tonight?" I asked. "You up for some Bond, maybe some takeout, or I can cook if you'd like. I bought a whole bunch of—"

"Let's go out," she said.

"What?"

"Let's go out to dinner. I feel like getting dressed up, going somewhere fun."

Wow. "Okay—that sounds great. Sure."

"But first I want to call your father."

"What?"

In my shock, I jerked the steering wheel and almost ended both our lives. I quickly righted the car, but not before frightening the poor driver in the next lane. He sped up and passed me, honking loudly.

"Be careful, Mara," Mom warned. Then she resumed the topic at hand. "I'm ready to talk to him. I've put this off long enough. Maybe he'll be able to join us for dinner."

She sounded as if she'd just said *maybe we'll have rain tomorrow,* instead of suggesting a get-together with her number-one-most-hated person.

"On second thought—I'd like to catch up with you tonight," she said. "I'll make plans to see him tomorrow. It's probably best if he and I talk alone anyway."

"Are you sure your doctor will think that's a good idea?"

"She said it would be fine—helpful actually. I'm ready, Mara." She smiled over at me from the passenger seat. "I'm ready to get on with my life."

I'd never believed in miracles before that moment.

* * *

Monday was interview day.

True to his word, Reid stopped stalling and instructed Lee to make the arrangements. He'd decided on his house in Eastport Bay as the sit-down interview location.

We would pick up a few more sound bites later as the two of us, wearing wireless microphones, walked and talked on his property and put out to sea on his yacht. We'd probably be able to knock out both locations today.

Then we'd film at his company's Providence headquarters tomorrow, taking an on-camera tour and getting a few more natural sound pops.

Sheldon started setting up the camera and stand lights in Reid's living room, even using reflectors to make sure the lighting was perfect.

To get out of his way, Reid and I went into the kitchen.

"You nervous?" Unbuttoning Reid's shirt all the way, I pressed my lips to his kissable chest before re-buttoning the shirt with the mic cord hidden inside.

He smiled down at me. "Now why didn't you do it *that* way the day of the first interview? I probably would have been in a much better mood."

He dipped his head, aiming for my mouth.

"Stop it," I hissed. "Sheldon is right in the next room."

I gave him a mock-severe look. "Be *professiona*l, Mr. Mancini, or all your private business is going to get out."

Reid's expression morphed into a seductive smolder. "We'll discuss my privates later, Miss Neely."

He laughed at my playful slap to his bicep. "Anyway, I don't care if people know about us. In fact, I want the world to know."

Lifting his chin like a Medieval herald, he cupped a hand around his mouth and raised his voice to a near-shout. "I have the most beautiful girl—"

I slapped my hand over his mouth. "Shhh—you idiot."

Sheldon appeared in the kitchen doorway, and I leapt back from Reid.

With a glance from one to the other of us, the photographer asked, "You guys ready? I'm all set up in here."

Straightening my outfit, I moved toward him with a confident stride. "Yes. Let's get started. A lot to get done today—no time to waste."

I glanced back at Reid, who'd fallen into step behind me. He gave me a wicked grin and made kissy-face lips at me.

The interview went smoothly. Reid seemed comfortable,

relaxed. He smiled at the right moments, came across as smart and sincere—all in all, he gave computer nerds a good name.

The only hang-up came when I asked him the big Whammy, the question that had sent him off the deep end during the first interview.

"What was your inspiration for starting your flagship company, StillYours dot com? I'm sure the site's users and our viewers have imagined you as quite a romantic, a believer in true love."

Reid returned my smile and opened his mouth as if to answer, but nothing came out. After a few awkward seconds, he said, "Can we cut?"

His hand went to his clipped-on microphone, not to rip it off this time, but to cover it.

"I don't like this question. I don't really have a good answer for it," he whispered.

I turned around and motioned to Sheldon to stop down before speaking to Reid in a low voice. "What's the problem? You know the answer to this one. I mean you have to know why you started the company."

"I don't want to talk about it."

"How can I do the story without this? It's one of the most basic things. Just be honest." I lowered my voice to a whisper. "You asked me to trust you—don't you trust me?"

He whispered back. "Of course I do—but that doesn't mean I feel like spilling my guts to the rest of the world."

Sighing, he rubbed the back of his neck. "Let me just have some time to think about it. I've got to come up with something good to say—you said it's the most important question, right?"

Now it was my turn to sigh. In defeat. "Right. Okay."

I turned back to Sheldon. "Well, I guess we're done with the sit-down. Want to gear up for outside?"

"Okay—let me check the batteries in both your wireless packs first, so we don't run into any problems."

As Sheldon filmed the two of us walking along the beach behind Reid's house, I actually had to remind myself not to reach for his hand. He glanced over at me once and grimaced, showing me he was having the same struggle.

Weird that it felt unnatural *not* to hold hands—we'd slipped so quickly back into our high school sweetheart roles. Of course things now were much more complicated.

When filming at the mansion was complete, we drove to the marina and boarded the yacht.

As I'd predicted, Sheldon absolutely loved it. He got some great b-roll of Reid piloting the boat, deep-sea fishing, and looking every inch the avid New England outdoorsman. A few whales even cooperated, breaching for the camera.

Back on shore, Sheldon packed up his gear, preparing to take the news car back to Providence. I helped him carry a few things to the trunk.

When we were beyond Reid's earshot and the trunk was lifted blocking his view of us, Sheldon gave me a goofy eyebrow-waggle.

"So?"

"So what?"

"So, it's obvious you two kissed and made up," he said. "Spill. What's the deal?"

"There's no deal. We just… did a lot of talking about the shoot, and he feels more comfortable now."

My friend and co-worker rolled his eyes up toward his bushy brows. "Right. I just spent a whole day around you two. I think you guys have been doing a *whole* lot more than talking."

Sheldon pumped his hips in a ridiculous little dance.

"You look like a new woman—I've never seen you like that around anyone. And dude is totally whipped."

Taking a step back, I shook my head and studied the gravel around our feet, trying to hide the deepening color of my face.

"Really, Shel. It's nothing."

"Okay, if that's the way you wanna play it, secret romance and all that. But when you guys announce your engagement… let it be noted that I *called it*."

His last two words were delivered in a high-pitched little sing-song, and his booty-dance resumed.

I couldn't help but laugh at his stupidity. "Go, Shel. I'll get a ride home with Reid. And I'll see you tomorrow at work."

He slammed the trunk and walked around to the driver's side of the news car. "Oh sure. He's gonna give you a ride all right…"

"Good *bye*, Sheldon." I'd never had a tormenting older brother, but for the first time I thought I could relate to girls who did.

THIRTY-TWO
Better Late Than Never

Mara

Mom got in from her dinner with Dad much later than I'd expected.

I met her at the door around eleven p.m. feeling like I was the worried mother, and she was the tardy teenaged daughter.

"How was it? Where'd you go? What did you talk about?"

She laughed as she hung her keys on the hook in the mudroom. "Hold on, hold on, Miss News Reporter. Let me at least take off my jacket and go to the bathroom before you quiz me."

When she stepped under the bright kitchen lights, I gasped. "Your lipstick's gone. Your makeup's all smudged. Oh my God—did you guys *kiss*?"

I felt a little dizzy, like I'd just fallen through a portal to a parallel universe.

She laughed again. "You *are* nosy these days. Give me a minute, and I'll tell you all about it."

I paced the kitchen, waiting for her to get out of the powder room. She sure was taking an extra-long time in there.

When she came out, her hair was neat, and she had on fresh lipstick.

I narrowed my eyes at her. “So what happened?”

Mom filled the teakettle with water and set it on the stovetop, then pulled the tea basket out of the pantry before taking the barstool next to mine at the kitchen counter.

“We talked,” she said. “We were very honest with each other. He apologized again, and this time I saw a real change in him. He even offered to drop out of the race for governor if I wanted him to. That’s big for him. He reminded me of the guy I used to know. And it was good.”

“Apparently so,” I said, my tone a bit surly.

Mom’s face brightened with amusement. “Look at you. What a face—you look like you did when you were eleven and I tried to pick out your clothes for you.”

“How could you kiss him, Mom? After all the things you said?”

“Well, I didn’t kiss him at the beginning of the evening, I’ll tell you that. But your dad’s a charmer, Mare-Bear. And we’ve got a lot of history between us. That doesn’t just go away, even after a separation.”

Tell me about it.

"So... what? You guys are getting back together after one heart-to-heart chat?”

In spite of my relief at seeing her act so much like the Mom I’d grown up with, I felt sort of... betrayed by her apparent forgiveness of my dad. What about *never need a man, you can’t count on anyone?*

“Of course we’re not back together, sweetheart. We’ll never be a couple again.”

“Oh. Why not?”

And now I felt a little disappointed. What a basket case—maybe *I* needed to be on some mood-stabilizing medication.

She paused and looked at me, tears forming in her eyes.

"Because I still love him. I *can't* be with him again because he still has the power to break my heart."

Ah... back at status quo. At least I knew what to do with this.

The teakettle whistled, and Mom got up to take two mugs from the cabinet, bringing them over to the countertop. I selected a bag of black tea and drank it strong without my usual cream and sweetener, for once craving its dark bitterness.

* * *

Once again, Sheldon was like a kid at an amusement park when we reached Reid's hi-tech company headquarters to film there on Tuesday. He even joined a pick-up game of basketball at the much-admired indoor court when we finished the shoot.

Afterward, as Reid and I walked together toward the building's entrance, I drew close and asked in a low voice, "Have you thought of an answer to that question?"

He gave me a sneaky grin. "Still working on it."

"Okay, but I have to start writing the story soon, and Sheldon's got to edit. In fact, we're heading back to the station now to start logging the footage and to pull some sound bites for the promotions department. Rob wants to get promos on the air ASAP for this. Sure you don't want to just wing it?"

He stopped at the door, turning to face me. "I'm sure. Tell you what—how late will you be at the station?"

I looked at my phone. "It's three now. I'll be there at least until news time—six o'clock—maybe later."

"Why don't I swing by there and pick you up for dinner? If I think of the perfect answer by that time, I'll just come in, and Sheldon can shoot that part of the interview there at the station. Would that work?"

"Uh, yeah, I guess so. You think you'll be ready by tonight?"

He gave a confident nod, a strange gleam lighting his blue-green eyes. "I do."

As Sheldon and I drove back to the station, I started to like Reid's idea more and more. We could wrap up the interview completely, and dinner with him afterward would give us time to talk.

I'd been thinking about what Mom had said last night. Even after everything my parents had shared, even though they'd had three kids together and were still attracted to each other, she was convinced it was best not to spend your life with a man you loved too much. The risk was too high.

It made a lot of sense.

Continuing to see Reid... did not. We'd had an amazing week together, but there was no reason to continue this... whatever we had.

Well, okay, there were a few thousand reasons I *wanted* to keep seeing him, but it was just foolish to indulge myself that way.

It couldn't become anything permanent, and every day I spent with him would only make it harder to do what would inevitably have to be done.

I had to leave him. Better now than later when I might have even less control over my own heart.

Whenever that heart started to rip open at the thought of being without him, like right now for instance, I'd sew it up with a thread of logic and good sense and carry on.

THIRTY-THREE
Two Words

Mara

Sheldon and I spent a long time logging the story footage, searching for just the right video and sound bites to make up the first part of our series of reports.

Once in a while, one of our co-workers would peek into the edit bay and squeal (if female) or curse (if male) at the sight of *the* Reid Mancini on camera and carry on about what an epic sweeps piece it was going to be and how lucky we were to be the ones doing it.

Someone from promotions also came by to ask Sheldon about a video clip so they could whip up a quick promo for tonight—apparently Rob and the GM just couldn't wait any longer—they were convinced these reports were going to launch us ahead of the other local stations for sweeps month.

Around news time Sheldon left me in the edit bay to go help with a live shot. I planned to stay and work until Reid called or buzzed at the front door. At six-fifteen, Shannon, one of our newsroom interns, came to get me.

"Miss Neely?" The awkward girl barely raised her voice above a whisper.

She wasn't exactly a go-getter, and though I kept encouraging her, she kept insisting she had zero potential as a reporter.

"You can call me Mara," I reminded her for at least the third time since we'd met.

"Uh, Mara… there's a guy here to see you."

"Okay, thanks, Shannon. I'll be right out."

I gathered up the memory cards containing the raw video Sheldon had shot and put them into a tote bag with my notes. Slinging it over my shoulder, I left the edit bay, planning to go by my desk and grab my purse and coat before meeting Reid in the reception area.

But when I walked out into the newsroom, Reid was there. And so was Sheldon, with his camera, along with Rob and my co-workers who weren't out on live shots or on the set doing the newscast.

They were all looking at me. Smiling.

I froze in place, a terrible sense of dread coming over me. The room was so quiet. The only sound was the newscast's live audio coming from a monitor on a nearby desk.

"Reid? What's going on? Did you decide to do the interview tonight, then?"

I glanced over at Sheldon, who was pointing the camera at me as Reid approached and dropped to one knee in front of me.

"Shel?" My voice was higher pitched now, bordering on hysteria. "Why's your camera on? What's—"

Time slowed to a crawl, the sights and sounds around me moving in slow-mo like video in our frame-by-frame digital editing program. My gaze left Sheldon's grinning face and dropped to Reid's, which was now at about my waist level.

As if in a dream, I watched him reach for my hand and take it between his. Every nerve ending in my hand registered his touch though I was unable to squeeze his fingers back or move even a muscle.

"Mara..."

Reid swallowed, his smile shaking a little along with his voice.

"I know I said I was a private person, but I couldn't let you put this story together without giving you the *whole* story. Last week, before I saw you again, I thought I knew who I was—a guy whose company meant everything to him, someone who couldn't be distracted by something as silly as love, because I knew that didn't exist. The truth is I wasn't really alive. All the money, the property, the toys, they meant nothing. I was on life-support, existing day to day, because when you left, you took my whole life with you. You were supposed to *be* my life —my partner. You were plans A, B, C... the whole alphabet. I'd never pictured life without you, so when I tried, it was like looking down a blank, empty hallway. I have loved you every day since I was a ninth grader with a squeaky voice and a face full of pimples. Even when you weren't around and I wasn't able to see you or hear your voice, I still loved you. I don't want to live another day of my life without you, because without you, I'm not really living."

Reid paused, maybe waiting for a response, maybe taking a breath. I couldn't say anything.

Perhaps I was in shock—I'd never felt it before so I didn't know—but all I could do was look at him. At that beautiful, tear-streaked face I'd loved for what seemed like my entire life.

And I knew what my answer *had* to be to the question he was undoubtedly about to ask. *Please don't, Reid. Don't ask it.*

He rose to his feet and picked up my other hand. "I know you're scared. But you don't have anything left to prove. You've already proved it—you don't need me or anyone."

Swallowing hard, he gave me a tremulous smile. "But *I* need *you*. And I'm hoping you'll *want* me enough to take a chance on me, to believe that there is at least one person in the world you can count on. Count on me, Mara. You used to. You could again. All you have to do is decide to. I'm asking you to count on me... and to marry me."

And then he stopped talking. And looked at me. Waiting.

No one moved, no one said a word. The sound of my breathing was magnified to my ears as if I were underwater and using scuba gear.

Every part of my heart screamed for me to say, "yes." I loved this man standing before me with hope shining in his eyes. This man who'd just put his own heart, his dignity, his very private reputation out there in the world's most beautiful proposal.

But the little voice in my brain was still there, still chanting its evil mantra, "It can't last. Nothing ever does. And you love him too much to be with him."

When I finally spoke, none of those twisted thoughts came out. Instead there were only two words...

"I can't."

THIRTY-FOUR

Promo

Mara

There may have been gasps from the onlookers around us.

There may have been loud boos and hisses and death threats. Explosions. I didn't know.

All I knew was I'd never seen anything like the look of crushing pain on Reid's face. He'd expected me to say, "yes" and jump into his arms, like any sane woman would do.

He'd expected the Happily Ever After and the sweeping end-of-movie musical theme.

But Reid didn't understand what happens after the credits roll.

He hadn't seen my mom slowly losing herself, falling apart, hadn't heard her weeping every night for weeks on end.

I could never adequately explain that to anyone, and I would never be able to forget it. Reid hadn't lived with her day after day as she slowly turned into a shell of the person she'd once been.

True love was responsible for that.

And after being at ground zero for all of it, I just wasn't capable of the kind of love and faith he was asking for.

Not anymore. I stared at him, unsure of what to say or do next.

In my peripheral vision, I noticed the small crowd around us dispersing, either too embarrassed or too disgusted with me to stick around for the fallout.

Slowly, like storm clouds gathering over the water at Narragansett beach, the hurt in Reid's eyes rolled and changed, expanding and darkening into something different.

Into anger.

Into hate.

His voice wasn't loud. It was very quiet, actually, but I cringed as if he was yelling directly into my face.

"You... you don't even have to think about it, do you?" he asked. "It's so *easy* for you to walk away. Did this week mean nothing to you? Did you not see *anything* that you wanted... about me? About this whole fucking empire I built? I mean, God—what does it take to impress you, Mara? I did all of it, everything, for *you*—to show you... but you don't even care. I was just an amusing little trip down memory lane for you. Or..."

His smile was a bleak sneer as another thought occurred to him. "Was I just another 'himbo'... a face you didn't mind looking at too much for a few days, a body you could use for a few hours until you got bored again?"

In the silence after his last bitter words, the desktop monitor blared audio from a station promo—a new one. The male announcer's deep voice boomed, intruding on our terrible private moment.

"Exclusively on Action News... reporter Mara Neely sits down with the intriguing creator of StillYours dot com. And you won't *believe* what she's uncovered."

Both of us turned toward the monitor as my recorded voice emanated from its speakers. There was Reid on the screen, sitting in his company's conference room, wearing the light blue shirt I'd so nervously buttoned for him during our *first* interview.

Oh God, no.

"How does someone so young decide to build an empire around reuniting lost loves?" I heard myself ask.

"I never talk about that," a very nervous-looking Reid replied.

"Why not?" My disembodied voice pressed him.

"Because no one would like the answer. The truth would be bad for business."

And then the announcer-voice was back, thankfully cutting Reid's sound bite off before it got to his damning tirade about *sentimental suckers who believe in love.*

"No other news team has ever gotten this close to the reclusive billionaire, and we'll share his *deepest* secrets with you. Starting next week at six and eleven... only on Action News Three."

I literally had no air left in my lungs by the time the horrific promo ended.

What had they done?

Where had they gotten that clip? It was supposed to have been destroyed.

When Reid turned back to me, the shock of ultimate betrayal had turned his face ghostly pale.

I lifted my hands to him, shaking my head. "Reid, listen. I don't know how—"

He clenched his fists by his sides, shaking and barely opening his lips as he ground out his accusation.

"Oh I see now... not an amusement, not a himbo... I was just another *story* for you. Well you got your story. Congratulations. And now you've got your greatest wish—you're on your own. You'll never have to count on anyone. Because you've managed to run off the last person on earth who would have ever hurt you. Enjoy all the *success* this *exclusive* brings you."

He spun around and charged out the door. My legs failing, I fell into a desk chair behind me.

Rob sauntered out of his office. The look on his face told me he'd heard everything.

"Well, I guess that takes care of your conflict-of-interest issue. Now you can just reap the rewards of your good work."

I glared at him, struggling to even speak. "Where did that interview come from? That was never supposed to air. That was supposed to have been trashed."

Rob's eyes darted off to the side. "I don't know anything about that."

I stood to face him. "And what the hell was that sensationalized crap—'deepest secrets'—it's not that kind of story, and you know it. It's not an exposé. It's a feature. That made it sound sleazy or something."

"Chill out, Mara. It's a promo. We need for people to watch. You didn't do anything wrong. He never said it was off the record."

I responded with only a nod.

Lifting my tote bag from the floor where I'd dropped it, I went back to the edit bay. I had some more work to do before leaving tonight—deleting every minute of the footage we'd shot with Reid from the editing system's digital memory.

When I finished, I grabbed my purse and coat from my desk. Into my tote bag I swept the framed photos from my desktop and the few personal items I kept at work.

I went to Rob's office and leaned into his doorway. He looked up from his monitor. "Leaving?"

"Yep. I'm all finished here, I think."

Maybe not—I still held a tiny bit of hope this thing could be salvaged. It was worth a try. "Rob? I need to ask you for something. I want us to pull that promo—and *never* run the rest of that sound bite. Can you do that for me?"

Rob pushed away from his desk, leaning back in his chair. "Why? He *said* it, didn't he?"

"That clip was not a fair representation of him, of what he's really like—he doesn't even believe that stuff he said. That day—that meltdown—was *my* fault. And I think you knew he asked us not to use it."

"It'll be fine, Mara. Let us handle promotions—you just work on the stories, do your job and let me handle mine."

My shoulders dropped along with my heart.

"Okay," I said. "But you may not have a job for much longer. You can expect to be served with a huge lawsuit—probably tomorrow morning. Reid swore he'd shut the station down if any part of that clip aired, and I'm betting he's got enough money and power to follow through on that. He's certainly angry enough to do it. I wonder... do you think the GM will take the fall for this—or pass it on down the line to the news department?"

Rob's answering expression was stricken.

I had one last thing to say before leaving. "And I don't *have* a job to do anymore, because I quit. Have fun in court."

Without another word, I walked out of the station, taking with me every one of the memory cards containing the raw interviews and b-roll of Reid Mancini. They were going to "accidentally" find their way into my microwave oven at home.

There was no way the powers-that-be at the station could do the story without them, even if they still dared to.

THIRTY-FIVE
Cardiac Care

Mara

Naturally, the series didn't air the next week when the ratings period began.

As far as I knew that promo never aired again either. But then, I wasn't spending much time watching TV. Or reading the paper.

Or talking to anyone, eating, getting out of bed...

I'd tried reaching Reid later that Tuesday night, but my calls went straight to voicemail, and he had not returned them.

Of course he didn't want to talk to me, and I knew he'd never forgive me. But I'd at least wanted to let him know that the sweeps stories we'd shot wouldn't be airing and he didn't have to worry about losing his privacy. I had no idea if his lawyers had, in fact, filed suit against the station.

It was no longer my business.

Late Thursday morning, Mom came into my room and opened the blinds, raising the light level in the room to full solar flare.

"Okay, this has gone on long enough."

I felt the depression of her weight on the mattress as she sat beside me. The coolness of her palm covered my forehead.

"Are you sick?"

I kept my eyes closed.

"No," I said, attempting to pull the covers up. But I was sick, and my disease was incurable.

I was in love with Reid. I loved him, and I could never have him. Every part of me ached for him, to see his face, hear his voice, feel his touch. And it would never happen.

Mom exhaled loudly. "Was this what I was like? I don't know how you stood it for one day. Mara. Work with me here, kiddo—open your eyes."

I begrudgingly complied. Her face was filled with tender concern.

"Sweetheart... I know things seem bad right now. But you can't just stop living. There will be other jobs, and eventually, another guy—"

"How did you find out?"

I'd told Mom about quitting my job, but I hadn't been able to speak of Reid's proposal, of my refusal. I didn't even want to think about it—thus, my attempt at sleeping twenty-four-seven.

"Sheldon called here looking for you. You were asleep so I didn't disturb you, but he told me what happened. And that boss of yours has called non-stop, looking for some video."

She ran her hand over my undoubtedly greasy hair. "You did the right thing, Mare-Bear. About the story, *and* about Reid—look how miserable he makes you."

Wrong. I'd done *that* to myself. He'd made me happier in the past week than I'd been in years.

"I know," I said. I rolled over to go back to sleep, back to oblivion.

Mom's weight lifted from the bed. I heard the sound of the blinds lowering again and then her sigh.

"I'll give you a couple more days to wallow. If I don't see some signs of life after that, I'm dragging *you* to see Dr. Weinberg."

* * *

As it turned out, I didn't even get that long to indulge in my pity party.

The door to my room burst open Friday morning, startling me out of sleep and into a sitting position in my bed. Mom was flying around my room, grabbing clothes out of my closet and throwing them onto my bed.

"Get up. We've got to go to the hospital. Dad's had a heart attack. I'm leaving right now. Get ready as fast as you can and meet me in the emergency room."

I lurched out of bed and ran to my bathroom, tearing off my pajamas, running a toothbrush through my mouth, and throwing my hair into a ponytail.

Though I hadn't eaten in days, I was charged with energy —I had to get there in time—had to tell Dad I forgave him for what happened years ago. I needed to tell him how much I loved him, how much I wanted us to still have a relationship.

God, what if this was his last day to live? What if it was too late already?"

I pulled on clothes without bothering to make sure they matched. I certainly didn't put on makeup before leaving.

Did it really matter if I looked like an unwashed zombie? My father might be dying. I broke the speed limit by, oh, thirty miles an hour or so getting to Rhode Island Hospital.

Mom was still in the ER when I ran in. She stood when she saw me. Her cheeks were streaked with mascara.

"How is he? What's happening?" I asked between sucking breaths.

"They took him to surgery in the cardiac unit. They said his arteries were almost entirely blocked. This is all my fault."

She flopped back into her chair and put her head in her hands, crying quietly.

I sat down in the plastic chair next to her. "Mom... how is this your fault?"

"I should have been taking care of him. Your father has always eaten too much fried food. I'll bet he's done nothing but eat out since I kicked him out of the house—and oh—the corn chips. I made sure never to keep them in the house because he couldn't resist eating a whole bag at a time. His condo in the city is probably overrun with them."

What is happening here?

As Mom wept, I sat rubbing her back in small circles and reeling from shock. She'd always exhibited strong emotions about Dad, but recently they'd been mostly negative.

It was surreal to see her so torn up now, so frightened for his health, and blaming herself for *anything* that had to do with him.

Next someone was going to tell me black was white, up was down, and caramel turtle cheesecake was health food.

"Whatever caused the heart attack... it had nothing to do with you, Mom. He's a grown man, and he's made his own decisions. Like you said, it's usually whatever he wants and lots of it, whether it's corn chips or something else. I'm sure he'll be okay. And... if not..."

I had to stop and swallow the boulder that had lodged in my throat. "If not... you'll be okay. You don't need anyone. You're a strong, independent—"

"No I'm not," she snapped, lifting her head to look at me. "That was a bunch of crap. I love him, Mara. I need him. It's impossible not to need anyone. And I can't imagine a fate worse than marrying someone you *don't* love... or not being with the person you do."

She stared at me for a minute. "I don't want that for you. The advice I gave you the past few weeks—I only wanted you to be safe—not to suffer like I did. But I was *wrong*. And you did suffer. I regret that I treated you like a friend or a therapist instead of like my daughter."

"No. It's okay. You didn't—"

"I did. I was hurting, and I was selfish. But you didn't need to hear all of that, see all of that. I blamed your father for ruining my perfect life—*our* lives. But I probably did as much damage to you as he did. I hope you can forgive me. And I hope I don't have to spend the rest of my life regretting that I didn't forgive your dad and give us another chance."

I sat hard into the back of my chair, breathless. Had I really just heard that? I looked over at Mom.

She was quietly crying again. I slid my hand over to cover hers, and she gripped it tightly. Maybe she'd said it out of emotional shock or something. Was she really ready to forgive Dad?

Was she really advocating for true love?

A few minutes later, someone came over and instructed us on how to get to the cardiac waiting area where we stayed for the next two hours.

Finally, a doctor stepped out of the door to the operating area. "Is the Neely family here?"

Mom and I both sprang to our feet. "Here," she said walking briskly toward the doctor. "I'm Mrs. Neely. I'm his wife."

I blew out a breath. *Okay*. So this was really happening.

As we listened to the doctor explain the procedure he'd performed on Dad, it was as if my entire lens on life had shifted. Up really was down, in was out, Mom didn't hate Dad.

I wasn't sure I could adjust to the change. I'd become so accustomed to viewing love as a dangerous thing, to seeing a need for someone as something poisonous, like a heroin addiction, which could only end in tragedy.

But over the next few days, as I visited Dad in intensive care and then in a regular room, as I watched my mother caring for him, being there through his recovery, forgiving old hurts and forging new ties, something inside my own heart began to heal.

I realized that I had hidden it behind an overgrowth of vines and thorns, just like that mythical princess in the fairytale.

I'd been sleepwalking through my life instead of truly living it.

When I got ready to leave the hospital on Monday night, Mom and Dad were laughing together, sharing a tray of rather unappetizing cafeteria food.

"Want me to bring you back some takeout, Mom? Or are you coming home tonight?" She hadn't left the building since Friday. I'd been bringing her changes of clothes.

She looked up. "I'll go home when he comes home."

Mom rubbed a hand through Dad's thinning gray hair. "We've spent enough nights apart already. And this food really isn't all that bad. You go on and get some rest. We'll see you tomorrow."

"Okay." I hugged her and kissed Dad's cheek.

The shock of seeing them affectionate with each other had started to wear off. Sort of. "I'll see you guys tomorrow then."

I did go home, but I didn't rest. Instead, I opened my laptop and logged on to StillYours.com for the first time ever. I glanced over some of the profile pages.

Many were private, of course, viewable only by those who'd been approved by the account holder. But others were open to the public.

The profile photos were of middle-aged people, old

people, college-aged kids, even some who looked like they were in high school.

There was page after page of desperate pleas, people searching for their long-lost loves, posting as much information as they knew, asking for help getting in touch.

In some cases, it was clear the account holder knew exactly where their lost love was geographically—they were just trying to make a connection, win another chance by pouring out their hearts online.

I supposed the network worked best when you were searching for someone and found they were also searching for you. The lining of my stomach trembled as I moved my cursor to the site's search bar.

Stalling, I got up and went to the refrigerator for a drink. When I sat back down, I typed in "Reid Mancini."

No results match your request

Of course. He wouldn't expose himself to the public by using his own site. Besides, I was sure he now wholeheartedly meant his original answer to my question about why he'd started StillYours.com. The one about sentimental suckers.

And as far as he knew, there *was* no true love out there to search for.

I briefly considered creating a profile for myself, just hanging it all out there for the world to see—my apology, my love. But I nixed that idea—it was too late.

Instead, I made myself some popcorn, poured a generous glass of wine, and curled up on the couch to watch my DVD of The Princess Bride.

Yep. It was that kind of night—if you're going to be miserable, might as well take it all the way.

THIRTY-SIX

Still Yours

Mara

The tears started even before the falling-in-love scenes really got going.

Whose terrible idea was this, anyway? I picked up the remote to stop the movie just as the baby-faced actor said to his lady love, "As you wish."

My heart went into fast-forward as I stared at the screen. I jumped up from the sofa and went back to my laptop, calling up StillYours.com again. This time I typed a different name into the search bar.

Farm Boy.

My stomach-trembling thing only got worse and was joined by a struggle for breath as I waited for the search to complete.

And then the page opened to reveal a picture of Reid. From high school.

It was the one of the two of us from our yearbook, but only his half. He must have snapped it directly from the page, because written inside a black magic-marker heart on Reid's chest were the words, "Mara, forever and always."

My heart stopped pounding and just... stopped. When had he posted this? Maybe a long time ago. Certainly not within the past few days.

Had he forgotten it was there?

There were no words on the page, no posts or comments... nothing but the name Farm Boy and that picture.

I started typing, my fingers flying over the keyboard, matching the pace of my pulse.

"Farm Boy—I lied when I said I couldn't remember my fortune. I didn't want to tell you what it said because I was afraid. But I remember every word—

LEAVE THE PAST BEHIND AND REACH OUT FOR YOUR FATE. IT'S RIGHT IN FRONT OF YOU.

You see, I didn't want you to be my fate because I loved you too much. And I knew I couldn't take it if you ever left me.

So I left you first. Then I ran and I ran until you caught me again somehow. The funny thing is—I turned out to be one of those sentimental suckers who believes in love and all that idiotic meant-to-be shit.

You are my fate, or at least you were, until I gave the world's stupidest answer to the world's most wonderful question. I may have lost my chance to spend a lifetime with you, but no matter what happens you will always be the love of my life."

I finished with the vow Buttercup made to Westley, "I will never love again," and signed it, "Still yours, Mara."

I hit the "post" button before I could change my mind and then tried to go back to my movie. But there was no hope of paying attention to the story. I checked my laptop once every ten minutes pretty much all night long and checked my phone several times to make sure it was charged and the ringer turned to full volume.

There was no activity from either electronic device. I finally fell into an exhausted sleep just before dawn.

My ringtone woke me a couple hours later. I was still on the couch and my phone was on the floor, where it must have dropped from my hand when I dozed off.

My sleep-weakened fingers fumbled for it, pushing it further away before I finally managed to grasp it and bring it to my ear.

"Hello?"

A chirpy female voice answered me, "Um, hi. This is Tanya Garcia at News Night America in New York calling for Mara Neely?"

"Yes." I cleared my throat. "This is she."

"Oh, hi," she repeated, even more chipper. "I'm calling to ask if you could come to New York this week and do an interview for us?"

I sat up, trying to clear my sleep-deprived brain. "What? Why would you want to interview me?"

News Night America was the country's premier prime-time news magazine. I half-suspected I wasn't actually awake, and this was some kind of vivid stress dream.

Tanya laughed, a bright, girly sound. "No. You're um, a reporter, right? They told me to call you and see how soon you could get here to do an interview for us with Reid Mancini—like *you* interview *him*—get it?"

Okay, definitely dreaming. "I think there's been some kind of mistake. I don't—"

"Well, this is the number they told me to call, and Mr. Mancini said it was the number for Mara Neely, and you're Mara Neely, right?"

"Yes..." Now I got to my feet and crossed the living room to my laptop. I logged onto Reid's website and went to his page—still no reply.

"Okay, well, I'm an assistant booking producer here, and

they said Reid Mancini… you know that super-rich StillYours guy?"

"Yes."

"Well, he called the network and said he would do an interview—he's never done one before, you know, and we've been trying to get him, like, forever—this is a huge deal."

"I know."

"Okay, well, he said he'd only do it if we got a reporter from Providence, Mara Neely, that's you, to ask the questions. I guess he's super-shy or something. And you know sweeps starts this week, so if you can make it, we'd really like for you to come. Oh, and he said you have some b-roll of his house and his company and stuff?"

"I um, lost it." *In an unfortunate microwave fire.*

"Oh, bummer. Well, we'll have to hire a crew to shoot some new stuff then."

"I know of a great photog here," I said. "He's with the local affiliate where I… used to work. I'm sure they'd be thrilled to let him shoot it if you'll give them access to some footage afterward. I'll give you his number."

Sheldon would *freak* when he got the call asking him to do something for the network, even though he'd be shooting basically the same video he'd gotten once before.

"Cool. So you'll do it then?" Tanya asked.

I took a beat to think. This was too weird. It didn't make sense. After all that had happened, why would Reid volunteer for another interview, with me of all people?

And then it hit me—he wanted to make me suffer. On national TV.

He knew the network was my ultimate career goal, and he'd arranged it so I would get a taste of it, but after the way I'd quit my job and destroyed the story footage, I'd never get hired there or anywhere else worth a damn.

Maybe he wanted to expose me on live television, tell

people I was some kind of predatory paparazzi journalist, or... he'd let me get out there on the set and then refuse to answer my questions and laugh in my face.

The possibilities for humiliation and career suicide were endless. Or maybe... no, I was too afraid to even let myself hope.

But I told Tanya I'd do it. After checking with someone higher up, she instructed me to be at the network's studios Thursday night. The show would follow their top cop drama and ensure certain ratings victory for the second week of sweeps. I gave her Sheldon's number then hung up and stared at my phone, contemplating calling Reid.

No. If he wanted to talk to me before the interview, he knew where to find me. Otherwise, we'd have our reckoning on live network television.

I had to give it to him—when he decided to start talking to the press, he didn't mess around.

THIRTY-SEVEN

Moment of Truth

Mara

"Miss Neely? You're on in ten. Follow me to the studio, please."

I stood and trailed after a short guy with a headset and a tablet he never stopped tapping from the green room down a short hallway to a door marked STUDIO: QUIET PLEASE.

When I'd arrived a couple hours earlier, I'd met the show's senior producer and the host, both of whom assured me of how unusual all of this was. I could tell from the look on the host's face that if Reid hadn't indeed been the "get" of the decade, there was no way she would've allowed such trespassing on her territory.

But, as we all knew, ratings ruled. And they were expecting an unprecedented audience to tune in tonight.

While the host went off somewhere to give her scripts a final read-through or meditate or something, the producer explained to me what would happen during my interview segment and went over the rundown with me.

"Is Reid here yet?" I asked, hoping for a minute alone with him before the show.

"Mr. Mancini is in a different green room. He's asked not to be disturbed until just before airtime. He's an interesting guy. Good luck out there, kid," the producer said and disappeared to go do whatever network producers do before airtime.

I was so far out of my league, I thought I might need an oxygén mask.

Short Tablet Guy led me to a chair on the set and handed me a lav mic to put on then plugged in my IFB cord, so I'd be able to hear the show's director cue me. The lights were on, and the camera operators were all in place, but Reid wasn't in the studio yet.

A terrible thought occurred to me—what if he'd lured me here under the pretense of doing the interview and then just didn't show?

The thought of it was worse than one of those dreams where you show up at school for the final exam and realize you forgot to study all semester. And you're naked.

The host would introduce our segment, the camera lights would come on, and it would just be me sitting there alone on the set with my mouth hanging open. Cue the crickets.

But at three minutes till airtime, the studio door opened, and Reid came striding across the floor toward the set. I hadn't been nervous on live TV since my first few weeks on-air. But now, adrenaline rocketed through my veins.

Reid wore a dark blue suit with a light pink shirt and a navy striped tie. He looked like every cent of a billion bucks.

Tablet Guy led him to his chair, helped him get his microphone on, showed him a glass of water that had been placed on a nearby table, and wished us both luck.

And then we were alone. Well, alone with a couple of camera ops, a floor director, and soon, an audience of millions. I finally dared to look at Reid's face. He gave me a little half-smile that caused the adrenaline jets to fire a new round.

"Two minutes," the floor director announced.

"What are we doing here?" I bit out under my breath, trying to keep our conversation private.

"I didn't get my fifteen minutes of fame. You know what a publicity hound I am," Reid said, following his droll statement with a dazzling grin.

"I don't understand." I was desperate for a hint at what he had up his sleeve. What he'd said so far wasn't helping much.

"When the reports didn't air, I had Lee call your station to find out why," he explained. "They told him you'd been fired because you refused to do the stories on me. And that you stole the video."

He lifted a brow, waiting for an explanation.

"Yes and no. I did steal the video. And I wasn't fired. I quit. I didn't want any part of exploiting you, or... us, or whatever."

His eyes narrowed. "Why not?"

"Because... that's not how you treat someone you love."

Now both Reid's eyebrows shot up. He leaned forward and opened his mouth to say something, but the floor director's voice cut him off.

"One minute. Quiet on the set, please. Your mics will be live in thirty."

The nightly news show's familiar music swept through the studio, raising goose bumps on my arm.

This whole experience was surreal. I was in New York City, on the set of News Night America, about to go live on network TV. To interview the man I loved, who may or may not still love me.

Who might, in fact, hate me.

The studio audio dropped out, and I listened through my IFB to the host's smooth voice welcoming viewers. She gave a preview of the night's top stories, and then she was introducing Reid and me.

"Mara Neely, formerly of our affiliate in Providence, Rhode Island, joins us to conduct the interview. Welcome to News Night America, Mara."

"Thank you for having me, Geena." I smiled into the camera lens behind the teleprompter. Turning to Reid, I said, "And thank you for joining us tonight, Mr. Mancini."

"Good to be here." He smiled, looking relaxed.

As I read over the obligatory facts about Reid and his background, his vast success, video rolled on the studio monitors, showing us what the rest of the nation was seeing. There was Reid at his company headquarters, out on his boat, walking along the beach behind his mansion—alone.

And finally came the moment of truth. I had to ask it—the question—because you just couldn't start an interview like this any other way.

"You've never spoken about the inspiration behind StillYours.com. There's been a lot of speculation, but you're the only one who can answer that question with authority. So tell us... what inspires someone so young to create a social network whose purpose is to reunite lost loves?"

Reid looked down and paused a few seconds before answering. It felt like an hour to me. He lifted his eyes to meet mine.

"I think it's pretty obvious." He grinned. "It was a girl. I loved her. I lost her. I had to get her back. And I realized there were a lot of people in this country, in the world, actually, in the same boat as me. I built StillYours.com for them."

He looked down and laughed softly, then looked up at the camera. "But I can't lie—I mostly did it for me. I was hoping the site might help me find that girl, that she might see my profile and want to reconnect with me."

And a nation swoons. Handsome billionaire bleeds from the heart on national television. Every woman in the country was probably licking her TV screen.

This woman, however, was doing her very best not to pass out.

Breathe. In and out. You're on live television, Mara.

"And did she?" I managed to get a bit of air and ask the natural follow-up question.

"No," he said. "Not until recently. Sometimes these things take time, so don't give up, everybody. There's always hope."

Reid laughed, his gorgeous white teeth and sparkling turquoise eyes surely winning over any remaining holdouts out there in living-room-land.

The interview continued, with Reid answering questions about his childhood, his personal interests, his charitable giving, which he still seemed reluctant to discuss. He talked about loving the ocean, the historic charm of Providence and Eastport Bay. I could picture the Rhode Island state tourism office erupting into cheers.

When the director gave me a two-minute warning in my earpiece, I started to wrap up the interview.

"People have called you everything from 'reserved' to 'arrogant' to a 'cut-throat businessman.' But with a business built on love, you sound like something of a romantic to me."

Reid grinned bashfully and held his hands out to the side in a mock-surrender. "You got me."

"Many people who have loved and lost might be scared to put themselves out there again. After the events in your own life that inspired you to start up your network, aren't you afraid of getting hurt, of being let down again by love?" I asked.

He considered the question for a few seconds. "Of course I am, but I have a philosophy—I believe it's a Confucius quote—leave the past behind and reach out for the fate that's in front of you."

The words from my fortune. There was no doubt now that he had read my post on his site.

My friends the butterflies were back, but this time they didn't attack. They settled sweetly around my heart, making it feel like *it* might grow wings and take off, too.

I stared into Reid's warm, smiling eyes. "But how can you be sure?" I asked, mimicking the question Buttercup asked Westley before he went off to seek his fortune.

And Reid answered in Westley's timeless words. "This is true love. Do you think this happens every day?"

I shook my head, fighting back tears and borrowing one more line from Buttercup. "I will never doubt again."

Reid got out of his chair, pulled me up from mine and clamped an arm around my waist, drawing me tight against his body before taking my lips in a kiss that may have been a *little* too hot for prime time.

"And we're out," called the floor director's voice.

In my IFB, Geena made a funny sound and ad-libbed, "Well, there's obviously more to *that* story, and News Night America will be sure to bring you the follow-up tomorrow night."

Reid stopped the kiss before I did—I might never have stopped it. He grinned down at me.

"So, I didn't get to ask *you* any questions."

I shook my head, smiling at him through tears. "That's not how it works."

"Still, there is something I wanted to know. How'd you like to go to Australia with me?"

I sucked in a breath. "That's where we said we'd go for our honeymoon when we were young and stupid."

"We're still young and stupid. But I guess you're right—we should probably get married first."

"Yes," I said, before he'd even finished the last word. "And I'll have plenty of time to travel as I am currently unemployed."

Reid tipped his head to the side, wearing a mysterious

expression. "I don't know—I've been thinking about buying a certain TV station in Providence. I hear the price might be quite reasonable, considering the massive lawsuit they've been threatened with."

"Poor Rob—I warned him."

"You like that joker? Because I was thinking of doing some serious housecleaning after I take over. Not that you need me to avenge your honor. You're a strong, independent woman—"

"I do need you," I interrupted. "And I *want* you, in every way, always and forever."

Epilogue

"I can't believe this, Mara," Heidi said. "Honestly, I thought you'd never get married."

My friend adjusted a tiny sparkling jewel in my updo as I sat in front of the mirror. "No offense," she said.

I gave the skirts of my wedding dress a shake and laughed. "No, believe me, none taken. I wasn't sure I'd *ever* be wearing the poufy white dress."

"It's not poufy—well, it's a little poufy—but it's gorgeous," Kenley said.

She smiled at my reflection with slightly dewy eyes, looking gorgeous herself in a sea-green dress that complimented her light blue eyes and blonde hair. Though I knew without a doubt she was happy for me, she'd been quiet all day.

This couldn't be easy on her, but thank God she'd come. I didn't know if I could walk down the aisle without Kenley and Heidi there.

Heidi had traded in her airline ticket to Atlanta for one to Rhode Island. I'd put my flight credit in Kenley's name, and both my best friends had flown in for several days' worth of pre-wedding festivities.

"I'm about to attend a star-studded wedding on the lawn of an Eastport Bay, Rhode Island mansion," Heidi said. "I feel like a Vanderbilt or a Rockefeller."

"Well, there might be a couple of those wandering around at the reception later. And if not, there are at least a few tech billionaires around here—we're going to locate one for Kenley before the day is through," I teased.

"Oh, not for me," Kenley protested. "I'm swearing off wealthy men. All my mama's been telling me since I was fourteen was that my looks were going to put me on a rich man's arm someday, and I'm sick of it. After what happened with Mark, I'm looking for some nice garbage man or a cute little fast-food worker. Anyone with money is *off* the list."

"Okay Kens," Heidi said. "But you're bound to run into a few rich and important types producing at WNN—Larson Overstreet for instance—so you'd better be on your guard. I hope you're taking martial arts or something because you may have to fight them off."

Kenley had recently accepted an assistant producer job at Worldwide News Network in her hometown of Atlanta, deciding to re-start her TV career behind the scenes instead of on-camera.

She got out of her chair and walked to the window, looking out over the expansive back lawn of Reid's mansion, where a gazebo had been erected and chairs had been arranged for the wedding.

"People are starting to arrive, Mara. I see your parents. They're holding hands."

Kenley glanced back at me and smiled then turned and gazed out the window as she responded to Heidi's teasing remark.

"I don't think fighting men off is going to be a problem. I

wanted to look nice for today, of course, but after this, I'm also swearing off makeup," she vowed. "And hair products, high heels—all that stuff. I've had it. I'm not on air anymore, so who cares? Mama's gonna flip, but that's too bad. I'm ready for a quiet, anonymous life. I want to find out what it's like to just be... me. For once."

Heidi and I shared a significant glance. Clearly, Kenley was going through a major crisis in the aftermath of her broken engagement. She loved cosmetics and clothes more than anyone I'd ever met. And she was good at all that beauty and fashion stuff.

But I sensed a pep talk wasn't what she needed right now.

I carefully moved across the room in my miles of white fabric and stood beside her, peeking down at the arriving crowd. My hand slipped around her back in a side hug.

"Hate to tell you this, babe, but you're beautiful even without it. It's your curse. But good for you—who needs all that crap? You're making me wish I had an off-air job myself."

"That's right," Heidi joined in, stepping to the window and putting an arm around Kenley from the other side. "The only problem's gonna be what to do with that extra two hours in the morning that you'll save by not fixing up."

We all laughed together and then cried a little as we embraced each other in a group hug. "This waterproof mascara had better live up to the hype because today's going to be the ultimate challenge," I said, and we laughed again.

We pulled apart, and Heidi's hands went back to my hair, smoothing it as Kenley fussed with the train of my dress.

"No way," Heidi said. "Crying time is all done. Now it's time to live happily ever after. And you look amazing... the perfect princess bride."

The door to my dressing room opened. The wedding planner peeked inside. "You ladies ready? It's just about go-time."

And with my best friends by my side, I set out to meet my prince—and my farm boy—the man who'd have my heart forever and always.

* * *

I hope you loved The Grumpy Billionaire! Want to read a bonus epilogue from Reid's point of view? Members of my VIP list get free bonus epilogues to all my books plus sneak peeks at upcoming books and a free novella set in the world of the Eastport Bay Billionaires. I'd love to have you join and give you all the goodies!

Have you read the other novels in the Eastport Bay series? Each book stands alone, and they can be read in any order, but they're interconnected in ways that make them even more fun when read together.

Here are the books in the series so far:

Bookworm and the Beast- A Beauty and the Beast story
Bargain with the Bachelor- A Snow White story
The Baby and the Blueblood- A Cinderella story
The Baby-whisperer and the Brute- A Rapunzel story
The Bombshell and the Bodyguard- A Frog Prince story
Scarlett and the Big Bad Billionaire— A Red Riding Hood and the Big Bad Wolf story
The Grumpy Billionaire- A Sleeping Beauty story (Reid's story)
The Merry Billionaire— A holiday novella (Hap's story)
The Sleepless Billionaire- (Tuck's story) Free when you join my VIP list!
No More Heartbreakers- A New Adult Romance
No More Billionaires- A New Adult Romance
No More Bad Boys- A New Adult Romance

Afterword

Thank you so much for reading The Grumpy Billionaire. I hope you loved it! If you did, I would be so grateful for a review on its Amazon page. And if your fingers aren't too tired, on Goodreads as well!

Reviews are so important for authors and they help other readers find great books.

There's more to enjoy in the world of Eastport Bay. Each book in this sexy small-town romance series stands alone, but they're interconnected in ways that make them even more fun when read together. And they're all available in Kindle Unlimited. I hope you'll check out the full series and have a blast reading them all!

Turn the page to check out my Also By page for a look at the covers and the links to download them.

And be sure to join my Tru Tales mailing list for notifications of new releases, free bonus epilogues, true stories of small town romantic comedy, excerpts, sneak peeks, giveaways, plus a FREE novella set in the world of Eastport Bay!

I'd love to have you join. Here's where to do that: https://trutaylor.com/tru-tales/

Also by Tru Taylor

Bookworm and the Beast- A Beauty and the Beast story

Bargain with the Bachelor- A Snow White story

The Baby and the Blueblood- A Cinderella story

The Baby-whisperer and the Brute- A Rapunzel story

The Bombshell and the Bodyguard- A Frog Prince story

Scarlett and the Big Bad Billionaire— A Red Riding Hood and the Big Bad Wolf story

The Grumpy Billionaire- A Sleeping Beauty story (Reid's story)

The Merry Billionaire— A holiday novella (Hap's story)

The Sleepless Billionaire- (Tuck's story) Free when you join my VIP list!

No More Heartbreakers- A New Adult Romance

No More Billionaires- A New Adult Romance

No More Bad Boys- A New Adult Romance

About the Author

Award-winning author Tru Taylor writes small town romance that's hot and sunny (and a little bit funny.)

She runs on Coke Zero and dark chocolate, lives for lunches with her girlfriends, and drives to the town beach several times a week to watch the sun set over the water.

She loves LOVE and will attempt to turn any show or movie she's watching into a romance whether it is one or not. Star Wars? A romance. Lord of the Rings? Clearly a romance. The Expendables? Okay, well not even Tru can redeem that one.

When she's not writing, Tru enjoys watching movies and reading books with happy endings, spending time with Mr. Tru and her two kids, and sneaking Hershey's Kisses from the top shelf of the freezer throughout the day. (Top shelf because... two kids. Enough said.)

Tru is the author of the Eastport Bay small town billionaire romance series and loves living in a small New England town where she's surrounded every day by the beautiful coastal setting you see brought to life in her books.

Want fun email from Tru? Join her Tru Tales mailing list for true stories of small town romantic comedy, free bonus epilogues, excerpts, sneak peeks, giveaways, and a free novella set in the world of Eastport Bay!

Here's where to sign up: https://trutaylor.com/tru-tales/

The Grumpy Billionaire is a work of fiction. Characters, names, places, brands, media, and incidents are either products of the author's imagination or have been used fictitiously and should not be construed as real. Any resemblance to actual persons, living or dead, events, or locales is entirely coincidental. It was previously published as Still Yours and Running from Romeo, and has been greatly altered and expanded, though some phrases and plot lines remained the same.

Oxford South Press July 2022

Cover Photographer: Scott Hoover

Cover Design: Emily Cover Design

www.ingramcontent.com/pod-product-compliance
Lightning Source LLC
Chambersburg PA
CBHW050823190726
48286CB00007B/1970

* 9 7 8 1 9 4 6 1 6 6 3 5 7 *